The Proxy Assassin

Book Three of the
American Spy Trilogy
by

John Knoerle

This is a work of fiction.

Published by **Blue Steel Press**
Chicago, IL
bluesteelpress@att.net
http://JohnKnoerle.com

Cover art and design by Katherine Bennett.

ISBN 978-0-9820903-9-8
Library of Congress 2008907387
Printed in the United States.

Also by John Knoerle:

"A Pure Double Cross,
Book One of the American Spy Trilogy"

"A Despicable Profession,
Book Two of the American Spy Trilogy"

"Crystal Meth Cowboys"

"The Violin Player"

The author would like to thank the following for their help and support:

Mark A. Ward
Sorin Crupa
Katie Bennett
Kelley Ristow
Professor David Anderson Heffner
Jimmy Higgins, Bobby Paladino and all the crew at Club Lucky in Chicago

And my wife Judie, without whom this labor of love would not have been possible.

For Jane,
the intrepid girl reporter.

"One of the things to be learnt about spying is that the least likely is the most probable."

-- Sir Dick White,
Chief of MI6, 1956 - 1968

It's November 1948 and I have somehow managed to make myself even more famous, though someone else performed my final act of heroism, someone more than happy to pass the glory on to me. You wouldn't believe how much crap you get credit for when you're a hero.

We do have a Central Intelligence Agency now, a one-year-old bouncing baby boy. But Great Britain's MI6, the dashing older brother of the OSS during the war, has fallen in with a bad crowd.

1949 is shaping up to be the worst year yet in the Cold War. Mao's People's Liberation Army is on the march in China and Stalin is tightening his death grip on Eastern Europe.

The CIA is fighting back, trying to foment revolution by 'indigenous anti-Communist insurgents' in the Balkans and elsewhere. We're not very good at it. Many a courageous ex-pat has paid the ultimate price for our bumbling.

Former OSS Director General William "Wild Bill" Donovan said it best…

"The newest weapons are falling before the oldest of them all – subversion. It's time to stop wondering if we will win the next war and find out why we're losing the one we're in."

Chapter One

The key number to remember when you parachute out of an airplane at an altitude of five hundred feet is two. You have two seconds to do two things. Get your feet down and your cord pulled. That's it, that's all you need to know.

I hadn't jumped since '44 so the flyboys thought it would be a good idea for me to take a couple low-altitude warm-ups from a C-45 at Andrews AFB. Shake off the rust after a four year layoff.

Sure. Why not *triple* my chances of falling five hundred feet in six seconds and smacking the sod at ninety miles an hour? I told them to get stuffed. I'd risk my tender hide only when it mattered. And I'd pack my own damn chute.

I was more of a jerk than I needed to be to those earnest young men who were just about my age but seemed like kids. It wasn't their fault I had fumbled and stumbled my way into another suicide mission.

The drop zone was located in rural central Romania. Transylvania, an area ringed by the thickly-wooded Carpathian Mountains. Which explained the tiny drop zone which explained the low altitude jump.

The mission wasn't a complete disaster. I jumped out the joe hole and into the night sky with one big improvement over WW II. It wasn't a blind drop, I had a group of resistance fighters waiting to greet me.

I executed a perfect two-point landing in a clearing between two mountains. My contact was Captain Sorin Dragomir, a large fortyish man with waves of thick brown hair. His well-upholstered gut and full set of teeth marked him as a man of stature.

That and his tasseled hessians and uniform jacket, buttons bursting, the gold braid above his breast pocket jiggling as he shook my hand. His dozen or so khaki-clad men were smaller and darker-skinned.

A dozen men. Christ. Joe Stalin must be quaking in his boots.

I got on my hotshot new Joan/Eleanor transceiver, rang the radio operator of the C-45 circling overhead and gave him the code for a safe landing. "Chaise lounge."

"Roger."

"Godspeed." With any luck the crew would reach their refueling strip in northern Turkey with a couple gallons left in the tank.

It was late, all I wanted was a quick snort and some shuteye. But the Captain made his men stand to attention around a guttering fire as he made a welcoming speech in English about the deep and abiding friendship between our two great nations. An elderly man stood beside him and translated his remarks into rapid-fire Romanian.

I guess I shouldn't have been surprised to hear that it sounded a lot like Italian. One thing I'd learned in my mission briefing was that, despite the vast expanse of pale and dour Yugoslavs and Hungarians separating them from Italy, Romanians considered themselves charter members of the Roman Empire. Which they were many centuries ago. Funny what people choose to take pride in.

The troops dispersed after the welcoming ceremony. The Captain and I retired to his little fortress at the edge of the clearing. It was a very old building. I had to bend at the waist to clear the doorway. The main room was lit by candles in an iron ceiling wheel. No fire in the fireplace though the night was cold.

Before the front door was closed I caught a glimpse of two of Dragomir's troops skittering by, headed home. It looked as though they had changed back into civilian clothes, which I took to mean that Captain Dragomir had not secured even this obscure slice of real estate.

The Captain and I seated ourselves at a table made from dark, foot-wide planks. The elderly man, apparently Dragomir's valet, went to a rough cupboard and fetched a bottle of twenty-year-old hooch and two crystal tumblers.

"I hate to look a gift horse in the mouth, Captain, but I don't drink Scotch."

"Why not?"

"It tastes like peat moss."

The Captain laughed at me. I knew the local drink was plum brandy so I asked for some. Dragomir laughed some more and issued instructions to his man.

We were served a delicious cold supper by candlelight. Three kinds of cheese, smoked ham, crusty bread, cucumbers in sour cream and sliced tomatoes. I should've stuck with peat moss, however. The plum brandy tasted like gasoline.

Frank Wisner, my boss, had set Dragomir and his men a task, which I relayed to him. They were to conduct surveillance on a Romanian Army encampment about ten kilometers to the southwest. This was to serve two purposes. To determine if the Captain's men could follow orders. And to assess the readiness and morale of the Romanian Army in a remote outpost.

The Soviet Army was spread thin throughout Eastern Europe. They had a base outside Bucharest, for instance, but they relied on the Romanian Army to keep order in the hinterlands. And the hinterlands weren't happy. The puppet government in Bucharest did as Moscow instructed. It collectivized farms and closed churches, which did not go over well with the locals.

Frank Wisner thought the Romanian Army would prove an unreliable ally for the Soviets, doubted they would open fire on their own people if push came to shove. How I was supposed to determine that by examining a remote Romanian outpost through binoculars was left to me.

Once I explained it to him Captain Dragomir agreed to Frank Wisner's assignment without hesitation. We would march tomorrow evening, zero hundred hours. And how was his old friend Frank coming along in his important new job?

"Fine."

The beeswax candles flickered in the drafty, heavy-timbered little fort. The old man cleared our plates and went away. The Captain poured himself another tumbler as the shadows danced.

"This building dates back to the 17th Century. It was a Swabian hunting lodge." He pointed to the stag horns mounted over the door, and the blackened hooks in the attic.

"That is where they smoked the meat."

Meat hooks, ugh. Hitler was fond of meat hooks.

Captain Dragomir was keen to tell me all about his elaborate plan to foment rebellion against Moscow's puppet regime in Bucharest but I was not, at this late hour, keen to listen to his delusions of grandeur.

That would have been a mistake under normal circumstances. If you are sent on a risky and expensive mission to gather intelligence you don't insult your source by saying, "I'm all in, Captain, let's discuss this tomorrow." That's because tomorrow has a way of scampering off down the road while you're lacing up your shoes.

But, as luck would have it, my bad attitude paid off.

Chapter Two

I returned home to Cleveland in July of '46 after my covert stint working for General William Donovan in Berlin. Returned to reclaim my room at Mrs. Brennan's rooming house and look for work. Being a hero doesn't pay well. I found a job as a research assistant in the downtown Cleveland Public Library. Not much of a payday but it gave me a chance to learn stuff. I liked it so far as it went.

Then I got a call from Frank Wisner, head of CIA's Office of Policy Co-ordination, inviting me to Washington for a weekend. I accepted. OPC was Wild Bill Donovan's dream come true – a well-funded, semi-independent covert operations org within the new CIA.

I was met by a driver at National Airport on Friday night, October 8th, 1948 and installed in a suite at the Mayflower Hotel. Nice digs. Wisner had left instructions at the front desk. Pack an overnight bag and meet my driver, Haskell, at 1300 hours on Saturday.

I did that. Haskell was a good hire, answering my probing questions with vague generalities. We drove three hours north to the Maryland shore. Sparse, wind-swept country with a tang of salt you could taste on your tongue.

Haskell perked up when we arrived at Locust Hill. "It's not a gentleman's farm, not a bit. They grow corn and sorghum and run livestock too."

We turned off the two-lane highway and jounced down a rutted dirt road between plowed-under fields. A man about forty and a boy about twelve were pitching silage into the back of a pickup, the boy straining to keep up. I asked Haskell if the man was Frank Wisner.

"Yes sir."

He had a high forehead, Wisner, a bulldozer jaw and dusty hair combed straight back. He looked like actor Van Johnson's tough older brother.

I climbed out with my overnight bag. Wisner greeted me like we were old pals and introduced me to Frank Jr. My driver turned around and headed off.

Wisner walked me over to a two-story brick house with creaky peg wood floors and bay windows with inch-thick glass. I met Wisner's wife and young daughter, Polly and Wendy, a pretty pair with matching cheekbones.

"Ellis and Graham are down at the crick giggin' frogs," said Wisner.

I smiled and nodded.

Frank grabbed me a beer from the fridge and led me out to the guest cottage in back. "Settle in, wash the dust off. You like gumbo?"

"If it's food, sir, I like it."

Frank Wisner was five yards gone before the screen door slammed behind him. I nipped at the beer and looked out the window, watched a stolid sugar maple shed red-orange leaves to the cutting wind. I flopped down on a saggy featherbed and wondered why I was here.

I would entertain any sort of stateside proposition Frank Wisner had to offer. But I wasn't going out again. I took a cat nap, washed up and reported to the farm house.

Wisner was in the kitchen, stirring a big cast iron skillet furiously. It was late afternoon but no other guests had arrived. Was I it?

"Schroeder, good timing. Take over."

Huh?

"When it gets dark brown turn the heat off. And watch yourself. It's roux, Cajun napalm."

I stirred the stuff, which looked like something you'd use to lube axle bearings. It went from light to dark brown in about a minute. I turned the heat off.

"Watch this," said Wisner and poured a cooler teeming with blue crabs into the sink. One scuttled up Frank's hard-muscled forearm. He brushed it back into the sink with a laugh.

Wisner put me to work chopping onions, the louse, then tossed the crabs into a pot of boiling water, cackling fiendishly. The mud-spattered boys, Ellis and Graham, trooped in with speared frogs and set about chopping off their legs. Dad scooped boiled crabs from the pot and hacked them apart with a cleaver.

Daughter Wendy poked her head in for a moment, gagged and went away. I saw her point. The kitchen looked like a battlefield surgery tent.

"We're draggin' our wagon here gentlemen. The distaff crew needs to get about the biscuits and dirty rice," said Wisner as he stirred the onions into the hot roux. He added okra and cayenne and garlic powder and dumped it all into a big pot of steaming soup stock.

Ellis and Graham floured and dusted a dozen frogs' legs. We had enough food to feed the Russian Army.

Wisner set the oven timer and told the boys to add the crab to the pot when it dinged. Then he took me by the elbow for a walking tour of Locust Hill Farm.

We passed a marshy pond rimmed by brown cat o' nine tails. Wisner pointed out the duck blind they used in season. "You a hunter?"

"Nazis count?"

A mild chuckle from Wisner. "I envy you. I wasn't privileged to see combat during the war."

"I don't know that it was much of a privilege. Sir."

"That's where you're wrong Schroeder. I was Navy before I joined the OSS, stuck in the New York Censor's Office, shuffling papers. I sprained my ankle playing touch football one weekend. So I was on crutches Monday morning when I climbed on a Manhattan subway car in my Navy blues."

Wisner winced. "And the good folks of New York City stood up and gave me a round of applause."

"Couldn't be helped, sir. And I hear you did great work in Bucharest."

Wisner did not reply. We walked on in silence, crunching dead leaves underfoot.

"Here's where we are," he said after a time, his Southern drawl making the sentence sound like one long word. "FDR thought that the Four Policemen – the U.S., Britain, Russia and China – would keep the peace in their four corners of the globe after the war. But that hasn't worked out so well."

"No sir."

Wisner picked up the pace. "I believe we can do a little something about that, Schroeder. I believe we can recruit, train and arm indigenous anti-Communist insurgents in Eastern Europe. I know these people. They're fierce fighters, sick to death of foreign occupation."

I was inclined to agree with him until he added, "You had some success in Berlin with this kind of thing."

"Mostly, sir, what we had was a lot of luck," I said, recalling how easily the Soviets had duped the White Russian resistance fighters. I continued. Shot my mouth off in fact.

"Sir I'm guessing the Soviets have already culled the herd in Eastern Europe. Anyone with military training has cast their lot with the Reds, or been executed. The leftovers, the shopkeepers, farmers and clerks, they're fine decent people who wouldn't know an M-1 from a licorice stick."

I hated hearing myself sound so candyass. Frank Wisner was a direct descendant of Wild Bill Donovan, whose wartime motto was 'try anything.' But, as I learned in Berlin, a cold war is a lot trickier than a hot one.

Wisner stopped and looked up at the purpled sky. A shadow of concern or disappointment flickered across his stony mug.

We turned and started back toward the house, footfalls in synch on the leafy dirt.

"We have made rookie mistakes, no question. I can't disclose details but we launched an operation in Eastern Europe earlier this year, with trusted foreign agents, ex-pats, from the OSS days. There were over a hundred of them all told. We inserted them into a controlled situation based on bad intelligence. And they were rolled up within a week. Prosecuted at show trials, executed at dawn," said Wisner in a husky voice. "We have got to do better."

Yeah, no shit.

I turned at the sweep of headlights to see a Cadillac limousine roll to a stop in front of the farmhouse.

A uniformed chauffeur opened the back door. A tall and slender young man with dark pomaded hair climbed out and leaned in to assist a tall and slender young woman. They stood in the dim light from the porch lamp and unrumpled their attire. His a belted tweed jacket and plus fours suitable for grouse hunting. Hers a brown cardigan over a white blouse and dark pleated slacks. They waited for Frank to greet them.

"Your Majesties, welcome to my humble abode."

Majesties?

His Majesty surveyed the old farmhouse with a jaundiced eye. "Just as you say."

Her Majesty smiled at Frank Wisner. "Ignore him. He's been like that all day."

The young man took this jibe good-naturedly. "A great pleasure to see you Frank. It's been too long. As you can see I have married well."

"So I've heard. Congratulations."

The young man nodded his appreciation, then grinned mischievously. "We have brought you an uninvited guest."

It was only then that I noticed the slight figure in the front seat. The chauffeur hurried to the passenger's side and opened the door. The woman who stepped out was short in stature.

Only her face was visible above the roof of the limo. Frank Wisner caught his breath.

"Your good friend, Princess Stela Varadja," said the regal young man. As if Frank Wisner didn't know.

"Hello Frank," she said in a heavy Eastern European accent. "You seem surprise to see me."

Wisner opened his mouth to speak but nothing came out.

Frank found his tongue once we were inside. He introduced me to his guests. Michael the First, King of Romania, and his wife, Princess Anne of Bourbon Parma.

"I prefer Prince of the Hohenzollern these days," sniffed the young king as he shook my hand. His grip was very firm.

"And you may call me Nan," said his wife.

The slight-figured Princess Stela hung back. She was one of those women you can't take your eyes off of for fear you'll miss something. Wisner stood to my left and vibrated with kinetic energy. A five-year-old could have told you they'd been lovers.

Frank ran down his exalted guests' genealogical charts, just to be saying something.

"Michael is the great-great-grandson of Queen Victoria. Nan is the daughter of Princess Margrethe of Denmark."

I smiled and nodded. Wisner cleared his throat. "And Princess Stela Varadja is a direct descendant of Prince Vlad Tepes."

"Vlad the Impaler," said King Michael, drolly. "Stoker's inspiration for Count Dracula, though Stela would prefer you didn't mention it."

I saw it instantly. Chalk white skin, devilish brows, a slender nose that dipped like a beak ever so slightly. Shimmering black eyes, purple lips.

"Vlad Tepes Draculea made Romania a country," said Princess Stela hotly. "And Bram Stoker was lying fool. Prince Vlad he lived in Wallachia, not Transylvania."

I kept my Bela Lugosi impression to myself and marveled at the cast of characters Frank Wisner had assembled in his rustic cottage.

Polly and the kids presented a welcome dose of down home when they entered a moment later, though I barely recognized the boys. They'd been scrubbed and shampooed within an inch of their lives.

The children were well schooled. They bowed and curtseyed as introductions were made and conversed easily with their guests. I was impressed. The loftiest visitor to ever grace our home in Youngstown was the parish priest. And he scared me to death.

Polly showed no sign of resentment or suspicion when she greeted Princess Stela. Of course she didn't. Frank Wisner hadn't come this far while married to a woman who didn't know how to play the game.

Princess Stela proved not so circumspect however.

Wisner pulled a jeroboam of champagne from the fridge and popped the cork off the kitchen ceiling to whoops of delight. Polly lined up six glasses on the kitchen counter. Frank filled them rapid fire, right to left, then added a blood red drop of Crème de Cassis to each glass.

"There," he said, "a proper Kir Royale."

The guests started forward to partake but Wisner waved them off. He placed the brimming champagne cocktails on a serving tray and handed the tray to Wendy, who was all of nine years old. We held our collective breath as she made her way from the kitchen to the parlor with short quick steps. She didn't spill a drop. Entertaining dignitaries was, apparently, a team sport in the Wisner household.

King Michael and his wife clucked and cooed at young Wendy's feat but Princess Stela looked cross. She hadn't suffered a tedious three-hour car ride to find her dashing wartime swain nestled in domestic bliss. He was supposed to be alone. No self-respecting European aristocrat carried his wife and family to his sporting lodge.

Wendy presented the Princess with her drink. Stela thanked the girl and looked up.

"Is no caviar Frank? We always had caviar."

The room got quiet. A gust of wind rattled the windowpanes. Polly Wisner's face froze in mid-smile as Frank did a slow burn. Graham, the youngest boy, broke the tension.

"We got frogs' legs. Right from the crick!"

After one of the most delicious, gut-busting dinners I ever set a tooth on Polly said good night and took the kids off to bed. Frank went outside to collect the chauffeur, depositing him on a stool in the kitchen with a cold beer and a bowl of gumbo.

Wisner ushered his regal guests to the parlor for coffee and cognac. As low scrotum on the totem I took the coffee orders – milk not cream for King Michael, one sugar for Princess Nan, black for Wisner, and cream, two sugars and a dash of Crème de Cassis for Stela Varadja.

I watched my footing carefully as I served them, aware that dumping a cup of scalding coffee on his or her majesty was just the kind of thing Hal Schroeder would do.

Frank sat next to the royal couple on a well-used chesterfield. Princess Stela and I sat opposite them in cane-back chairs. The fire in the rough stone fireplace burned bright.

Princess Stela, who looked more gypsy than vampire now that she'd had a few champagne cocktails, began to spin a spellbinding tale.

She told how King Michael staged a daring *coup d'etat* against pro-Nazi strongman Ion Antonescu in 1944, throwing him in prison and declaring war against the Axis. She recounted how the King fought Soviet control almost single-handedly after war's end but was finally forced to abdicate in 1947

Princess Stela husked her voice as the fire grew low and smoky. She told how the Red Army had rounded up eighty thousand *Volksdeutsche*, mostly Saxons from Transylvania, in January of 1945. And packed them off in boxcars to Stalin's work camps to slave and die.

Stela paused to brush back a damp strand of hair that was plastered to her forehead. She grabbed it between thumb and forefinger and returned the errant tress to its proper place before she concluded her story. How Frank Wisner had racketed around Bucharest like a madman trying to stop the roundup, trying to save anyone he could.

This was all for my benefit, had to be. Everyone else knew the story. I asked Wisner if he'd had any luck.

"Well, I saved Hugo."

The chauffeur hoisted a beer from the kitchen.

Chapter Three

I slept late Sunday morning, swallowed up by the featherbed in the guest cottage. Frank Wisner and family had just returned from church when I joined them in the kitchen. Polly was frying up cornmeal mush in bacon grease.

"Your timing, Schroeder, is first rate," said Wisner with a bright-eyed grin, showing no ill effects from the late evening.

I'd said goodnight once the second bottle of cognac came out and, feeling like a hushed kid at the top of the stair, watched from the window of the guest cottage as Frank Wisner and his royal pals hunkered down for grown up conversation punctuated by peals of laughter.

"I've got a nose for grub sir."

"But you don't show it," said Wisner, patting my flat belly. "What's your secret?"

"What's yours sir?"

"Me? I'm fat as a lord," he said, pooching out his gut.

Polly laughed at him. "Did you know that Frank was invited to join the U.S. track team for the '36 Olympics?"

"Wow."

"But his daddy didn't cotton to such foolishness and marched him off to work. And Frank's been trying to cross that finish line ever since."

Frank and Polly exchanged a sweet, knowing look. I answered his question.

"It's true I eat like Henry the Eighth, sir, but I worry like Anne Boleyn. That's my secret."

Wisner shook his head. "Worrying's my job Schroeder."

Frank Wisner walked me to my waiting Chevy Fleetmaster after breakfast.

"I have been in contact with the leader of a Romanian anti-Communist cell, a man I know from my time in country. He claims to have a worked-out plan to foment insurrection, claims a secret ally that he can't divulge."

"Do you trust him?"

Wisner gave me a side door answer. "I was impressed by him. But I don't know how capable a field leader he is."

We walked to the rear of the Chevy, Wisner bent over and put his foot on the bumper. "Romania is critical, it's the beating heart of the Balkans. A successful uprising there would radiate out in all directions – Bulgaria, Yugoslavia, Hungary, even the Ukraine."

I nodded, dumbly.

It was then that Frank Wisner popped the question. Popped the question after just one date. Would I consider parachuting into a remote mountain camp to liaise with the Romanian resistance group?

"I'd want your positive assessment before we got involved."

"Why me, sir?"

"I don't have anyone else with your behind-the-lines experience."

I asked him why that was just to hear him say it.

"They're all dead."

I had already survived two suicide missions in my lifetime, a third did not appeal. But I told Frank Wisner I would need a few days to think it over. I had some sightseeing to do.

We listened to the Cleveland-Baltimore game on the drive back to D.C., Haskell the driver and me.

Haskell was a serious Colts fan. He didn't like me so well when I told him I was from Cleveland. The Browns had shut out the Colts last season. Twice.

Haskell didn't like me any better when the Browns beat the Colts in Baltimore on that crisp October Sunday, 14-10.

Chapter Four

Top secret overseas junkets on USAF aircraft differ from commercial flights in one important respect. There is no scheduled return flight. The airline determines when, and if, you get to return home. I only knew where they would land. OPC had access to a secret airstrip in central Romania near Sibiu.

Soviet radar and air defense systems were plain lousy in that part of the world so the USAF wasn't too worried about getting blown out of the sky by ack ack or scrambling Yak-9s. The problem was establishing a line of communication to my hotshot new Joan Eleanor transceiver in order to arrange the time of my retrieval, which depended on how things went with Captain Dragomir.

We were fighting the last war with new tricks. Himmler's spycatchers, the *Sicherheitsdienst*, were expert at triangulating and tracking down alien transmissions. But my hotshot new Joan/Eleanor used a much narrower VHF broadcast band which made intercepting signals next to impossible. Take that, you dirty Krauts!

Here in Romania, however, where there weren't any SD trucks tracking and triangulating alien broadcasts, the snappy new technology was more trouble than it was worth. The receiving plane had to be in a narrow overhead window to take my call. Why not use an old fashioned broad-range transceiver just this once?

I asked the USAF that very question and given a lollipop and a pat on the head.

A de Havilland Mosquito would fly overhead at high altitude at zero dark thirty in three days' time so I could tell them when to come fetch me. If the weather didn't permit a flight they would come the following night, and so on. But the real nut cutter was what happens when the flyboys get their wheels down.

'Falling down is easy, it's the getting up that's hard,' as the old song says. No one has yet devised a way to shoot a ground agent onto a low-flying airplane. You have to land the damn thing, which tends to attract attention. You can't fly over enemy territory in broad daylight and the night has a thousand eyes. The Reds might have lousy radar in this part of the world but once the plane is on the ground it's a sitting duck.

I was an experiment is what I was. A guinea pig for both Frank Wisner and the United States Air Force.

My sister Beth kept a pet guinea pig when she was eight or nine. It was too big for its little glass cage and spent its days pacing back and forth through the tangle of wood shavings, going *eep, eep, eep.*

My sentiments exactly.

The Captain was gone when I rolled out of bed the next morning. His valet told me he would return that afternoon and asked me a silly question. Was I hungry? He served a breakfast much like supper save for a fried egg with a golden yoke. Best egg I ever ate.

I wandered outside and enjoyed the sunshine. Golden birch shimmered amidst the black firs that crowded the mountain-sides. The calendar said fall but it felt like summer.

I had supposed we were in the middle of nowhere so the rumble of a truck engine pricked up my ears. The road noise led me down a dirt path that led to a dirt road that led to an excavated roadway that may have been paved at some point but was now mostly dust and gravel. And busy with traffic.

Parked on a tree stump I watched the parade. In the space of half an hour I saw four trucks, half a dozen hay wagons, a babushka lady leading a donkey piled high with bundled sticks, a group of men, scythes slung over their shoulders, smoking and singing as they strode along, two frighteningly pretty gypsy girls in long bright skirts and flowing scarves - hitchhiking - and a man peddling his bike down the road with his horse trotting happily alongside.

Oh, and a huge bull ox meandering along the shoulder – on the proper side of the road, in the direction of traffic – making his way back to the barn all by himself.

I walked back to the little fort, wanting to wash off the dust, but found no tub or shower, just a wash basin with a pump handle. I remembered hearing a mountain stream nearby.

It was down a steep bank, not twenty yards behind the building. I wound my way down a rocky well-worn path, watching every step. I wasn't going to march ten klicks to an army camp on a twisted ankle.

The stream roared along at a good clip but I found an eddy pond behind a boulder. I stripped down and jumped in. *Damn* it was cold. I splashed around for as long as I could stand it then scrambled out, catching my foot on a taut lanyard.

What was this now? I hauled in the sunken treasure, hand over hand. It was a canvas bag containing a quart of milk and four bottles of beer.

I didn't have any cash to place in the sack, I was traveling light. Gun, knife, L-pill.

While Hal the Younger would have filched a beer in a heartbeat, Harold the Elder, sadly, couldn't bring himself to take what didn't belong to him.

But wait. The old man had served me a glass of cold milk for breakfast though there was no fridge in the little fort. This was *his* stash, the cold beer was meant for *my* enjoyment. I was simply saving him the tedious chore of fetching it.

I shook myself dry best I could, got dressed, uncapped a beer against a rock shard with a smack of my palm and climbed back up the river bank. A wooden stool sat outside the front door of the little fort. I moved it onto the scrubby grass and let the beating sun dry my clothes.

The beer, *Ursus*, was crisp and cold. I stretched out my legs and felt, for a man on a suicide mission, quite relaxed.

I watched a gray-white stork swoop in with a beak full of rags and sticks, which it used to feather its nest atop the fireplace chimney of the little fort. It was big nest, about two feet high. Which raised a question.

What was a bird's nest doing on top of a fireplace chimney at a time of year when the nights got cold? And where had Captain Dragomir got to? Probably visiting his actual residence, a house with running water and a furnace.

Wise up, Schroeder. The little fort is a prop.

Thanks to Bram Stoker, gullible tourists like me pictured Transylvania as a blood-soaked land of dark castles and vampire bats. But what I'd seen on that main road looked about as scary as Amish country.

Captain Dragomir, the big man in the little uniform, was simply trying to give the customer what he paid for.

The Captain returned late that afternoon, looking pleased with himself. His cheeks were flushed but he didn't smell of booze. An invigorating interlude with his mistress perhaps.

I was halfway to cheesed off until he opened his leather satchel to reveal a bottle of homemade red wine and two fat hero sandwiches like you'd find at an Italian deli. My mood improved.

We talked about that night's march to the Romanian Army camp. "It's recon, not combat," I reminded him. "No rifles, mortars or machine guns. Nothing more than sidearms."

"This would be foolish."

"That's the way Frank Wisner wants it."

"But there are many Magyars in the area. And they are well armed."

"What's a Magyar?"

"A tribal group, Huns," sneered Dragomir. "*Hungarians.*"

"Okay. And what tribe is your group?"

The Captain reared back, insulted. "We are Romanians!"

I was surprised to hear Dragomir faced armed opposition from other natives. My OPC mission briefers said that, in Transylvania at least, the storyline was simple. Oppressed peasants versus hated Reds.

The Captain nibbled at his sandwich and wiped his chin with a tiny napkin. "The Huns claim they are seeking revenge for Iron Guard atrocities during the war."

I remembered that the Iron Guard were Romanian Nazi sympathizers who murdered Jews and suspected Communists during the war. Magyars too for all I knew.

"But what does that have to do with me?" said the Captain, pouring red wine with abandon. "I worked for King Michael, the courageous young patriot who had Ion Antonescu arrested."

"The leader of the Iron Guard," I said, hopefully.

Dragomir drank wine and nodded. "The Magyars are Hungarian nationalists and nothing more. They seize hold of any slander against us and use it to advance their goal."

"Which is?"

I feared the Captain was going to perform a spit double take. "To forcibly return Transylvania to the Hungarian Empire!"

Guess they have long memories in this part of the world. If I remembered my high school history correctly the Austro-Hungarian Empire went bye bye a long time ago.

I asked the Captain an embarrassing question. "Were any of your men members of the Iron Guard?"

The Captain shrugged. Maybe, probably, didn't matter now. "We are monarchists, not fascists."

"Admirable, sir. But I have met King Michael."

"Is that so? And how did you find him?"

How did I what? Oh. "I found him well, happy with his new bride."

"Princess Anne, I haven't had the pleasure," said Dragomir, stiffly.

"King Michael didn't express any interest in returning to Romania."

"Why would he?"

"I'm sorry?"

"He was forced to abdicate. And he is a Hohenzollern, whose mother was a Greek."

"So you are a monarchist...who doesn't care if your monarch returns to his kingdom?"

"That is not true," said Captain Dragomir, wiping his mouth. He had somehow managed to munch his sandwich down to a nub during our brief conversation.

"Then I'm confused."

Captain Dragomir gave out with a deep-chested snort and raised his glass. "Welcome to Romania!"

Chapter Five

Haskell the driver returned me to the Mayflower Hotel after my visit to the Frank Wisner's Maryland farm. I was having a Sunday evening beer in the Towne and Country Lounge - a thousand square feet of low lamped, leather upholstered, walnut paneled heaven - when a big-gutted man with thyroid eyeballs took the barstool to my right. William King Harvey, terminated by the FBI, now working for the CIA. I'd heard him described and there couldn't be two.

The Negro bartender looked to Harvey who nodded, then ticked his head toward me. The bartender got busy. Harvey lit a cigarette and gave me a pop-eyed once over.

"You take that Romanian job Wisner's been shoppin'?"

"No comment."

"I'm Bill Harvey." He had a Midwestern handshake, firm, quick and dry.

"I know."

"Interesting that Wisner invited the Romanian royals out to meet you."

This got my full attention, but I was wary. I had never heard of an FBI agent going to work for the CIA. Word was that Hoover had forced Harvey out for some minor infraction - showing up late, wearing his tie loose - but for all I knew Bill Harvey was Hoover's mole. He sure didn't look CIA. He looked, in fact, like J. Edgar Hoover's fat bastard son.

"Thank you Winston," said Harvey as the barkeep served him a brimming Manhattan. I was surprised to see Winston serve me one as well. "Drink up," said Harvey, "the man's a genius."

I took a bite. *Yeow.*

Harvey didn't find an ashtray handy so he flicked his cigarette ash into his cupped left hand. "What do Commies hate worse than capitalists?"

"Beats me. Fascists?"

"Monarchies. Ask the Romanoff's, you don't believe me."

"That would be difficult."

"You in a yank?"

"Nope."

Winston the barkeep slid a clean ashtray Bill Harvey's way. Harvey dumped the ashes from his cupped hand and leaned his bulk on the bar.

"Bulgaria was ruled by a boy king during World War II. His uncle Prince Kirill was installed as regent to cover the king's tender ass seein' as how the king's tender ass was about six years old at the time. After the Red Army rolled in the Prince was executed, along with the royal staff, hundreds of people. This was early '45."

"What's your point?"

"Bulgaria's neighbor to the north is my point. Why was the King of all Romania permitted to remain in power till late '47, and then allowed to pack up his gold cufflinks and leave? Why didn't the Reds give *him* a cigarette and a blindfold?"

"Because he stood up to the Nazis?"

"He was the monarch of a Balkan republic that's been conquered more times than....shit, I dunno, what's been conquered more times than a Balkan republic?"

Harvey laughed at my reply. "Mount Campbell, tallest peak in Ohio, 1550 feet."

"Small country monarchs can't afford to stand up, not for long. Some people of an overly-suspicious nature might wonder what side the Romanian royals are really on."

I nibbled my perfect Manhattan and waited to hear what Harvey was after.

"There was a woman in the front seat I couldn't make."

I didn't hesitate. Wisner hadn't sworn me to secrecy, and I was aggravated that he'd asked me to go all the way on the first date. "Princess Stela Varadja."

"Ooh la fucking dah. Bet that was fun."

"It was all pretty civilized."

Harvey snorted. "Well it would be, wouldn't it?"

"You gonna give me something now?"

"You first."

"I just went first."

"That's just bullshit backstopping. Tell me something worth hearing."

"I don't have anything, I..."

Harvey waggled his caterpillar eyebrows.

What the hell, in for a penny, in for a pound. "Wisner said they ran an operation in Eastern Europe earlier this year, ex-pat agents from the war, blown from day one."

Harvey flicked ashes in the general direction of the ashtray. "That must have been Bucharest, mid-June."

"Bucharest? Bucharest, Romania?" Harvey didn't answer my dumb question. "Are you shittin' me a pound?"

Harvey drained his Manhattan. "I never lie when I'm drinking, too complicated."

"Wisner wants me to find out if his Royal pals are playing both sides?"

"Sure. But he won't say that out loud because he wants to deny ever giving that order if they come up clean." Harvey stubbed out his cig. "He's an honorable guy, Wisner. A gentleman of the old school in the wrong line of work."

Harvey looked at his watch, threw down a fin, nodded and waddled off. I got to wondering.

Princess Stela had taken pains to portray Frank Wisner as a lonesome hero fighting to save the *Volksdeutche* in 1945. I didn't doubt it, though the story of the Russians rounding up ethnic Germans was new to me. What got me to wondering was how Princess Stela knew I was important enough to

Wisner to make that effort. She was a surprise guest, she and Wisner didn't have a moment alone.

Step back, Schroeder. Stop speculating. They teach you at spy school that speculation is akin to masturbation. You get where you want to go far too quickly. I wasn't the person Princess Stela was trying to reach with her adoring tale of Frank Wisner's heroism.

Princess Stela was addressing herself to Frank Wisner.

Chapter Six

The troops filtered back to the little fort after dark, wearing civvies. They changed into their olive drab in a low-roofed outbuilding, an old hog pen or hay shed.

The Captain made them stand to attention on the grass in front of the little fort at 2300 hours. Dragomir had equipped them well. They held recent vintage Lee-Enfield repeating rifles at present arms. He walked the line, inspecting them as if they were Beefeaters guarding Buckingham Palace.

When the inspection was complete the Captain told the men to stand down and addressed them in their native language. The part of his speech where he said they would not be permitted to carry their rifles was evident from their furrowed brows.

I'd told Frank Wisner I had doubts about his well-intentioned campaign to support indigenous anti-Communist elements in Eastern Europe – good intentions being the paver stones of the road to hell. This was a good example. OPC wanted to avoid a bloody international incident so they gave me strict instructions. 'No heavy or long range weaponry permitted on the reconnaissance probe. Self-defense weapons only.'

The OPC meant sidearms. But none of the Dragomir's poor peasants owned anything as exotic as a Mauser or a.38 Special. A self-defense weapon to them was a knife. Or rock.

We would be marching into what I had recently learned was hostile territory with what I had even-more-recently learned would be soldiers carrying no weapons of any kind.

We had half an hour to kill so Captain Dragomir invited me inside for a libation. The elderly valet must have seen the empty bottle I'd left outside because I wasn't offered peat moss or gasoline. He poured me a cold Ursus beer with a wry smile.

I drank thirstily, waiting for the Captain to finally unveil his master plan to overthrow the puppet regime in Bucharest. But he remained silent as he used a bootjack to pull off his tasseled hessians, then stepped into a pair of lower-cut boots more suitable for a long march.

He was worried about his men, what else? He hadn't refused Wisner's no-rifles' decree but it had to piss him off.

I felt a pang of sympathy for the man. It had to do with his socks. He had been doing his best to maintain his appearance as a well-appointed potentate, field marshal, kingfish and all around Big Chief Itch and Rub. But his socks told a different story. They had been darned so often it was hard to tell if their original color was brown or green.

My money was on brown. The toes and heels were mostly green.

There might be safety in numbers in combat but not in espionage. The only reason I survived behind German lines in World War II was that I operated solo. And I had a trick. I would dig a three-foot hidey hole not 100 feet from my recon post. If spotted I could be in that hole in five seconds flat with a neatly trimmed cover of peat pulled over, the cover sprayed with a canister the OSS gave me to put off the German Shepherds. I'm not sure what was in it but you'll never hear me speak ill of skunks.

But Frank Wisner wanted the Captain's men put through their paces. So we would skip down the road together, hand in hand.

We set out promptly at zero hundred hours. The men were skilled, they knew to march in twos, widely spaced. And to keep their yaps shut.

The night was fine, cool and starwashed. The road twisted up the mountainside, perpendicular to the main road I had visited earlier. It was gravel at first, then packed dirt as we climbed higher.

The foliage crowded in as the road narrowed. It grew cold. Animals scurried in the brush as we passed. Captain Dragomir led the procession, I brought up the rear.

We kept up a good pace until a single rifle report rang out. A nearby tree trunk took the hit.

Dragomir and his men hit the dirt as one. I took a knee and listened.

Don't prone yourself out in a combat zone, if you want my advice. It limits your mobility, and sightlines. I learned this important lesson from observing a young woman in the farm country outside Karlsruhe.

She was herding a few scrawny goats down the road when she heard the scream of a P-51 Mustang swooping down for the kill. She bit the dust. The P-51 flew past.

Well done and executed. Except the young goatherd kept flat a moment too long. Two five-ton German half-tracks, the Mustang's intended prey, roared out of a stand of trees they'd been hiding in and ground the poor girl to grist under their caterpillar tracks.

Combat is fight or flight. I'm partial to flight myself but it's hard to do either when your nose is in the dirt. Keep a knee up, keep your head up. We'll all be prone soon enough.

Chapter Seven

No more rifle fire commenced. I got my trusty Walther P-38 in hand and listened hard.

No sounds of motion, whoever took a potshot at us remained in place. I fired twice in the general direction of the rifle round. Someone took off through the underbrush.

We had crossed some perimeter most likely and a lone sentry had cranked a round at the sound of marching feet. A polite warning as these things go. But we had been found out, the road was not our friend.

I had followed my OPC instructions to the letter so far but I wasn't going to march Captain Dragomir's men into an ambush just to prove they could follow orders. I would do it my way from here on.

Dragomir climbed to his feet. His men followed suit a moment later. He dusted himself off furiously, his dignity offended.

I told him in a whisper that he was to take his men back to the little fort, that I would slog through the underbrush to the Romanian Army encampment with a guide of his choosing.

The Captain responded with something no red-blooded American wants to hear. "Let's wait, be patient. We will try again in a day or two."

I knew something about making my way through heavy brush so I pulled rank and insisted. Dragomir shrugged, and assigned me two guides. "My most trusted men."

"Why two?"

Dragomir didn't mince words. "One is your guide, one is my spy, who will follow at a distance. If you and Spiru are killed or captured my spy will report back."

"It wouldn't hurt, Captain, if your men made a little noise on the march back."

I was about to explain that this would telegraph to any sentries that the troops were now in retreat, but he cut me short with a brisk, "Of course."

Smart fellow, this Dragomir.

He issued instructions to Spiru, an elfin little guy with big ears.

I followed Spiru into the woods. Man, it was thick. What wasn't trees was bushes. Spiru had a little flashlight that helped us scratch our way through the thicket at a snail's pace.

My best guess is that we were still a couple miles from the army camp. It would be broad daylight before we got there at this rate.

I tapped Spiru's shoulder. We stopped and listened. Dead quiet. If Dragomir's spy was tailing us he was doing it on the road.

Could be it was time to rethink this fighting-our-way-through-brambles-with-a-flashlight idea. The night was still moonless, we were only two. We would walk down the road, not march. Flatfooted. No one would know we were there.

But someone did know.

When Spiru and I climbed out of the brush and started down the road another shot rang out. A pistol round, small caliber, close by.

Then three more in quick succession.

Spiru pitched forward, fell on his face and stayed there.

I was twisting around to confront our attacker when the lights went out.

I woke up with a thudding headache and a mouthful of mud, which I took to mean that someone had turned my head to the side so I didn't drown in the shallow puddle I had fallen into.

I spat out the mud and looked around best I could. My hands were tightly bound behind my back. Ankles too. An apple in my mouth was all I needed.

Poor little Spiru was not where he had fallen. A bloody trail in the dirt road indicated that his body had been dragged into the woods to be disposed of by bear, wolf and fox. I would say a prayer for him when I could but I had by more immediate concerns.

My captors were standing above me speaking a language that wasn't Romanian. It sounded odd, woozy-making, like English played backwards on a tape recorder.

Hungarian, what else? These were Magyars, half a dozen or so.

I heard the wheeze of a rattletrap car or truck behind me. How the hell had they gotten the drop on us so quick, just as we stepped out of the woods?

I had my answer a short minute later when two men hauled me up at knees and shoulders and dumped me into the back of a flatbed truck that reeked of pig manure. The men climbed in on either side of me. They didn't wear uniforms like Dragomir's boys but they looked much the same. Short, dark, taut. They had sidearms holstered to their belts, some Great War relics I didn't recognize. But these weren't the men who ambushed Spiru and me.

No, that would be the surviving member of Captain Dragomir's 'most trusted men,' the one who was supposed to be his spy.

The moon had put in a late night appearance. I could see him trudging along behind the sputtering truck, avoiding eye contact with the prize porker in the flatbed.

An enterprising young man. He must have been highly motivated to sneak a concealed weapon past Dragomir, kill his comrade in arms with four quick rounds from a snub nose and then conk me out with the butt of same.

If he was one of the Captain's most trusted men it didn't speak too well for the rest of his crew.

We turned left off the main road and climbed a serpentine trail that wasn't much more than a cow path with tire ruts. My guards had to jump out and help push the truck uphill when we hit a muddy patch.

We weren't headed to a Romanian Army camp, that was sure. While I had not been looking forward to interrogation by some self-important base commander with a swagger stick, we would at least speak the common language of military protocol and strategic interests.

He'd know he'd bagged a valuable asset in other words.

It was doubtful that my strategic import would impress whatever tribal chieftain I was being carried off to. Hal Schroeder wouldn't be a captured knight on the Cold War chessboard to him. Hal Schroeder would be a foreign interloper sent to help a hated rival.

Fun.

We reached our destination before dawn. A few moth-eaten pup tents clustered around a fire pit, an open air latrine stinking to high heaven and a listing-to-port hunter's shack with papered-over windows that stood above the perimeter, twenty yards uphill. The imperial palace of the King of the Magyars.

"What is your name American?"

"Puddintane. Ask me again and I'll tell you the same."

It looked like Captain Dragomir had himself a formidable opponent. A gargoyle head on a fireplug body, a brawler. A brawler with a steady pilot light burning behind pale gray eyeballs.

I had been untied and stood on my hind legs to greet the boss man, my guards bending my arms behind me. The boss man didn't bust my lip for mouthing off for some reason.

Apparently Captain Dragomir's most trusted weasel had already sent word that an American had dropped in to see the Captain, and that the troops had been called to assemble late at night. The weasel would not have had time to relay our exact plans since Dragomir didn't reveal them till the last minute. But the boss man knew we'd be on the move.

It would never have occurred to him that the head of a U.S. covert operations agency would send an agent halfway around the world to conduct a training exercise. That Captain Dragomir had called off the march or attack or whatever it was after one warning shot had to puzzle the crap out of him. That I had continued on almost alone made no sense either.

So the boss man hadn't slugged me because he wasn't sure who I was or what I was up to. But he was chewing on it.

He barked an order. My guards sweep kicked my legs out from under me and dumped me on my back. The knot on the back of my head sent thunderbolts down my spine.

The boss man bent to one knee and patted me down, intimately. He looked in my mouth with a flashlight and ran his finger around my teeth. He pulled off my boots and socks and searched inside. No joy. He was looking for a hidden cyanide pill that would positively identify me as a spy.

But why did he give a shit? Unless he was working for the Romanian Army. Or, more likely and far worse, the sadistic little brother of the Soviet Secret Police, the Romanian *Securitate*.

I held my breath as he examined my boots with care. Leonid Vitinov, my archrival in Berlin, had a rule. 'Do not use gadgets - dart guns, mini-cameras and the like. If you are captured with them they cannot be explained.'

L-pills deserved a mention.

The boss man drew his knife and jabbed and pried at the heel of my right boot. The spring-loaded cavity popped open. He removed the little blue pill and held it up for me to see.

I was fresh out of wisecracks.

The boss man stood up and gestured for Dragomir's traitor to step forward. He counted out a small stack of local currency and handed it to him.

That was it? The traitor shot his comrade in the back and betrayed his tribe for beer money?

My opinion of Benedict Arnold improved a moment later when a woman of middle years emerged from the hunting shack leading a frightened little girl. They made their way across the moonlit compound gingerly.

Benedict Arnold sank to his knees. The little girl flew into his arms.

"*Nusa*," he sobbed, "*Ó mea Nusa.*"

Chapter Eight

The traitor, Captain Dragomir's spy, took his daughter in hand and walked on down the road. I lay on my back in the mud, waiting to learn my fate and wondering what the traitor would do next.

He would take his daughter home of course. But if he later reported to the Captain that I had been killed in a Magyar ambush then Dragomir, and Frank Wisner, would observe five seconds of silence and move on.

But that would be a hard story to sell. Even at a distance Dragomir would have heard the four pistol shots ring out in the dead of night. The Captain would want to know why it had taken his spy several hours to report back.

More likely Benedict Arnold would tell the Captain a slight variation of the truth. Spiru and I had been ambushed by Magyars, Spiru gunned down, me captured. Benedict Arnold had followed at a distance for a time but had been spotted and had to flee. That would explain his tardiness, and why he didn't know where I'd been hauled off to.

A nice yarn. The only loose brick was the little girl.

Would little Nusa do as Daddy said and stay quiet about her ordeal? If she didn't, word would spread quickly through her tight-knit village and Dragomir would hear the scuttlebutt in no time. Little Nusa had not been off visiting her maiden aunt, little Nusa had been kidnapped by Magyars.

The Captain would then assume the story of my capture was cooked up to cover the time it took the traitor to return home with his daughter. I hadn't been captured. The first two pistol shots had been for Spiru and the next two for me. Dragomir would likely conclude that I was beyond rescuing.

I didn't have any illusions about the Captain mounting a successful rescue in hostile territory. But Frank Wisner just might be able to move some chess pieces around the board to get me sprung. I hadn't killed anybody, not yet anyway. So long as Dragomir didn't tell him I was dead I had a chance.

So please, little Nusa, do as Daddy says and keep your adorable yap shut.

They didn't hogtie me for my next truck ride. I was given the royal treatment now that they knew I was a gen-u-ine secret agent – cuffed and blindfolded and deposited in the cab of the boss man's pickup. My guards rode in the back where they belonged.

Gargoyle Head drove for two hours or so. My Teutonic gyroscope said north and west, mostly north. They removed my blindfold once the boss man parked his truck in front of a high, carved wooden gate across a dirt driveway.

There were no sentries and only a three-wire fence on either side of the gate, intended more to keep livestock in than intruders out. We were, apparently, deep in Magyar country.

One of the guards jumped down and opened the gate. We drove in.

Expecting some version of Dragomir's fort, I was surprised to see an orange brick house with a corrugated tin roof, a barn, a hog pen and a few acres of hilly farmland dotted with yellowed tomato plants and a small vineyard.

Four young men played cards around a table covered in oilcloth. They gave me a quick once over and went back to their game. Two heavyset older men sat smoking on fold-up chairs next to the side entrance to the farmhouse. They found me considerably more interesting. The bald one said something to the hairy one that made him laugh.

None of them wore uniforms, no one was armed, yet none were dressed for farm work. They were soldiers, if not as spit-and-polish as Captain Dragomir's men.

They didn't need to be. You don't need white glove inspections to instill military discipline at platoon level when you've got *Securitate* goons and Red Army regiments to back you up.

I was, I understood, up to my chin in shit. They wouldn't have removed my blindfold and allowed me to eyeball their layout if they thought I was going to leave here alive.

My guards cinched me up under both arms and walked me into the orange brick farmhouse, blood hammering in my ears. The two heavyset men got up and followed us inside. To my surprise the boss man swung his truck around and headed back up the road. I took that to mean I was about to meet the boss man's boss.

I didn't have any illusions about my ability to stand up to torture. I'd spill my guts at the first sight of alligator clips attached to crank generator or a filet knife dipped in lye.

The only good news was that I didn't know a damn thing worth knowing. They would know all about Dragomir and his little fort. They already knew I was an American spy. My chain of command in D.C. didn't figure to interest them much. What they'd want to know was why I was here. What diabolical plot had Captain Dragomir cooked up that was worth the CIA sending me halfway round the world.

I didn't know. We had never gotten around to talking about it.

It was quite homey for a torture chamber. A country kitchen with a wood burning stove, a table draped with a colorful, hand-stitched tablecloth and framed religious icons on the walls. I recognized Saint Michael the Archangel. Bet they didn't know he was the patron saint of paratroopers.

There was a platter of food on the table. Quartered tomatoes, sliced cukes and chunks of soft cheese.

What was it about the Magyars and the Romanians? They ate the same food, they looked alike, their families had shared the mountains for umpteen generations. Why the savage enmity?

The power of words maybe. Magyars and Romanians spoke different languages and called themselves by different names.

The boss man's boss was a leathery old man with stooped shoulders and a big narrow head that, as he leaned his elbows on the table, made him look like a buzzard sizing up a meal.

There weren't any telephone lines in this part of the world that I had seen and I hadn't used my real name to anyone but Dragomir. Beats me how the old buzzard knew to say, in good English, "Welcome to Transylvania, *Domnule* Schroeder."

They dumped me in a barn stall when they were done with me. My interrogators were dumb thugs, unskilled in the black arts. Getting beat up hurts of course but it isn't *terrifying*. And they didn't know how to mete it out, take a breather, give me a sip of water. Let me ponder what was coming next.

They just beat me up. And, I'm happy to report, the body protects the brain under those circumstances. I went into shock after the first few haymakers. And then I blacked out.

The real pain comes later. When you roll over in your bed of straw and groan, feeling every thudding bruise on your body. They must have worked my gut some too.

Maybe they did understand the black arts. My tormentors had thoughtfully provided me with a bowl of cold beans and crusty bread. I was starving, I dug in. Hard to do with loose teeth.

I ate what I could then lay back in the straw. A horse snorted from somewhere close. Any minute now I would get up and mount him, bust through the barn doors and ride bareback into the Carpathian hills. Any minute now.

In the meantime I tried to get my brain to work. My tormentors barely had time to ask me any questions before they put me out. Maybe that was the plan, to introduce themselves good and proper.

They figured to take it slower the second time. They'd want to hear all about Captain Dragomir's nefarious plot. Did it involve other partisans in the mountains? What level of munitions? How much cash in what currency? What were the ins and outs of the operation and did it roll all the way down the hill to Bucharest?

I didn't know any of that, save for the last question. Neither Frank Wisner nor Sorin Dragomir would be satisfied with lighting a few bonfires in the mountains. Bucharest was their ultimate destination.

I had a decision to make. They had tossed me in the barn stall unconstrained. No cuffs. I didn't have any illusions about escaping the compound. Guards were afoot and I had nowhere to go. I wasn't keen on starring in the Punch and Judy show every day and twice on Sundays, not when I was dead meat at the end of the run.

The only way to win was to beat them to it. Every barn has a few tools scattered about. A rusty saw I could use to cut my wrists. A length of rope.

I was going to get my woebegone carcass off this straw and rummage around the barn for a suicide weapon while there was still sunlight leaking under the eaves. Any minute now. As soon as I convinced myself not to be a hero.

The real heroes, the ones who did what they didn't have to do, are all dead. That I was about to cross the Stygian Ferry didn't make me a hero. I got caught.

What might make me a minor league hero would be to absorb enough abuse so that my tormentors might believe my elaborately fabricated version of Captain Dragomir's nefarious plot, so that they and the *Securitate* goons they reported to would waste time and troops on a wild goose chase.

Elaborate fabrication. That would require ten dollars' worth of concentration at a time I didn't have a dime in the bank. But I'm a good bouncer-back. I could probably muster it after a couple hours sleep.

The question I had to answer was straightforward. Was I willing to get thumped like a bass drum in the St. Paddy's Day Parade to advance the cause of freedom and democracy?

No, I was not.

Would I suffer abuse to help decent and courageous men like Sorin Dragomir and Frank Wisner fulfill their admirable if farfetched schemes?

Yes, I believe I would.

Shuteye, Schroeder, you need sleep. You're talking crazy talk. I got my ragged breathing smoothed out and drifted off in the scratchy hay.

Chapter Nine

I was halfway out the door of my Mayflower Hotel room the morning after I returned from Frank Wisner's farm, looking forward to a day of sightseeing, when the phone rang. The hotel operator wanted to know if I would take a call from Senator Daniel Conklin's social secretary.

"Sure. I guess."

Senator Conklin's social secretary wanted to know if I was indeed Harold Schroeder.

"None other."

"Please hold."

I held. Another lady got on the blower. "Mr. Schroeder, this is Winifred Conklin. I'm sorry to be so last-minute but the Senator and I are hosting a cocktail reception this afternoon and we would be ever so pleased if you would accept our invitation to attend."

Not one to turn down free food and drink, I accepted Mrs. Conklin's invitation.

Georgetown is hilly, with brick sidewalks and two and three story shoulder-to-shoulder, 19th-century homes painted in bright yellows and pale blues. A pleasant change from the limestone monoliths downtown.

Senator Conklin's house on P Street didn't rub shoulders with its neighbors, however. A three-story white colonial with a red door and black shutters, it stood alone on a double lot, with a narrow circular driveway and a tall flagpole in front proudly flying the stars and stripes.

I looked up at the big handsome house. There were powerful people inside who wanted to make my acquaintance. It would be interesting to find out why. I wasn't nervous. If my debut on the Georgetown circuit was a flop I would take the bus back to the Mayflower Hotel, pay a lengthy visit to Winston at the Towne and Country Lounge and charge it to my room. I walked up the driveway.

Senator Conklin hailed from the Northern Plains. Why else have a snarling, eight-foot stuffed grizzly bear in your entry hall? Though the bear's head and paws did serve as a handy hat rack for those tall enough to take advantage.

On the wall to my right hung a framed and matted photo of Teddy Roosevelt on horseback, leading mounted men into battle. It was signed by TR himself. Had Senator Conklin been a Rough Rider?

You'd never know it to look at him. The Senator was a bald, gaunt old gent with one foot in the grave and the other wrapped in gauze and stuffed into a quilted house slipper. He didn't want to be seen hobbling around on a cane apparently so he used his wife's shoulder as a crutch as he stumped forward to greet me. His hand was soft, and cold as ice.

"You must be Harold Schroeder." I said that I was. "Meet Harold Schroeder, Winnie. The hero of Muhlendamm Bridge."

The what?

Mrs. Conklin looked as if she had stepped out of a 1920s' tintype in her violet dress ringed with matching fringe, her iron gray hair set in concentric curls. A *marcel* I think they call it. Age is a terrible thing. No doubt the Conklin's cut a dashing figure twenty-five years ago.

"Senator, permit me," I said, offering my arm. "We'll pretend we're war buddies from way back."

The Senator accepted my offer with a dry laugh or cough, it was hard to tell. His wife thanked me with a look. And thus I made the circuit of a jam-packed cocktail reception on P Street with the senior senator from North Dakota on my arm.

Conklin was a tough old bird. His foot was bunged up pretty bad, judging by how hard he yanked on my arm every time we had to step up or step down. Something we had to do often in the sprawling house with all its added-on rooms. But he kept a game smile on his mug as he worked the crowd.

At each stop the Senator would introduce me as Harold Schroeder, the hero of Muhlendamm Bridge. And at each stop the cluster of guests would go *Ohhhhh*.

The bridge in question spans the river Spree in East Berlin. It's the place where the Mooney boys and I – and Eva Litinov, God rest her soul – confronted a truckload of duped White Russian freedom fighters intent on attacking a Soviet armory. It was a clever NKVD ruse intended to justify a Soviet invasion of West Germany. A moment both proud and bitter for me. And largely ignored by the American press who, in 1946, still called Stalin 'Uncle Joe.'

We wound our way back to the high-beamed parlor. At the center of the room was a compact, pipe-smoking gentleman I had never met. Allen Dulles, General Wild Bill Donovan's second-in-command at the OSS. We stumped over to greet him.

Dulles wore gold-rim spectacles and a little feather duster mustache. He shook my hand and said he had heard so much about me. I blushed seven shades of crimson and dug my toe in the dirt. Then I asked him what he'd heard from our mutual friend General Donovan.

Dulles gave me a quick 'not too much' and changed the subject. I took this to mean that Allen Dulles, a Republican and a prime candidate for CIA Director if Dewey got elected, considered Wild Bill more rival than friend.

I didn't much like Allen Dulles to start with and his answer didn't improve my opinion. I didn't like him because he was snug as a bug in Bern while I was hiding behind hedgerows in Nazi Germany. I didn't like him because he was a Wall Street lawyer who, unlike Wild Bill, never tasted battle. Mostly I didn't like him because he was one of those posh gents who sail through life on a smooth line of patter and a wry smile.

I was jealous maybe.

Dulles carried me along to an imposing Englishman of about thirty-five. I'm not sure how I knew the man was a Brit exactly. The equine face perhaps. I read a quote somewhere about how to spot a British aristocrat. 'He'll either look like his dog or look like his horse.'

Dulles introduced me to the Englishman. It was Harold 'Kim' Philby, MI6's liaison to OSS in London in '42. I'd heard tales of young OSS staffers gathering in Philby's office after hours, sitting at his feet, inhaling g&t's and the great man's wisdom.

"Mr. Philby did brilliant work against the *Abwehr* early on, in concert with the Soviets," said Dulles. "Top notch, schooled us well."

Dulles gave Philby some softsoap about my important mission behind German lines but we didn't buy it, Philby and me. I was transmitting weather reports while Philby was running a Continental spy ring that broke Nazi codes and foiled sabotage that targeted Great Britain's all important lifeline. Shipping.

We chatted a while till Dulles and Philby inclined their heads. Time for the chiefs to powwow. I excused myself, grabbed a glass of bubbly from a passing tray and headed off to the kitchen to mingle with the help.

A man of middle years wearing Royal Navy ducks hovered above a tray of popovers fresh from the oven. He snagged a morsel between long fingernails and popped it into his mouth, steam leaking through his gappy teeth. "It's only hot if you think it is," he said, chewing.

"I'll keep that in mind."

The man washed it down with very tall Scotch and soda. "You don't recognize me," he said in a proper British accent.

"No, I don't. Give me a hint."

"*Ernstrasse.*"

Oh yeah. He was one of the 'handsome lads' who flocked to Col. Norwood's salon in Berlin in '46, though he looked like he'd aged ten years. He asked me if I'd heard from the Colonel.

"Not a word."

"Pity. His wife and daughter are bereft."

"Sorry to hear that," I said.

Col. John Norwood was Berlin Bureau Chief for MI6. He was also a double-dealing rat I foolishly allowed to flee to the South Seas. I turned to go but the young-old man stuck out his hand.

"Guy Burgess, Second Secretary, British Embassy," he intoned, snootily. His breath was hundred proof.

We exchanged a handshake. His hand suited him. Hot and greasy.

"Hal Schroeder," I replied, snootily. "The hero of Muhlendamm Bridge."

I fought my way back into the fray, looking to make a quick exit. My hosts stood in a corner to my right, by a table that had been pushed against the wall. On the table were three silver chafing dishes wafting meaty aromas that made my nose twitch and my mouth water.

The Conklin's were chatting with Allen Dulles and a ruddy man with a mane of white hair who had Chief Justice or Treasury Secretary written all over him. I sidled up to the chafing dishes while I waited for a lull in their conversation.

The third dish looked promising. Swedish meatballs swimming in a dark tomato sauce. I tried to spear one with a toothpick but they were tough little buggers. I'm not a man who's easily discouraged when it comes to meatballs, however.

I was about to enjoy the fruits of my labor when I noticed that I had attracted the attention of the august group in the corner.

I hoisted my meatball in salute and popped it in my mouth. It didn't taste right, but damned if I was going to spit it out in front of Allen Dulles and the Chief Justice of the Supreme Court. It took a good deal of chewing but I managed to get it down, then ankled over to say goodnight.

"Did you enjoy Danny's legendary concoction?" said Dulles from behind his spectacles.

"Delicious."

"Most people prefer them fried," said Mrs. Conklin, "but the Senator likes them stewed."

"*Them*?"

"Sheep testicles," smiled Senator Conklin.

I cringed, tasting the spongy texture on the back of my tongue, feeling the eyes of my betters upon me. They were awaiting a snappy comeback.

"I suppose it's customary to eat two."

My poor quip drew hearty laughter. Which must have caught the attention of Guy Burgess because he stumbled up and flung his arm around my shoulder.

"Is this our debutante's coming out party? I feel so underdressed!"

Burgess wasn't wearing a jacket with his navy whites and his tunic looked like a crime scene.

"Not that Harold ever seemed to mind," he leered.

I slipped my finger inside his belt and gave him a quick backward tug as I twisted out from under his arm.

Guy Burgess fell flat on his back and stayed there. We stood around and looked at him, his eyelids fluttering like moth wings. Mrs. Conklin wondered if we oughn't do something.

"Don't concern yourself," I said, "he does this all the time."

I thanked my hosts for their hospitality and, with the briefest possible nod to Allen Dulles, walked out the front door and down the steps. I waited at the northwest corner, across the street, behind a street lamp. Out of habit. Guy Burgess would get the heave-ho soon enough. It wouldn't hurt to know where he went next.

Imagine my surprise when, a short time later, prim and proper Kim Philby helped the drunken Burgess down the steps, and walked east with him on P Street. I followed.

They walked a long while, not stopping to hail a cab on busy Wisconsin Ave. Drunk or sober the Brits love their constitutionals.

They turned south on a quiet residential street. I crossed to the far side and darted from one parked car to the next, startling a young couple who were steaming up the windows of a Studebaker.

I scurried down the sidewalk, wishing I was that lucky bastard in the back seat of the car, burying my face in perfumed mounds of...oh, can it, Schroeder. Your surveillance targets just disappeared!

I beat feet down the sidewalk, head low. I almost raced past them as I scanned the intersection ahead.

Philby and Burgess had climbed the stoop of a four flat across the street and were standing by the first floor unit on the right. The light-reflecting marker was easy to read. *4001 Nebraska Avenue.*

Guy Burgess was a happy drunk, honking with laughter at his botched attempts to fit his key in the lock.

Philby showed no reaction. Was this the elder statesman frog marching his misbehaving subordinate home? Or a homosexual tryst?

I was pretty sure Kim Philby was married, not that it mattered. Being married hadn't bothered Col. Norwood much.

I had my answer in short order, down on my knees behind a Dodge coupe, squinting across a waxed hood that splintered the light from the streetlamp. Philby elbowed Burgess aside and opened the door with his own key. They went inside and shut the door.

Kim Philby and Guy Burgess were roomies.

Chapter Ten

I'm a Kraut, I'm supposed to be good at directions. But it took me almost an hour of wandering downtown Washington's circular maze to find my way back to the Mayflower. I washed up in the men's room and made a beeline for the Towne and Country Lounge. I was in luck, Winston was in residence.

"And what will you have this fine evening, Mistah Schroeder?"

"Oh, I think you know, Winston."

He flashed his blazing grin and got busy with the cocktail shaker. I suppose it's a courtesy to recognize hotel guests by name but it made me twitchy. Why was I so all-fired important all of a sudden?

Winston served me a perfect Manhattan. My mood improved. I was about to order another when a young lady took the stool to my left. We made a show of ignoring one another.

She asked Winston for a glass of rosé. He grabbed a bottle from the cooler. She asked me a question.

"Did you have a good time at the Conklin's party?"

"Why? Were you there?"

She nodded. I hadn't seen her. I would have remembered a tall shapely girl with auburn hair and Betty Boop eyes.

"My name's Julia Hammond. I'm what they call a 'stringer'."

"What's that?"

"A freelance reporter. I sell items to papers and wire services."

"That pay well?"

"Five bucks a pop."

"You make five bucks at the Conklin party?"

She shook her head. "Just another G-town shindy. You were the only one I didn't recognize."

"And that's why you're here?"

She sipped her wine and didn't answer. I wasn't going to give her a five buck item but it was pleasant to have company. Washington D.C. is a lonesome town.

"I heard you introduced as the 'hero of Muhlendamm Bridge.'"

"But my so-called heroics were more than two years ago. Why now?"

Miss Julia regarded me as if I had said something very stupid. "We're in the final weeks of a fierce campaign, the Red Menace is issue number one. And you're the blue ribbon hog at the County Fair that every pol wants to pat on the haunches while he gets his picture took."

"I didn't get my picture took."

"And how do you feel about having your haunches patted?"

I lowered my voice. "That depends?"

She lowered hers. "On what?"

"By who and how hard."

She laughed. I asked a question. "Any particular reason Allen Dulles was at the party?"

Julia hesitated. She was not in the business of giving away free information. "Winston, Miss Hammond is on my tab. Bring her another glass of wine when you get a chance."

"Yessuh."

Winston took his sweet time. Ten seconds.

Julia plucked a Salem from her purse. Winston leaned over to light it with a gold Ronson. She appreciated the attentive service. I could tell by the contented little sound she made as she feathered her hand through her long hair. Did I mention it was auburn?

"That was a Dewey crowd," she said. "Allen Dulles wants Senator Conklin to head the National Security Council in the Dewey Administration."

"Why? Conklin's an old man, just hanging on."

"That's why."

We kicked it around for a while. She was a farm girl from southern Virginia who lost her mother to cancer. She fled to the big bad city because her daddy and three younger brothers expected her to cook, clean, do the wash and milk the cows.

"I didn't fancy being Ma Kettle."

I sat back and surveyed her, north to south. "Not the least resemblance."

"Gee, thanks."

Miss Julia kept her notepad in her purse. I liked her for that. Hell, I plain liked her. She was smart and good lookin', kicking her slender strapped ankle under the bar and smelling like a hay ride through heaven.

A burst of rowdy laughter broke the spell. I looked around.

"That's the men only bar."

"Men only?"

Julia ticked her head to the left. "Over yonder. There's a sign above the mirror."

"I'll be damned."

"You don't have men only bars where you come from?"

"Sure, we have men only bars in Cleveland. But we don't need a sign." I hesitated. Would she laugh at a crude joke? "Green cigars and beer farts work just fine."

She would.

I asked Winston for a second Manhattan. We watched him work. Two jiggers of Jack, a half jigger of sweet vermouth, dash of bitters. Shaken in ice and served in a chilled martini glass with a maraschino cherry.

We made pleasant conversation as I made Winston's Manhattan go away. She didn't talk too much or laugh too loud. I was in a mellow mood when she asked me who I liked for President.

"Not Truman."

"Why not?"

"Because Truman disbanded the OSS in late '45, with ten days notice. He thought spying was un-American. And we've been at the back of the parade marching through horse flop ever since."

"So we're losing the Cold War?"

I told myself to shut my yap. But I was drunk and smitten enough to tell the truth.

"If this were a prizefight the ref would've stopped it two rounds ago."

Room service woke me the next morning at an ungodly hour.

"I didn't order room service," I croaked.

"Roomey service, Meester Schroeder, roomey service!" insisted the high-pitched voice.

I got up and padded to the door, expecting my Jack Daniel's hangover to catch up to me. But Winston, bless him, had let my ill-advised third Manhattan mellow in the ice of the cocktail shaker.

I threw open the door. "I did not...oh shit."

Bill Harvey bulled his way past me carrying a white bag and a folded up newspaper. He handed me the bag. "Heller's Bakery, best doughnuts in town."

I grabbed a warm cruller from the sack and took a bite. Delicious, but no coffee. Who eats doughnuts without coffee?

"I hope you're good with a dueling pistol, Schroeder, because you just spit a wad of tobacco juice in the eye of a Southern gentleman by the name of Frank Wisner."

He handed me the newspaper, folded to page three. **Uncle Sam a Punch-drunk Pug, says Cold War Hero.**

Byline, Julia Hammond. Five buck item my ass.

"Why would Wisner give a shit what I say?"

"Because he's Cold Warrior Number One," said Harvey. "And he's paying for your hotel room."

Bill parked his rear end on the side of the bed and bit off half a sugar doughnut. When he was done chewing he said, "There are only two men in this town with hard power."

I had to wait another half a doughnut to find out who they were.

"J. Edgar Hoover and Frank Wisner."

"Not the President?"

Harvey snortled, which is somewhere between a chortle and a snort. "The President's naked to the world – photographers, stenographers, biographers. He tries to have you clipped and it comes back to bite him."

"Clipped? Frank Wisner's going to have me *killed*?"

"Unlikely. But the thing to remember about the Director of OPC is that, even more than Hoover, he's unsupervised. The higher-ups don't want to know. We've never had a government official that powerful in the history of the United States."

True enough. I had done my due diligence in the back stacks of the Cleveland Library after I accepted Frank Wisner's invite to D.C. I read the charter of his new Office of Policy Co-ordination and remembered one chilling line in particular.

It said OPC operations must be conducted so that the President and the executive branch *could plausibly disclaim any responsibility.*

Harvey stood up and brushed powdered sugar off his front. "Lay low, don't answer the phone, don't call room service. I'll try to smooth out the wrinkles."

"And what do I do for food and drink?"

"You got doughnuts and a water faucet."

"Very funny," I said, moving to block the door. "Fork it over, I know you're packin'."

Harvey grumbled and reached inside his coat. He handed me a shiny silver flask.

"I am eternally in your debt," I said, "but one last question. Why all this room service? What makes me so goddamn special?"

Harvey looked out the window. The dawn was pink and gray with fog. "Though it pains me to say so, Schroeder, you're my hero."

"Good one Bill."

"No, it's true," said Harvey, nodding his great bovine head. "You made that sonofabitch Hoover look stupid two years ago and you have lived to tell the tale. So far."

Chapter Eleven

I got hungry and bored hiding in my room at the Mayflower. It was 5 p.m. on a Tuesday, who's gonna know? I took the service elevator to the lobby. I saw no sign of newshounds, just a few well-fed gents bellied up to the Towne and Country Bar. Their name badges read *Iowa City Chamber of Commerce*.

I was pleasantly surprised to see Winston behind the bar. I ordered dinner and a beer. I didn't need any more hard stuff after nipping at Harvey's flask all afternoon.

With the slightest twitch of an eyebrow Winston indicated I had company. A large man wearing a floppy black hat took the barstool to my left. He wore an expensive pinstriped suit.

"You are Mr. Harold Schroeder?" lisped the man. He was about forty, with a flat pale face and a wide clownish mouth. He spoke with a Russian accent. "You are heem?"

"Yeah, yeah, I am heem." I asked how he knew where to find me.

"Everyone says you are here."

And here I was, parked on my barstool in the Towne and Country Lounge, the Harold Schroeder anti-Communist Command Center.

I leaned over and grabbed the Russian's wrist, hard, felt his pulse hammering. I suppose it was rude of me to be so rude but I have a checkered history with Russians in Savile Row suits.

"And who are you, comrade?"

He said his name was Nikolai Savayenko, that he was an attaché to the Russian Ambassador here in Washington.

I released his wrist. He slid a photograph my way – a little girl sitting on a woman's lap – as his eyes searched the mirror behind the bar.

"Who is this?"

"My wife Maria and my daughter Tina. We want to defect to your country."

This got my attention. "Why come to me, Mr. Savayenko? Why not go..."

"My wife is ill with heart condition, very rare. There is surgeon, at the Georgetown Hospital, who can help her."

"Why not just check her in?"

"She is in Leningrad."

Well it's never easy, is it? This was a lot to chew and digest on short notice. I didn't know who or what this guy was. With the Reds you never know where the real power lies. The Ambassador's chauffeur might outrank the Ambassador.

"I'm not a government official, Nikolai."

"This is why I come! You are a man of action, not talk! The others I know, the diplomats, I cannot trust their indecision."

I took a closer look at the photo, my eyes drawn to little Tina, a bright-eyed cutie with ringlets shooting off in all directions. I could act as an intermediary with Wisner I suppose. But...

"We still use the barter system over here, Nikolai. You give me something of value, I give you something back."

"I will give you a complete lisstt of Soviet agents operating in USA," said Nikolai, leaning in, spraying saliva.

"Legals?" I said. "Or illegals?"

The CIA knew who the legal Soviet agents were. Anyone who worked for the Soviet Embassy. Illegal agents posing as everyday citizens did the real damage – the clerk in the State Department mail room, the typist in the DoD secretarial pool, the lab tech at Los Alamos National Laboratory.

"The illegals," said Nikolai, just like that.

Good God, the motherload! We studied the mirror behind the bar. No one was paying us the least attention.

I gave Winston the nod. He stepped forward to take Nikolai's order. Shot of Smirnoff. And again.

The preferred method of exfiltration of foreign assets was submarine. Not possible in the northern Baltic this time of year. Nikolai's wife and daughter couldn't escape overland through a thousand miles of Soviet checkpoints and we wouldn't violate Soviet airspace to snatch them. There was a slim chance Wisner could engineer a swap, but first things first.

"We need to get you out of here, Nikolai. Too public. Let's go up to my room and..."

He shook his head. "I need first to speak to your Mr. Vizner."

"Fine. We'll go up to my room and call him."

But Nikolai was eyeing the mirror again. I followed his look. A familiar face, wearing a rumpled suit, straggled up to the other end of the bar as if climbing a steep hill. Damned if it wasn't Guy Burgess.

Nikolai turned his face away. He had recognized Kim Philby's friend.

I caught Winston's eye and inclined my head.

A good bartender is a rare and glorious thing. Winston quick stepped down the bar and greeted the disheveled Brit like a long lost friend, giving me a moment to issue instructions.

"Tomorrow, Lincoln Memorial, nine a.m."

Nikolai Savayenko squeezed my hand before he turned and hurried off, the brim of his floppy black hat pulled low.

Chapter Twelve

If you ask me Abe Lincoln drew the short straw in the monument derby. The Washington Monument soars high above the D.C. skyline. A bronze Jefferson towers above the visitors to his memorial dome. Only the rawboned rail-splitter sits on his marble keester, deep in shadow.

I gaped up at him. He looked depressed.

Honest Abe had drawn a fair crowd of visitors for a Tuesday morning in October, mostly school kids on a bus tour. I looked around for Nikolai.

Ah, there he was, his back to me, about ten yards away. There was no mistaking that dumb floppy hat.

Only he had shrunk a few inches. And dropped fifty pounds.

I felt a clutch of dread in my gut as I approached the hat wearer. He was a boy about fourteen. His teacher reached him before I did.

"Donald, what in the world?"

"It was just sittin' there, Miss Hazelton, on the bench!"

"Well you put it back where you found it."

Young Donald galumphed over to the marble bench by the front entrance and threw down the hat.

He needn't have bothered. Nikolai Savayenko wouldn't need it anytime soon. The message from the NKVD was clear. The greatest potential catch in the history of American intelligence was now deceased.

I felt cold eyes watching as I ankled out the entryway. A thick line of trees bordered the reflecting pool straight ahead, convenient cover for watchers.

I didn't give the Blue Caps the satisfaction they sought, didn't run down the steps in a panic. I took my time, then turned at the bottom of the stairway to stare up at the pillared edifice in which the proudest son of the heartland sat parked on his duff.

As a fellow Midwestern bumpkin I couldn't help feeling I had let the great man down.

I strode the length of the National Mall on a windswept day that couldn't make up its mind – cloudy one minute, sunny the next. I was angry with myself. I shouldn't have let Nikolai walk even if it meant putting him in a hammerlock and marching him upstairs.

The NKVD knew that Nikolai was ripe for 'imperialist conversion' because of his wife's illness. That his family didn't accompany him to his foreign posting indicated his superiors didn't fully trust him. He would have been under surveillance. His unauthorized visit to a decadent D.C. watering hole was all they would need to know.

Maybe. But it was thin gruel. Even the Blue Caps needed more than a visit to the T&C Lounge to justify a wet job in a foreign capital. Someone must have informed the NKVD that Nikolai was headed to the Mayflower in an attempt to establish contact with yours truly.

Nikolai was dead when he walked in the door. Or, more precisely, when I let him walk out.

I was Nikolai's proxy assassin. He was snuffed for the crime of speaking to me. But his real executioner was the person who sent him my way.

My question to Nikolai had been right on the money.

Why come to me?

Nikolai was steered, that's why. Sidled up to at a diplomatic reception by someone who knew he was frustrated and ripe to cross over, someone saying, 'I can't help you personally but may I make a suggestion? Take your case to Hal Schroeder, he has the ear of Frank Wisner, he's easy to get to. And, by the way, it would be better if Mr. Schroeder thought this was your idea, not mine.'

A twofer. Eliminate Nikolai and reduce my reputation to a smoking hole. Guy Burgess appeared just in time to flush Nikolai from the plush confines of the Harold Schroeder anti-Communist Command Center.

Burgess wanted the Russian neutralized because he feared Nikolai would expose him. Burgess wanted me discredited because I knew he was an intimate of Col. Norwood, who fled Berlin after I caught him working both sides.

Of course the person who sidled up to Nikolai couldn't be on Nick's list of known Soviet agents, as Burgess likely was. Burgess would have needed a front man.

Hard to see how it could be anyone but his roomie, MI6 legend Kim Philby. Philby was beyond reproach. If Philby was dirty Nikolai wouldn't have known. If Philby was dirty only Lavrenty Beria and Josef Stalin would know.

Guilt by association, assassination by proxy.

Well, two can play at that game. The apartment on Nebraska Avenue would be watched. Beria, in his dark and devious heart, had to suspect that this decadent British aristocrat was playing him, that Burgess was that rarest of birds, a triple agent. Reporting to Burgess' apartment immediately after my big meet went bust would confirm that suspicion.

Yes, this was a wonderful plan, the new way of the world. Don't get your hair mussed or your hands dirty, young fella, become a proxy assassin. Enlist today!

I stopped at a newstand. It was possible I had gotten ahead of myself. Nikolai had been found out but it didn't necessarily mean he was dead.

The story on the front page of the *Washington Times-Herald* quoted the Soviet Ambassador. Embassy attaché Nikolai Savayenko had thrown himself into the Potomac river upon learning of the death of his wife in Leningrad. She had died of heart failure.

Sure she had.

This is what we were up against. An enemy willing to kill an invalid to justify the murder of her husband.

I muttered dark curses and swore bloody vengeance. And not for the Soviet diplomat who had been bundled into a car by NKVD goons and dumped off a pier in the dead of night.

Anyone who's tasted combat enjoys poking fun at the blue-sky cookie-pushers in the State Department. There are, however, no blue-sky cookie-pushers in the Soviet diplomatic service. There aren't even any diplomats, not really. They're all members of the *Cheka*, an acronym for Committee to Combat Counter-revolution or somesuch. Imagine the FBI, CIA and State Department all rolled into one tight-knuckled fist.

So I didn't swear vengeance for Nikolai Sayavenko. I was angry for the bright-eyed girl in the photograph, little Tina, now consigned to some dreary Soviet orphanage to be fed a diet of cold porridge and correct thinking.

I dumped the paper in a trash can and continued walking east. Guy Burgess figured to be sleeping it off at half past nine in the morning. Could be he'd slam the door in my face. I *had* dumped him on his backside at the Conklin's party.

Then again I had maintained decorum by not shoving his mug into the tureen of sheep testicles.

It's been my experience that scumbags generally keep a strict ledger of these things.

4001 Nebraska Avenue NW was a leg-stretcher and then some. I stood on the sidewalk and stretched my back when I arrived, stood there long enough for the NKVD to get a few snaps from whatever apartment window they were holed up in.

I climbed brick steps and knocked on the door of the apartment I had seen Philby and Burgess enter two nights ago. First floor, on the right.

I knocked again. No answer. Burgess was probably zzz'ed out with a pillow over his head. I crowded closer to quick pick the cheesy lock while pretending to wait for the door to open.

I opened the door, made gestures appropriate to being welcomed, entered the apartment and closed the door behind me.

The parlor was a mess, stuff everywhere. I went to a back bedroom. Chaos. The place had been tossed!

Maybe not. I heard a toilet flush. My first instinct was to bolt but I told myself to grow some gonads. It would be swell if they got pix of us leaving the apartment together.

Guy Burgess stepped out of the bathroom in his boxer shorts. His hair and face were wet.

"Oh good, you're here," I said, cheerily.

Burgess, bleary-eyed, was speechless.

"I wanted to give you a heads up in case you hadn't heard. Nikolai Savayenko - Soviet attaché, guy I was trying to recruit in the Towne and Country Lounge yesterday - he was fished out of the Potomac this morning. We were among the last people to see him alive. I'm afraid the cops will trace his steps back to me."

Burgess shook his head to clear the cobwebs. "What are you doing here?"

"I just explained that."

"Well say it again. Slowly."

I walked him through it again, admiring the gutsiness of Burgess' plan. His walking in on my confab with Nikolai had risked raising my antennae. He covered that by pretending to be a hungover zombie. Well, he *was* a hungover zombie, but a timely one.

"I don't remember any of that," said Burgess.

"The point is we need to come to an agreement."

Burgess went to his dresser and grabbed a starched and folded dress shirt. From his closet he selected a charcoal gray suit and a red bowtie. The dark suit was a good choice. He could spill food down his front and no one would notice.

Burgess didn't speak till he had assembled himself in front of the dresser mirror. "What sort of an agreement?"

"An agreement that we never saw Nikolai Savayenko in the Towne and Country Lounge."

"How does that work?"

"The other patrons were tourists and the barkeep was Winston."

"The Negro?"

"The same."

"And he'll keep his mouth shut?"

"He will."

Burgess affixed black pearl cufflinks and a matching tie tack, chewed up a breath mint, then turned to face me with a smile thin as shaved ice.

"And pray tell me, Mr. Schroeder, why I should give a flaming fuck?"

I hung my head. "As a favor to me," I said, simpered. "I don't want to be known as the man who let Nikolai Savayenko get dumped in the river."

This was all terribly complicated. Me, hat in hand, attempting to win the co-operation of my adversary in order to derail a smear attempt against *myself* that my adversary *himself* had engineered. Would Guy Burgess recognize the irony, walk it back and glom that I was in on the joke and messing with him? Or would he simply bask in my humiliation?

It didn't much matter, he'd be fish food by tonight. But I wanted to know if Burgess was any good.

It takes patience. Imagine looking at the reflection of a pleasant someone in a standing full-length mirror, in a long hall of standing mirrors that stretch to infinity. The pleasant someone appears identical in every diminishing reflection until, suddenly, at reflection number thirty-two, say, his appearance changes, his affable grin becomes a fanged snarl.

Guy Burgess didn't have the patience for it. He nodded smirking agreement to my pathetic plea, then looked at his watch and cursed.

"You have a car?"

"Got a cab waiting," I lied.

"I need it."

"It's all yours." Burgess started for the door.

"Shoes," I said, drolly.

Burgess looked down and busted out laughing.

We spilled out of the flat, cackling merrily. My non-existent taxi wasn't there. I cursed the wretched driver and stood on the corner to hail another. Now that Burgess and I were best pals I ventured a question.

"Frank Wisner is after me to background his Romanian royals, King Michael and Princess Stela. You got anything?"

This was supposed to be a standard mirror read. The Romanians were dirty in inverse proportion to the degree that double agent Burgess defended their honor. Only he didn't. Not hers anyway.

"Stela Varadja?"

I nodded. He snorted.

"Better watch yourself with her pretty boy. She'll suck your blood down to the marrow and you'll enjoy every delicious moment. Just ask Maurice Thorez."

I suppose I could have asked who Maurice Thorez was but I had humbled myself enough for one day.

A taxi driver saw my raised hand and slid to the curb. Guy Burgess piled into the back seat. I waved him an affectionate farewell as the hackie sped south.

If you listened hard you could just about hear the NKVD camera shutter clicking below the telephoto lens.

Chapter Thirteen

My internal alarm clock failed me. I slept like the dead in the barn stall until my cold shower at the break of day - a bucket of water dumped on my head by one of the young soldiers. He was gone before I could thank him.

It's showtime, guv'nor, rise and shine now. No need to memorize your lines because that other Mr. Schroeder, the playwright, 'e never got round to writing 'em! 'Fraid you'll have to bail him out again, seat-o'-your-pants like.

I wasn't sure why an imaginary cockney gentleman was giving me a pep talk just then but it did the trick. I knew what I had to do. When asked a specific question by my interrogators I would deny knowledge, suffer punishment, then cough up some nonsense that I would try to remember for next time.

I was free to make shit up. They wouldn't have any NKVD fact checkers up here in the hills.

A few minutes later I was handcuffed in front and escorted to my customary seat at the table in the country kitchen and given a cup of coffee so strong I couldn't blink for an hour. The old buzzard, the boss man's boss, sat at the head of the table, his two heavyset armbreakers stood on either side of him.

A tableau worthy of a Renaissance master. They looked at me and said nothing.

Guess it was my turn. I wanted to establish my bona fides to make them more inclined to believe my disinformation so I volunteered intel they already knew, or would figure out.

"My name is Harold Schroeder. I am a special agent of the Office of Policy Co-ordination, which is a semi-independent covert operations arm of the CIA. I report to Frank Wisner, the director of OPC. I was sent here to liaise with Captain Sorin Dragomir, to assess the readiness of his squad in the event that OPC might want to offer logistical support for a future, yet-to-be-determined mission."

I paused to see how this was going over. Blank stares from the armbreakers. Doubtful they knew more English than 'okay' and 'Mickey Mouse.' But the old buzzard seemed to understand some of what I said. I concluded with, "And that is all I'm prepared to say."

The old buzzard used his long ropy arms to push himself up off his chair. His legs were little more than bowed sticks but his upper body was still strong, as if he'd been on crutches most of his life. I saw that his black eyes were afire as he slowly made his way to my end of the table. His armbreakers started to follow but he waved them off. He wanted me all to himself.

I felt a strong and visceral dislike for this old creep. I knew I should submit to abuse in order to win the opportunity to sow disinformation. I also knew that if this son-of-a-whore raised his leathery mitt to smack me I would jump up, lock my cuffed hands behind his neck and use the peak of my brow to drive his nasal cavity deep into his forebrain which, according to Fearless Dan, our hand-to-hand instructor at spy school, usually does the trick.

But the old buzzard hadn't made it to a ripe old age by pushing his luck. He stopped short of throttling range and cleared his throat by way of a ragged cough followed by a putrid belch. He showed me black gums and yellow teeth.

"Do not concern yourself, Mr. Schroeder, with your preparation."

I didn't take his meaning, looked confused.

"Your preparation to speak, that is our task."

Oh, shit. I pictured pliers and power drills, serrated knives.

But it wasn't like that. The armbreakers merely cuffed me to the back of the chair and took turns slapping me silly when I declined the answer the old buzzard's questions about Captain Dragomir's nefarious plot.

They paced themselves this time, dumping water on my head when I pretended to pass out. I would come to and beg for mercy, absorb a few more smacks then blurt out some bullshit the old buzzard wrote down on a pad of paper.

The whole thing felt like an act, like a dress rehearsal for the real thing. I suffered the abuse okay. It stung like hell until it didn't. They weren't doing any permanent damage, that's all I cared about.

And laying on a beating isn't like twisting the dial of a generator that's alligator clipped to your scrotum. It's personal, your tormentors feel the impact of each blow. And they get tired.

The armbreakers ran out of steam after an hour or so and looked to the boss man for further instruction. He had filled three pages of note paper with my ramblings. The old buzzard answered by stumping over to a sideboard and grabbing a bottle filled with dark purple liquid.

My torture had just begun. The bottle was filled with plum brandy.

I liked the boss man a lot better after a few pops. He even allowed me a chunk of cheese to quell the bonfire in my empty gut started by the purple gasoline. My ears rung and my cheeks burned but I was okay.

Come to find out the old buzzard had learned some English during World War One when he worked with the Central Powers against Great Britain and the U.S. He learned some more English in World War Two when he worked with Great Britain and the U.S. against the Axis. But the political winds had shifted once again. The fascists had been defeated. The Yanks and Brits were the new-old bad guys.

I asked him why that was, why the Magyars subscribed to Marxist-Leninist ideology. He didn't seem to know what that was so I asked him why his people sided with the Communists. His explanation was straightforward.

"When *Nazişti* took power the Iron Guard killed our families. Now it is our turn."

He recounted grisly tales of Iron Guard atrocities during the war as we drank *ţuică*. I only remember one story. How they rounded up folks in one village and used the electric saws at a meat packing plant to process the entire population, men, women and children.

Man oh man.

Frank Wisner's worldwide clash of ideologies seemed a distant hum out here in the Carpathian Mountains. It seemed to me the real conflict was tribal hatred, and the settling of old scores.

I was encouraged by our conversation. Why would the old buzzard tell me his people weren't fire-breathing Bolshies unless he wanted me to pass it along up the chain of command? He was reaching out, he wanted to bridge the gap between the fierce Magyars and the buttoned down warriors of the Central Intelligence Agency. I wasn't going to be dragged out into a field and forced to dig my own grave.

That's what I told myself in my plummy haze. It was a good feeling that lasted until the old buzzard poured himself a fresh one and crowbarred himself off his chair. The armbreakers stood with him. They hoisted their glasses. I hoisted mine in response.

The old man said something in Hungarian. The only word I recognized was *Securitate*.

I drained my glass because that's what you do when somebody makes a toast, but it made no sense. The infamous greeting to the Emperor given by Roman gladiators as they entered the Coliseum came to mind.

We who are about to die salute you.

I ate a last supper of cold beans and crusty bread. And more plum brandy. I was permitted a spoon this time. Then they dumped me in a swayback bed in a tiny upstairs bedroom, cuffed to the bedposts wrist and ankle.

I should have killed myself when I had the chance. I should have made a mad dash for it and got myself shot, or wrestled the gun away from my pursuer and done the deed myself. The *Securitate* weren't going to play patty cake like the Magyars. They would get down to business.

The human body is such a cantankerous machine. The brain can't make the heart or the other vital organs stop producing consciousness. The brain needs the co-operation of the extremities to do that via gun, knife or L-pill. Kinda makes you wonder who's in charge.

I would have one last chance. They had to uncuff me in the morning. I could follow Fearless Dan's instructions for quickly debilitating an opponent. Simultaneous knee to the groin and under-the-chin palm shot followed by a two-thumb eye gouge.

Yes siree. And I would do the same to the other half a dozen security goons in attendance provided they waited their turn.

Fearless Dan also taught us how to painstakingly roll a newspaper into a lethal dagger. Perhaps I could ask for the latest edition of The Times of London when served my morning tea.

I rolled over and passed out.

God bless plum brandy.

Chapter Fourteen

My proxy assassin gambit was a bust. Guy Burgess' NKVD minders didn't know, or care, that I'd paid him a visit.

I checked the papers the following morning, had a late breakfast, then called the British Embassy about eleven. Posing as a reporter I asked to speak to the Second Secretary. Guy Burgess was on the line in no time, sounding decidedly undead. I hung up in his ear.

I couldn't figure it. I *knew* Burgess was a two-timing rat.

Smarten up, Schroeder, the Blue Caps knew it too, knew that Burgess was, in fact, a human train wreck. They would take what he gave them with a fat grain of salt and wouldn't bother with surveillance. If my suspicions were correct they had someone else to keep an eye on him. His roommate, Kim Philby.

I was now, it must be admitted, a complete and utter screw-up. Nikolai was dead, Guy Burgess free as a bird. I could slink back to Cleveland and hide in the back stacks of the Public Library. Or I could confess my sins to Frank Wisner and take the Romanian job as penance.

I suspected it had to be the second option. I had sworn bloody vengeance for Nikolai's bright-eyed young daughter. But I wanted to butt heads with Bill Harvey one last time. Maybe he could talk some sense into me.

Harvey hadn't been in touch since he left my hotel room to try and patch things up between me and Frank Wisner. I had no way to call him. He wouldn't want me calling through the CIA central switchboard and he hadn't given me his private line.

I found the D.C. phone book in a desk drawer and paged through on the off chance that Harvey's home number was listed.

An instructor at spy school enjoyed telling the story of a Turkish agent for the Axis powers whose cover was professor of archeology at some prestigious university in Constantinople. The *Abwehr* provided him with elegant, gilt-edged business cards to that effect, which he passed out enthusiastically. The Professor could not, however, resist adding a sticker on the reverse side of the card that promoted his real business. Ali Babba's Carpets.

The moral of the story was don't assume your adversary isn't an idiot.

Sadly, William King Harvey was not. He wasn't listed in the phone book. I would have to get to him some other way.

Harvey worked in counterintelligence but I had no idea where the CI unit was housed. They wouldn't be in the phone book either. I sat at the desk in my room at the Mayflower and stared at the telephone and spun fanciful scenarios. The phone stared back at me. It had nicely labeled buttons. Front Desk. Room Service. Bellhop. Concierge.

I wasn't sure what a concierge was but it was the only one with a red button so I picked up the receiver and pushed it.

"Good morning, Mr. Schroeder, how may we assist you?"

I had the address of the counterintelligence offices of the CIA twenty minutes later.

I got dressed and went down to the lobby at a quarter to five, shielding my eyes as I passed the Towne and Country Lounge. Executing proper tradecraft, I zigzagged several blocks on foot. Didn't matter. No one liked me anymore.

I hailed a taxi at the corner of 17th and N Street. I gave the hackie the address of the CI building and waved a five dollar bill at him.

"Hope your wife can wait dinner, Mac, I might need you for a while."

The driver, a slight man with greasy salt and pepper hair, said, "My wife's been waitin' dinner since we got hitched."

"You log a lot of overtime?"

"That's one reason."

"What's another reason?"

"She can't cook."

We found the address on Euclid, an old box that looked like a leftover army barracks. We turned left, saw the parking lot in back and set up shop on the far curb. The street was one way with corner stop signs as far as the eye could see. Excellent.

I shot the breeze with my driver and settled in for a long wait. Harvey didn't figure to be the type who clocked out at closing time.

But he waddled out the back door not ten minutes later and motored out of the parking lot a minute after that. He drove a black Cadillac Fleetwood, the Stars and Stripes flying from the radio antenna.

"Okay, Mac, here's the drill. We tail the Caddy at a distance for two blocks, then close in quick at the third stop sign and lean on the horn. Our guy will turn around to look and I'll jump out."

"Sure thing."

In fact Harvey gunned his V-8 down the one-way street and slid through the first two stops sign so quick my driver had to floor his old Plymouth to keep pace.

Apparently Harvey remembered his training. Wanna know if you're being tailed? Start running!

Harvey busted the third stop sign completely and fishtailed right. A slow-moving sedan that followed him through the intersection kept us at bay for precious seconds. I stuck my head out the window when we made the turn. The Fleetwood was gone.

My driver was game, preparing to whip around the sedan and continue pursuit. But we weren't going to run Harvey to ground in this heap.

"Forget it, we lost him."

He eased up on the accelerator and slumped back. "What now?"

"My fin get me back to the Mayflower Hotel?"

"Sure."

The cabbie started to swing a U-turn and almost got broadsided by a fast-moving Caddy flying the American flag.

Crap on toast. I would never hear the end of this.

I gave the cabbie the fiver and climbed into the front seat of the Fleetwood. We drove north.

"Nice shag job," grunted Harvey.

I gave him a minute to gloat before I said, "Does the most powerful man in America plan to have me clipped or doesn't he?"

"No. As it turns out, your quote about us losing the Cold War strengthened Frank Wisner's hand."

"Nice of you to let me know." We struggled through cross traffic for two blocks, half the town going home for dinner, the other half going out. "I'm taking that Romanian job."

"Suit yourself," said Harvey, left hand on the wheel, right hand drumming against his thigh. "But don't forget the Cold War is fought mostly on the front page. The Reds have a fairytale they want to peddle to the poor and miserable the world over. Only Commies care about proles, peasants and peons."

"Bill!" I said at the sight of a teen girl crossing in the middle of the block.

"I see her."

Harvey laid on the horn. Or horns. The Fleetwood sounded like the Queen Mary sailing into New York harbor.

The girl flapped her arms and ran screaming across the street. We drove on.

"You see what I mean?" said Harvey.

"Not really."

"If I had run over that girl in my big black Caddywacker while gassing about my heartfelt concern for the little people, you'd think me a fat bag of wind."

I bypassed the obvious reply and thought it through.

"You're saying Frank Wisner plans to cram local freedom fighters into the Red Army meat grinder just to score a PR coup?"

"I'm asking a question," said Harvey. "Does he back every wild ass bomb thrower who comes along? How is anyone, even a God-fearing man like Frank Wisner, supposed to make the right call about supporting anti-Communist insurgents when he knows that he wins a military victory if they win and a propaganda victory if they lose?"

Bill Harvey had a valid point. A point of morality. Not what you'd expect from a drunken wildebeest.

He punched the cigarette lighter, fished out a crumpled pack of Pall Malls and tossed them over. "There's one left."

"I don't smoke."

Harvey's irritated wheeze rumbled deep in his chest. "Extract the last remaining cigarette, Harold, straighten it up and hand it back."

"Oh. Sure."

Harvey lit his wobbly Pall Mall with some difficulty and settled back at the wheel. We drove a block at twenty-five miles an hour.

"I'd bypass all that in-country horseshit if I was Director of OPC," said Harvey. "You're not gonna beat the Red Army in their own backyard. The better way to play it would be to round up some poor dumb ex-pat bastards, misbrief them and drop 'em in."

I understood the misbriefing reference. USAF daylight B-17 bombing runs over Germany in '43 had no cover, the distance to target was too great for the fighter planes of that time. The result was a brutal rate of attrition. There were rumors that bomber crews were given phony intel about future targets in the likely case they were captured and interrogated.

"That's poor dumb bastard, singular. I'll be the one with the parachute."

Harvey checked his watch. "Better hurry over to Frank's office then, don't want to be late for your misbriefing."

"You're a riot, Harvey. Maybe you can drop me off on your way to your daily squeal session with J. Edgar Hoover."

Bill didn't like my joke for some reason. He smoked the Cadillac to a stop in the middle of the street. Horns honked.

"Out of my car asshole."

I climbed out and leaned down. "Sorry Bill, I…"

He sped off. I hoofed it back to the Mayflower, thinking that Harvey hadn't talked any sense into me whatsoever. He'd given me a reason to go, not stay.

I might save some lives. Wisner's Romanian resistance group wasn't going to get a thumbs up from me unless they were crackerjack and battle-tested, unless their leader was up to the task.

I wouldn't say no just to say no, they deserved the benefit of the doubt. A scrappy middleweight can KO a top-ranked heavyweight every once in a great while. Ask Gene Tunney about Harry Greb.

But I didn't expect to find a scrappy middleweight in Romania. I expected to find a money-grubbing fight manager touting a flyweight with a glass jaw.

Chapter Fifteen

I was hauled into the backseat of a khaki-colored four-door sedan the following morning by three *Securitate* bruisers. They cuffed me behind my back but didn't bother with a blindfold. We drove further north, deeper into the mountains, crawling up gravel roads beneath sheer rock walls papered with gray-green lichen.

My minders, two in front, one in back, acted as if they were on a ski vacation, passing a thermos of spiked coffee around, laughing and joking, oblivious to the plunging canyons that crowded the narrow road and scared the bejesus out of a flatlander like me.

I was being taken to a remote location. A place where my screams would not be overheard, a place where my corpse would draw no notice. A grim prospect to be sure. Why then did the bruiser in the passenger's seat, when we reached a lush green valley on the other side of the mountain, twist his hairy neck around to give me a wink?

My question was answered a short time later when we turned into a well-maintained, down-sloped driveway lined with trees. We drove a bit before rounding a bend and pulling up to a most unexpected structure. A stone cottage. A one-story building with walls of pink granite veined with gray and a roof of black slate, a small blue lake shimmering behind it.

The driver parked the car. His pals smoothed their hair and made themselves presentable. They walked me to the rounded oaken door and used a heavy iron door knocker to announce their presence.

The woman who yanked open the door wore the drab uniform of a domestic. She was broad-shouldered and sour-faced. She said something curt in Romanian. The men shrugged and shuffled, then snapped to when the lady of the house appeared.

I can't say I was expecting her exactly but a pink granite cottage on a lake was clearly not a *Securitate* holding pen so I didn't faint over when the lady of the house, looking splendidly relaxed in open-toed sandals and a mid-calf dress with diagonal stripes that highlighted her tiny, belted waist, said, "*Monsieur* Schroeder, hallo. It is again my pleasure to see you."

"Thank you, Princess Stela, but I beg to differ. The pleasure is entirely mine."

Chapter Sixteen

Princess Stela regarded me with frowning concern. I must have looked as bad as I felt. The driver pulled a folded paper from his coat pocket and handed it to her. I was a package that had to be signed for.

She said something to the man in Romanian, her tone sharp. He patted his pockets furiously. So did his comrades. No pen.

The hardbitten *Securitate* thugs squirmed under the gimlet stare of a young woman who couldn't ring up 110 on the bathroom scale if she jumped up and down soaking wet.

The maid produced a pen from somewhere. Stela unfolded the paper and spun her finger in a circle, slowly. The driver grumbled and turned around. The Princess used the back of his coat as a desk.

Well, well. It looked as if I was going to be spared Lavrenty Beria's iron fist in favor of Princess Stela Varadja's velvet glove. No complaints here. But knowing the how and why of this stunning turn of events would have to wait. The last few days had suddenly caught up with me. It was all I could do to keep vertical until the *Securitate* handed over a manila envelope and lumbered off.

The broad-beamed maid must have seen my knees a-knockin' because she took hold of my arm and half-carried me through the living room, down a hall past the kitchen and into a small bedroom on the left. A small bedroom with a big window that looked out over the blue lake and the green and purple mountains in the distance.

The maid - Ilinca I think Stela called her - plunked me down on the foot of the bed and set about unlacing my boots. Stela breezed in and asked if I needed anything.

"Glass of milk," I wheezed. "Biggest glass of milk you ever saw."

Stela breezed off, leaving Ilinca to the task of stripping my clothes off and rolling me into bed. I tried to help but I was spent. You don't realize how much energy it takes to hornswaggle yourself into believing you've got a shot at survival until you actually *do* have a shot at survival and you feel your body shed its armor and collapse in a heap.

A man appeared with a tall glass of milk after I was tucked in. Though he wore a white chef's tunic, a stained apron and blousy checkered pants, he didn't look like a chef. He was skinny and pale, with cold eyes that took pictures of everything they saw.

Time to armor up again, Schroeder. The chef is an NKVD agent. So's the maid. Bill Harvey's suggestion that Princess Stela had Communist sympathies was correct. It's why I was here. Stela Varadja was a Soviet Mata Hari.

Princess Stela breezed in again, in that gliding ballet slipper way she had. She sized up the situation. Me casting a wary eye, the chef proffering the glass of milk, the maid hovering.

Stela stood behind them and held a white finger to her purple lips. She flicked a glance at the dome light on the ceiling.

I was to shut my yap and keep cool. We were being listened to. She was not a Red Mata Hari, she was on my side.

I sat up and drank the glass of milk. It smelled funny but tasted great, warm and creamy. Goat's milk maybe.

Stela ushered her minders out of the room and closed the door behind her. I conked.

I woke up at dusk, feeling like a new man. Like I say I'm a good bouncer-back. I gazed out the window as the last of the sunset gilded ripples on the lake.

What the hell was Princess Stela doing here? Had Frank Wisner sent her on ahead to act as my guardian angel in the event I was collared? That would mean Wisner was running his former mistress as a double agent and had orchestrated her surprise appearance to his Maryland farm so that we could get acquainted.

That, it seemed to me, was too cute by half. Then again Wisner hadn't asked me to jump out the joe hole until after Stela's surprise appearance at his Maryland farm.

Speculation, Schroeder. Stick to what you know. Princess Stela ran some sort of salon in Paris. And a beautiful royal would never want for dough. Why return to the wilds of Romania unless she was a Commie zealot? A Commie zealot with a taste for caviar and champagne cocktails.

There were, no doubt, a host of Commie zealots in Paris with similar tastes. And in Paris they happily remained.

I looked up at the dome light on the ceiling, the one Stela indicated held a hidden microphone. Her bedroom would have another such device. This charming stone cottage had all the markings of a classic honey pot, a secluded place where fetching young women extract state secrets from lust-drunk government functionaries. Why would Princess Stela need to stoop that low?

Bucharest was notorious as a den of prostitution. One of my mission briefers had quoted Churchill. 'Romanian is not a nationality, it's an occupation.'

Princess Stela might well be selling her services to the Communists but I didn't think that's why she was here.

I got out of bed to see about some grub. And a shower, I stunk to high heaven. Getting up exposed a problem, however. Ilinca had taken all my clothes. I poked my nose into the small closet. Empty save for a couple blankets and a long wool coat. I squeezed into it and buttoned up. The sleeves barely covered my elbows.

An oval mirror hung on the back of the closet door. I took a look. My face was swole up like a black and blue bullfrog. And me with a hot date.

The bedroom door, to my surprise, was unlocked. I padded up the hall to the kitchen whistling "Swanee River," not wanting to startle anyone. The wool coat itched like a sonofabitch.

No one intervened and the kitchen was empty. Some security. Okay, I wasn't likely to flee barefoot over snow-capped mountains. But what was to stop me from grabbing a kitchen knife and committing *hari kari* before they could wheedle highly classified intel out of me?

Well, the bounty piled high on the kitchen counters and chopping block for one. Roasted game birds, candied fruits, pickled vegetables, pink salmon in mayonnaise, sesame cakes, two kinds of pâté and three kinds of caviar.

I glanced out a kitchen window that overlooked a back courtyard framed with chestnut trees, and saw reason number two.

The Princess had been skinny dipping in the lake. I knew this because her hair was wet and she was shivering most fetchingly. And she was nude when she shed her silk robe, stood gloriously still for a moment, stretching her back, then stepped down into some sort of hot spring steaming away in the courtyard.

I had never seen a woman so perfectly naked before, perfect as a marble statue in the Louvre. So perfect as to be almost beyond carnal desire.

Almost. Did I dare join her? I needed a good soak. And we could have candid conversation. There didn't figure to be a hidden mike on the patio. It would be rude and presumptuous of me of course but when had that ever stopped me?

I let myself out the side door to see Ilinca the maid sitting on a stone bench, smoking a cigarette. Damn. She shot to her feet, a pugnacious look on her mug. I raised my hands in surrender and summoned my best *please don't hurt me* smile.

It worked. Try as she might Ilinca couldn't squelch a laugh at the half-naked bullfrog that stood before her, bundled into an ill-fitting coat.

Princess Stela called to her from around the corner to my left, saying the Romanian equivalent of 'What's so damn funny?'

I turned the corner and answered her question.

Princess Stela, sunk up to her neck in a stone pit of steaming water that smelled of sulfur, was not amused. Or shy. She stood up, put her hands on her hips and rattled off some rapid fire Romanian

Ilinca led me back into the house. I was still hungry and smelly but in a better mood. It had to do with what I saw below Princess Stela's perfect breasts. The silvery stretch marks across her belly. She had been pregnant, presumably given birth.

I had done my homework on the Romanian royals. Stela had been married but there was no mention of offspring. She wasn't tending to a precious bundle in Paris, Bill Harvey would have mentioned it. But those stretch marks might explain why Princess Stela had returned to her family's ancestral cottage in Romania. She wanted to search for her child.

Ilinca took me into Stela's gauzy boudoir with its four-poster bed. She opened a standing closet in the corner. Judging by the jumble of styles and sizes crammed into the wardrobe Princess Stela had entertained a number of gentlemen visitors here over the years.

Unfortunately there was only one set of duds suitable for a big galoot like me. A pair of moleskin pants, a flannel shirt and a tan hunting jacket with a corduroy collar and deep pockets for dead game.

I tried them on and looked at myself in the full-length mirror and wondered why this getup bothered me so much. I didn't want to look like a bumpkin of course but it wasn't that. The trousers were a tad short, yet the jacket sleeves met my wrists because the shoulders were so broad. Could be I was wearing the hunting outfit of a gentleman visitor by the name of Frank Wisner.

Weird.

Ilinca marched me outside to a wood frame bathhouse where guests washed off the smell of sulfur from the hot springs. I took a cold shower under her watchful eye, which annoyed me no end and which was, I suppose, the point. To make me feel like a small boy.

Ilinca gave me a rough towel to dry off with and wrap around my waist. My grooming was not complete, however. She snatched at my chin spinach and shook her head. A scraggly beard was not acceptable at milady's table. Or, presumably, in her bed.

Ilinca pointed me toward a cold water basin with a pockmarked tin mirror and handed me a rusty Blue Blade. No hot water, no shave cream. Nope, ain't no days like that.

I handed her back the razor. "No dice, Ilinca."

She blinked at me, confused. Was I refusing a direct order?

I was. I picked up my borrowed duds and marched back to the house in search of some socks and underwear.

The dinner bell rang about an hour later. Yes, there was an actual dinner bell and I was Pavlov's dog. The dining room table was covered with a lace tablecloth and set with enough china, silver and crystal to make Marie Antoinette blush.

The NKVD chef, in a crisp white tunic, seated me at the side of the table. The chair at the head of the table was empty, as were all the plates, bowls and goblets. There was a pot of soup simmering on the stove and something dark and meaty in the oven, spitting and crackling.

I sat and waited for the lady of the manor to make an appearance. I sat and waited and listened to my stomach growl.

The night got started once Princess Stela, wearing a dark red dress with a cinched waist and a full skirt, took her chair. Her shoulders were bare. Were they ever. Wine was poured and food was served, course after delicious course.

I was surprised at how much I enjoyed caviar, though I learned it's best to spread it lightly on a cracker. Spooning it directly into your mouth is frowned upon.

Polite conversation was had. I enjoyed myself completely, but a thought nagged. Why the half-ass security? I wasn't a lust-drunk government functionary, I was an experienced agent trained to kill people. Where was Ilinca to keep an eye on me while the chef was busy? Where were the armed guards patrolling the perimeter?

I had noticed an old carriage house behind the cottage when I was out in the courtyard. Presumably it housed a car or truck. Escape was not impossible.

I couldn't figure it. It sure as hell wasn't going the way Lavrenty Beria would've drawn it up. Or Frank Wisner for that matter. It was rinkydink.

Princess Stela got up to powder her nose. The NKVD chef slid a frosty look my way. I raised my glass to him. Hell of a cook for a skinny guy.

Then it struck me. Lavrenty Beria would never have signed off on this cozy arrangement in the first place. Perhaps a superior had counseled patience. All capital cities run on gossip and rumor.

We don't want to transport this American to Moscow where his presence will be quickly known. It is better to deal with him in the hinterlands.

Beria had only one superior that I was aware of. Holy shit. Could be it was the *Chateau Lafite* '33 talking but it was possible that I was enjoying a candlelit feast with a Romanian princess thanks to political interference from on high. Thanks to Joe Stalin.

I gnawed on the tiny drumstick of a pheasant or squab or quail. We were rapidly approaching the third act of this production. The prospect was daunting. I was drunk on food more than wine, in no condition to spew semi-believable bullshit to a hidden mike while nestled in Stela Varadja's four-poster. Not without a walk through.

I needed to get Stela someplace where we could talk. A cup of mud on the veranda maybe. What was the drill? Was I supposed to moan and groan and whisper sweet nothings to the light fixture? It seemed so silly, and dispiriting. Making fake love to a beautiful woman.

Princess Stela returned to her seat at the head of the table, smiling pleasantly. "You are enjoying the repast, *Monsieur*?"

"Not sure," I said. "But the food's great!"

No laugh from the Princess. I titled my head toward the courtyard, mimed holding a coffee cup. But Stela was watching the chef in the kitchen. She reached over and took my hand. Hers was warm, silken. Mine clammy. She gave me a squeeze, whispering, "Crepes Suzette."

The NKVD chef wheeled a cart to the head of the table. The cart held a sauté pan heated by a can of Sterno, inside the pan were thin folded-over pancakes. He poured in a glug of brandy which he ignited with a long-snouted lighter apparently invented for the purpose of serving *Crepes Suzette en flambé*.

Communism, it seemed to me, was rife with contradictions.

After dessert we sat and drank coffee. The chef remained in the kitchen, stacking dishes for the maid. We drank more coffee.

Stela excused herself once more to freshen up. I thought this odd so I titled my chair back and watched her. She didn't duck into her bedroom. She slipped into the bedroom across the hall. She returned a minute later, her face a mask of grim purpose.

Princess Stela resumed her seat. "And what is news of your American election for President?" she said apropos of nothing.

I told her what little I knew about the Truman-Dewey race. Governor Dewey had a good lead heading into the home stretch. President Truman was banging on about a 'Do Nothing' Congress.

Stela reached into her beaded purse while I was talking and removed something you don't expect to find in a beaded purse. A leather sap. She slid it to me under the table and looked at me, meaningfully.

"Dmitri is busy. Please to fetch me fresh cup."

I slipped the blackjack into the game pocket of my hunting jacket. "My pleasure."

I ambled over to the coffee urn on the kitchen counter. Dmitri, to my right, cranked his pale face in my direction, eyes narrowed.

Perhaps he noticed I was carrying the cup and saucer in my left hand. So I used both mitts to set the cup down and said, "Excellent meal, Dmitri, best I've had."

Dmitri grunted and turned away. I filled the cup with my left hand, dug out the sap with my right, stepped back and crowned him a good one.

He was out on his feet. His forehead would have smacked the counter on the way down so I grabbed him from behind and laid him out on the floor, face up. I owed him that for the good eats.

I opened his eyelids. His pupils were rolled up and blank. I patted his pockets. No gun to steal.

I stood up. Stela was gone.

Then she was back, lugging a suitcase. She hurried to the side door, opened it and snapped, "Are you coming?"

No, your highness, I think I'll remain behind, take long, moonlit walks around the lake, work on my memoirs.

"Gimme a second." I inspected the carving knives tucked in a wooden block. I selected one with a five inch blade, wrapped it in a linen napkin and put it in my pocket with the leaded sap. "Let's go."

We crunched across gravel to a sturdy old carriage house made of planed and varnished tree trunks. Behind the garage stood a newer, smaller stucco building with narrow pillbox windows and a flat roof sprouting a six-foot antenna. The radio room. The comm center. The transcribing-Stela's-nocturnal-adventures general HQ.

The slotted windows were dark. I pointed. "Anyone in there?"

Stela shook her head, and opened the swinging doors of the old carriage house to reveal an amazing sight. A groundbreaking automobile I first read about in the pages of *AutoCar*. A Soviet-made GAZ-61, the very first four-wheel-drive passenger vehicle that wasn't a Jeep.

I prowled around her with a low wolf whistle. The four-door body sat jacked up half a foot above the chassis and the rugged cross country tires. The 61 was designed to scale mountain passes and ford streams and was the favored Command Car of Red Army brass during World War Two and beyond. She was, to put it bluntly, a two hundred and twenty cubic inch, four stroke, six cylinder piece of ass.

"You can drive this?" said Princess Stela, a question she should have asked before now.

I knew that GAZ manufacturing had begun as a joint venture with the Ford Motor Company in the early 30s, when the Yanks and Reds were on better terms. Ford had since been shown the door. But motor vehicles don't give a shit about politics.

"Sure," I said, "I can drive it."

"Make yourself acquainted," she said. "I am needing to change for our journey."

Journey to where, I wondered as she hurried back to the cottage in her full-skirted red dress. I put her suitcase in the back seat.

Chapter Seventeen

Stela returned to the carriage house in traveling garb – black slacks, sheepskin boots, a dark gray greatcoat over a white blouse, her black hair piled up under a woolen cap. She looked like a very cute boy.

I had checked the fluid levels and inspected the tires while she was gone. We were gassed up and ready to rumble up the gravel drive.

The GAZ-61 was light on its feet for a car stuck atop a truck bed. When we reached the road I asked Stela which way to turn, thinking she would say 'right,' the opposite direction from whence we came.

She pointed left.

"Why? Where are we going?"

"Drive the car," she said, "and I will answer."

I turned left. The night was clear and moonless. It figured to be about eleven. The stone cottage, like me, was clockless.

I drove a while, getting the feel of the stiff gearbox, enjoying the car's surefootedness on the twisty road, waiting for Princess Stela to say her piece.

"Sorin Dragomir was Captain of Palace Guard in the time of King *Mihai*," said Stela. She sounded weary, not keyed up as I was at our daring escape.

The manila envelope handed her by the *Securitate* would have briefed Stela on my Captain Dragomir connection. Her news about Dragomir's job didn't surprise me. He was a spit and polish kinda guy.

"I have a son," she said. "He was stolen away."

I drove on as the road climbed, jouncing over potholes.

"He was stolen away when Red Army deposed our king, as the tanks they come along *Calea Victoriei*."

"To the Royal Palace?"

"Of course. At that time I am supposing some member of staff has taken him, to keep him far from *Sovietici*."

"Okay. And then what happened?"

"Nothing then happened!"

"No ransom note? No indication that your son had been kidnapped?"

"No!"

Stela Varadja fell silent. I filled in the blanks best I could. She figured her son had been kidnapped by some member of the royal staff who planned to use him as a political pawn. When she learned that Captain Dragomir and Frank Wisner had big plans, the tumblers clicked. She knew who the kidnapper was.

Frank Wisner told me his contact in Romania had a 'secret ally' who was integral to his plot to overthrow the government. Sorin Dragomir said he was a monarchist who didn't care if King Michael returned, since he was a Hohenzollern descendant with a Greek mother. It looked like Dragomir had a better, purer candidate for King of all Romania. It looked like his secret ally was the three-year-old direct male heir of Vlad the Impaler.

It occurred to me somewhere after the second harrowing mountain switchback that I didn't have to do this.

"I was not sent here to rescue your son, Stela. I was sent here to assess Captain Dragomir's operational readiness."

"And kidnap of young boy is part of this…readiness?"

"I don't know. Where I come from kidnapping is as bad as murder."

"But you are not, now, where you are from," said Stela, tartly.

"No, ma'am. Not by a long shot."

My statement was punctuated a short minute later by a sphincter-puckering wolf howl. And not one of those Gene Autry movie wolves neither, keening mournfully from a distant ravine. This sucker was close.

I gave the car some gas and leaned into the curve. It was better driving these mountain roads after dark I decided. You couldn't see the jagged tombs awaiting you below every turn.

"What is it you expect to happen here?" I said.

"We will go to Secaria, to Sorin Dragomir."

"Secaria?"

"To the south."

"How do you know that Dragomir lives there?" She flicked her hand at me, silly question. "Okay, and then what?"

"You will tell Sorin Dragomir to return to me my son."

"Okay, and then what?"

"You will have some plans, plans to return to USA. We will join you so far as Paris."

Provided I had a flight out. Plan A was contact the flyboys with my J/E radio. I counted Dragomir as my plan B since he had a back channel to Wisner. If the Captain had headed for the hills after my capture, however, and taken my J/E with him, I was screwed, blued and tattooed.

I had assumed Princess Stela had an escape plan up her sleeve when we piled into the GAZ-61, some romantic anti-Commie underground railroad that smuggled fugitives to freedom across the Balkans to the Adriatic Sea.

Guess not, kinda pissed me off. I kept my eyes on the road and asked PS a rude question.

"Why did you go into Ilinca's bedroom?"

"I am sorry?" she said, deep in thought.

"You went into Ilinca's bedroom after dinner. Why?"

"I went to make certain she was passed away."

"Passed out?"

"*Da.* I had given to her soup dose of Nembutal."

"And how did that work?"

"Ilinca was, how you say in States, *a gone goose*."

This was one cold chiquita. I waited until we reached a straight stretch of road to turn and ask another, ruder, question. One that William King Harvey would approve of.

"Stela, do you know anything about the arrest and execution of a large number Romanian expatriates in Bucharest earlier this year?"

"Everyone in Romania is knowing about it."

"Did you have anything to do with it?"

Princess Stela gave me a stare worthy of her murderous ancestor. "What…are you saying?"

I stopped the car and met her look. "You have been working with the *Securitate* and the NKVD. You have high-level contacts in U.S. intelligence. It's a logical question."

"This, in Bucharest, this was something to do with Frank Wisner? How would I know such a thing? Frank Wisner would tell me?"

She had a point.

"The Blue Caps, they use me as whore," she said, her lower lip trembling, "to take secrets from important men."

"Okay, sorry I brought it up," I said. But she wasn't done.

"You are stupid man. Do you not see where I am living? The men they send to me are all *român*, all *Comuniştii!*"

I wound my way up the mountain, feeling dumb as dirt. What she'd said made sense. The Soviets deployed much more secret police manpower keeping their satellite countries in line than they did worrying about us stumblebum Yanks.

We made the long journey to the town of Secaria without incident, and in stony silence.

There had been no checkpoints on the mountain roads and precious little traffic. But at some point Dmitri or Ilinca would come to and sound the alarm from the radio room. The GAZ-

61's distinctive profile would be easy to spot, even now. Come daylight we would draw stares.

So I was puzzled at PS's insistence that we pull off the main road and onto a lightly-wooded country lane. "Why are we stopping?"

"I am need to sleep." And with that Stela curled up like a cat inside her fur-lined greatcoat and dropped off.

I fought off the tug of slumber for the better part of an hour by keeping an eye out for traffic on the main road and listening to the howls of a distant wolf pack and the hoot of a nearby owl. Every once in a while the gleaming eyes of a nocturnal beast would flit my way. I hated not having a gun.

Stela stirred just before dawn. She opened the passenger's side door and tumbled out. Apparently even princesses needed to pee first thing in the morning. But that's not what she did. She retched, heaving violently three times, then coughed and spit to clear her throat.

She climbed back in the car, took off her woolen cap and shook out her hair.

"Are you alright?"

"Now I am fine."

She told me to return to the main road and turn right toward the village. I did that, the GAZ drawing a stare from a peasant woman emptying a chamber pot into the culvert below the road.

All of the houses in the tidy village of Secaria were crowded up against the road, offering no inconspicuous place to park. But Stela directed me off the main road and up a big hill. Captain Dragomir's brick one-story commanded the high ground.

I turned off the headlights for stealth as we approached, as if that would do any good. The GAZ-61 sounded like a twenty-ton bulldozer grinding up that hill.

I parked. A light went on inside the house. An electric light. *The good Captain is not in residence.*

So said the sleepy gray-haired housekeeper to Princess Stela when we knocked at the door. Or so I gathered from the housekeeper's head shakes and hand gestures. The answer was much the same when Stela demanded to know where Sorin Dragomir had gone. Or so I gathered.

I wasn't any use in this fandango so I slipped past the housekeeper and cased the joint. It was sparsely furnished with bare walls, more like a safe house than a home. There were scant clothes in the bedroom closet and bureau but I scoured the place on the off chance the Captain had left my J/E transceiver behind.

No such luck. I did spy something that Stela would find interesting. In the far corner of a back bedroom stood a hand-hewed bed suitable for a small child. The bed had been stripped and there were no stuffed animals or toys in the room.

But I kept at it. The bureau drawers were empty, ditto a knotty pine toy chest. I got down on all fours and looked underneath it. A small, brightly-painted wooden soldier, his hand raised in salute, looked back at me.

Had the kid done this on purpose, to leave a marker?

Sure he had, Schroeder, kid's a three-year-old superspy. I snatched up the wooden soldier and went to show Princess Stela what I'd found.

She thanked me with a quick squeeze of her hand and shoved the wooden soldier at the housekeeper with a torrent of angry words. The housekeeper responded with Romania's national gesture. She shrugged.

My job description didn't include browbeating elderly housekeepers but it was obvious that Princess Stela had not cowed this obstinate woman. I looked over to Stela but she was out the door.

She returned a minute later holding a drawstring jeweler's bag. She reached in and removed a folded sheet of muslin. She unfolded it slowly as the housekeeper and I watched with rapt attention.

What Princess Stela revealed to us was a small cross, not much larger than a rosary crucifix but considerably thicker, heavier. It looked like silver but it was badly tarnished and old, very old. Not sure how I knew that exactly. The dark green pits in the metal maybe. The uneven edges indicating it was forged before die casts were mass produced.

The housekeeper took a long look at the silver cross that Stela Varadja held in the palm of her hand – the cross bar was inlayed with elaborate curlicues of mother of pearl – and fell to one knee, her head bowed. The housekeeper spoke briefly.

She must have told Stela what she wanted to know because PS turned on her heel and, with a tug at my elbow, marched back to the car.

I got behind the wheel. Stela took her seat. "He is in Sibiu. With my son."

"How far is that?"

"As far as it takes."

This was not a helpful answer. We were low on gas after the long trek and stopping at a petrol station would just give the locals time to stare and ask questions.

But wait, the house had electric lights. I climbed out and looked around for power poles. Not a one. Captain Dragomir had himself a gas-powered generator.

I found it in a tool shed behind the house, complete with a five gallon can of petrol which I promptly added to our tank. Then I fired up the GAZ and rolled down the hill toward the main road.

"What is that?" I said, pointing to the ancient crucifix she still clutched.

Princess Stela declined to answer. I stopped the car at the main road. "The crossbar's engraved with a strange design," I said, putting the car in neutral, waiting, wasting precious fuel.

Stela sighed. "Wings of *dracul*, to protect the cross."

I kept my yap shut and waited for more.

"Vlad Tepes Draculea died fighting Ottoman Turks. They take his head as trophy." She rubbed her thumb gently along the edge of the silver cross. "This cross, from his breastplate, this was all that was left…"

"To identify his body?"

"*Da.*"

Nice touch that, the trailing off, leaving me to complete the thought. I found it hard to swallow all this historical humbuggery of course, but Princess Stela did sell her part convincingly.

And you can't ask a spy to do any more than that.

Chapter Eighteen

My few days in Romania had given me the impression the entire country was a backwater and driving through the outskirts of Sibiu confirmed that view. Stores made of concrete block huddled next to crumbling gray stucco houses with broken windows.

My impression changed when we reached the center of the ancient walled citadel with its cobblestone streets, broad plazas and brightly-painted buildings with foot-thick walls. Some of the tile roofs had ventilation outlets that looked like oversized eyeballs keeping watch on the bustling crowds below.

Central Sibiu was alive. Gypsy girls in long cotton dresses stood on street corners selling flowers and cakes. Men sold live chickens in cages hung from yokes across their shoulders. A hand-painted banner proclaimed *Recolta de Struguri Fest* which, Stela explained, was the annual grape harvest festival.

It was unlikely that Captain Dragomir had traveled all the way to Sibiu for fun and frolic. More likely he had something planned for the festival crowd.

I asked Stela a dumb question. "Captain Dragomir is a capable leader, and a patriot. Would you consider remaining in Romania to work with him?"

"No. Sorin Dragomir is wanting to make Regent, guardian of my son and ruler of Romania. This I cannot be. *Poporul român* will not accept a female sovereign. But, in time, they will accept my son. I seek for him proper education at fine university."

A lovely sentiment. But Frank Wisner would not be reassured to learn that the boy king would send the Reds packing in about twenty years. Still, I wasn't going to stand between a mother and her kidnapped son.

"Follow my lead when we confront Dragomir. I will see to it that you are reunited with your boy."

"Thank you, *Monsieur* Schroeder."

"Hal."

"Hal."

"And what is your son's name?"

"Vlad."

Of course it was.

I followed PS's directions to the address the housekeeper had given us, treading lightly on the gas pedal. The GAZ-61 wheezed, sputtered and died as I parked it on the street.

The house was a show horse amidst nags. It sat on the corner of a narrow side street lined with nondescript stucco boxes, their windows shuttered against the cold. Its black-tiled roof had upturned edges that made it look like an ivy-covered pagoda. In my research Romania was often referred to a 'the furthest outpost of the Orient.' This was the first I'd seen of it.

I turned to Stela. "I need to talk to Dragomir alone, before you start in with the flying cookware."

A blank look.

"Frying pans, plates…never mind. We need to discuss strategy, the Captain and me," I said. "Anything I need to know that I don't already?"

Another blank look.

"For instance, how did Dragomir and Frank Wisner get along?"

PS fielded this one without difficulty. "Sorin was always, how you say…?" She puckered up her lips.

"Kissing Frank's ass."

Stela's smile flickered and was gone. She soothed her brow with her palm, pushing her shiny black hair back then lowering her head to let it fall forward. And again.

"Anything else you'd care to tell me?"

She worried her lips before she spoke, testing words. "Frank Wisner, our...romance. It was cause of my divorce. And humiliation."

"That's a pity," I said, without sufficient concern apparently because her face curled into a sneer.

"Go!" she said. "Take yourself to your meeting!"

I was eager to do that but it seemed obvious that Princess Stela had another shoe to drop. I waited patiently but she declined to co-operate. I asked the question.

"Your romance with Frank Wisner led to your divorce and humiliation. Why is that important for me to know?"

"Perhaps it is not."

"Then why did you mention it?"

Her fluted sigh indicated that the Princess was disappointed in me. Well, take a number honey. And spill it already.

She said what I should have guessed. "Frank Wisner is the father of my son."

A pretty young maid escorted me into the study lined with leather bound books where Captain Dragomir was seated at a heavy desk, writing furiously with a fountain pen.

"I knew you would come, I *knew* it!" he said, bolting to his feet.

I found this a surprising statement given that I'd been rotting in a barn stall two days ago thanks to one of Dragomir's most trusted men.

"How in the hell did you know that?"

The Captain crossed the floor to greet me. "I knew that Princess Stela had rescued you. I have spies among the Magyars!"

"And they return the favor," I replied, acidly. "How'd you know I'd bust out and come here?"

Dragomir holstered his outstretched hand, his smile fading. "It was the logical conclusion."

Logical, that was a good one. If the good Captain wanted me to come find him he would have instructed his housekeeper in Secaria to fork over his address without hesitation. Yet he seemed genuinely pleased to see me.

As a smartass youth I believed that life was something like a long column of numbers. While it would be difficult and time consuming, once you toted up that long column you'd arrive at a perfect sum. I have since come to understand that life and mathematics differ in one important way. Life makes no sense.

I didn't ask the Captain about the fancy digs, didn't ask him if he was the kidnapper of Stela's boy. I asked Dragomir if he had used his back channel to Frank Wisner to inform him that I'd been captured.

"I did not. It's a cumbersome process, fraught with peril."

He could speak the King's English, this guy. But here's what he was really saying: *I weren't gonna deliver no bad news to my butter'n'egg man. I planned to hang fire and hope the Vampire Princess would work her magic.*

"Well, I need you to use your back channel now, Captain, to arrange my return flight."

"You can't leave us now, we're just about to get underway!"

I let my mug do the talking.

"Your face is a ruin," said Dragomir after a time.

I liked the way he said it. Straight up, without sympathy.

"And yours is a vision of loveliness."

We laughed.

"When the time comes to arrange your departure, *Domnule* Schroeder, why not use your radio?"

"You have it?"

"Of course."

"Great, glad to hear it. But the J/E has a limited range and the Air Force is expecting me to contact them from my original drop point."

"That's quite a distance."

"That's okay, Captain, we have a car."

"*We?*"

"She's outside in the car, waiting to talk to you."

"Excellent!" grinned Dragomir after a freighted pause. "I am sure Princess Stela will enjoy hearing of our plans."

Sure she will, Captain. You can run down the details while she's slamming your head against the wall.

"Why don't you run them by me first."

Dragomir did that. He was scheduled to make a standard patriotic speech Saturday night, at the end of the week-long harvest festival. He would use the opportunity to incite the crowd against the hated invaders, then conclude by presenting the boy king to the cheering throng. He and his men would then lead the mob to storm the office of the Mayor.

"He is a toady, a collaborator of the vilest sort."

"You intend to kill him?"

"No, no. He would not be in his office on that night. This will be a symbolic act, to stir the blood of the people."

Dragomir went on to say that this symbolic act would be followed by a more serious late-night attack on a nearby Romanian Army garrison.

"I have men inside. The troops are conscripts, they will not resist once their officers are seized. We will commandeer their trucks and weapons and ambush the Red Army outside Sighisoara as they roll tanks to quell the revolt."

"Why not make your stand here in Sibiu? I saw lots of old towers and ramparts you could use for cover."

Captain Dragomir drew himself up to his full height and puffed out his chest. "That would be a strategic, and a symbolic, mistake."

I was tempted to laugh at his pomposity but his fierce gaze shut my yap. It made me realize the chasm between us. Captain Dragomir's campaign to reclaim his homeland was essentially an abstraction to me, a small part of a much larger game. To him it was life and death. I used to hate the big brass way back when. The Generals pushing toy tanks across a table map as poor slobs like me froze, starved and died. Now, five years later, you could make a case that I had crossed over. How in the world had that happened?

"There is a narrow gorge the Red Army must pass through, where Prince Vlad massacred the Turks," said the Captain. "That is where we will make our stand. And where your help would be most welcome. We need anti-tank weapons, and gold to pave the way. Sighisoara is Magyar territory but they have no great love for Russians. They can be bought."

This was all news to me. I asked Dragomir how much he would need in gold.

He paused, he fidgeted. "Twenty-five thousand dollars."

My half-lidded reply drew a nervous laugh. "Those are some high-priced Magyars you got there, Captain."

I told Dragomir that $25,000 might be feasible provided I had a way to ask for it in a timely manner.

"We have an airstrip nearby, which is known to Frank Wisner. It is where your return flight was meant to land."

He gave me a look that said 'you see what I'm saying?'

I hate that look.

"If the Air Force cannot receive your transmission from the spot of your original drop, they would, it seems to me, attempt to monitor your landing strip."

Oh. Yeah. I might be able to get a message to Frank Wisner after all.

"We will need something else from your government," said Dragomir.

I was about to call him a greedy bastard when he said, "Announcements on Radio Free Europe about the success of our operation. The Red Army is stretched thin, holding the Balkans with sixty thousand troops. What they most fear are simultaneous uprisings. There are small but powerful resistance movements in Serbia, Hungary and Bulgaria. If they hear of our success they will be inspired to act!"

My goodness, a worked-out plan. Just the sort of indigenous anti-Soviet resistance that Wisner wanted to encourage and support.

A flurry of angry shouts interrupted our powwow. Stela had grown tired of waiting. She burst into the study a moment later, trailing the frantic young maid who had tears in her eyes and one bright red cheek. Princess Stela fixed her gaze on Captain Dragomir who, for once, looked unsure of himself.

"Where is my son?" she demanded.

"He is here. In good hands, well taken care of."

"*Where*?!"

The Captain looked to the maid, who was hovering behind Stela.

"He is upstairs, taking his afternoon nap," she said.

Stela turned to go upstairs as the Captain put his foot in his mouth.

"You should thank me. I took the boy only to save him from the Red Army."

"You did not tell me!"

"You fled the city! The next day!"

"I had no choice!"

Dragomir showed his palms and lowered his voice. "Princess Stela, I beg of you, stay. Together we can inspire a glorious revolt against the invaders. Some dare call you a fellow traveler but I know you to be a true patriot."

The Captain turned quickly to me. "When the first German officers arrived in Bucharest the aristocracy feted them with lavish parties, toasting the handsome new conquerors of the world." Dragomir gestured to PS. "But Princess Stela refused all invitations and stayed at home."

Nice touch. But I was dead on my feet and not interested in refereeing a ten rounder.

"Here's how it's going to be, Captain. If Frank Wisner authorizes a flight to deliver supplies to your airstrip, I intend to be on that plane when it takes off. And I won't back support for your operation unless you allow the Princess and her son to go with me."

"Princess Stela can choose to join you of course. But her son's place is here, with his subjects."

I expected this answer but I made a show of arguing with him while I shot Stela a quick look.

She understood. She waited for the proper moment to hang her head and say, resignedly, "It is all right, *Monsieur* Schroeder, we will stay."

Great, fine, well done and executed.

Now all I had to do was contact Frank Wisner from the middle of nowhere, convince him to mount an expensive, big deal supply operation in enemy territory then find a way to smuggle the Princess and her son aboard a supply plane at a secret, heavily-guarded airstrip.

A ludicrous mission, yet one that had to succeed. That was made clear a short time later when I witnessed the regally cool Stela Varadja, eyes abrim, tenderly stroking the head of her long lost son, Prince Vlad.

Chapter Nineteen

That night one of Dragomir's men, Lucian, drove me to their secret landing strip in a narrow valley about twenty miles north of Sibiu. Only it wasn't. It was a plowed-under ag field with a stand of tall trees at the far end.

I asked Lucian to explain.

"I will show to you."

He drove his small hay truck toward the far end of the field, wallowing through the furrows in low gear. This was a job for the four-wheel GAZ but we'd decided to garage it. Too conspicuous.

The truck got stuck in the furrows so we climbed out onto the half-frozen sod and started to walk. "Lucian, here's an idea. Why not just tell me what we are going to see?"

Lucian waved me on happily. "Come, come!"

I slogged along behind, grumpy as a socialite at the Loyal Order of the Moose Friday Night Smoker. Lucian led the way with his flashlight as we wandered into the tall trees and down a crude road covered in pine needles. He pointed excitedly to a small clearing, to a massive hulk covered with a tarp. Lucian ran to it and lifted up its skirt, revealing the rusted front drum of a very big and very old steam roller.

So. We didn't have a landing strip. What we did have, given enough time, good weather and an enormous supply of coal or logs to stoke the boiler, was a potential landing strip.

"*Este bun,* yes?" beamed Lucian.

"It's better than *bun,* Lucian. It's what we Yanks call *tarfu!*"

"*Tarfu?*" said Lucian. "*Da!*"

Lucian's smiling face reminded me of those beardless youths at Andrews AFB who wanted me to take a few practice jumps from a C-45 at five hundred feet. I didn't tell him that *tarfu* is Army shorthand for 'things are really fucked up.'

When had all young men the world over become idiots?

I walked the length of the ag field, counting steps, one long stride to a yard. I stopped counting at five hundred figuring that was enough runway to accommodate a twin-engine C-45. I tramped back to the truck, climbed into the truck bed, switched on my J/E transceiver and waited for the tubes to warm.

The beauty of the J/E is that it uses a UHF frequency with limited range. You can talk with an overhead plane without being overheard even twenty miles away. Which meant I didn't have to transmit in code. By rights I should, but I didn't have to. Which was good seeing as how I had no verbal code training whatsoever.

The de Havilland Mosquito has a ceiling of thirty-thousand feet. If it was up there I wouldn't be able to see or hear it. I was a stranded freighter firing distress flares in a heavy fog.

But I kept at it every ten minutes or so, hoping Frank Wisner hadn't written me off, saying, "This is TIMBER calling STINGRAY, come in STINGRAY."

Flyboys always get the cool code names.

Lucian busied himself digging the truck tires out of the furrows with a garden trowel, smoothing the dirt into little ramps for our escape. In between transmissions I took time to curse our shoddy tradecraft.

I had met STINGRAY at Andrews AFB. Nice chap. But he wouldn't be able to positively ID my voice at 30,000 feet.

We should have agreed on a threshold question before the mission. A way to establish I was who I said I was. My knowing the proper code names wouldn't be enough for Frank Wisner. Could be the bad guys had beat that out of me.

But Wisner would know that I would never conduct a phony broadcast even with a gun to my head. So there would be a threshold question only I could answer.

Finally, in a burst of static, came the response from high above. "Roger, TIMBER, this is STINGRAY, over."

I keyed the J/E. "Nice to hear a friendly voice."

"Roger that."

So much for chitchat. He asked me the threshold question. What was the proper name for 'Cajun napalm'?

Christ. I remembered stirring the red hot flour and oil mix at Frank Wisner's Maryland farm but the name of the stuff escaped me.

"Don't recall, what's the backup question?"

Frank Wisner was a pro. There would be a backup question.

No response from up top. I tried again. And again. I heard a garbled response. I tried again.

Came the reply, loud and clear. "What local delicacy...was served at dinner?"

I pictured Wisner hacking up Maryland blue crabs to toss in the pot, but that was too easy. Blue crabs was a guess anyone who knew I'd been to Wisner's farm could make. Frank was testing me. Saying, in effect, 'You don't get this one right you're not worth retrieving.'

I'd thought of that memorable Saturday any number of times, remembered his boys had been down giggin' at the crick.

"Frogs' legs," I said to the J/E. "But they were served as an appetizer, not dinner."

No response. Shit, Schroeder, can the wisecracks for once, will ya?

Then, from on high. "Roger."

Once I passed muster with STINGRAY I told him that a major operation was afoot, pending developments. I relayed Dragomir's request for infantry anti-tank weapons - bazookas and sticky bombs - and twenty-five thousand dollars in gold.

STINGRAY didn't laugh out loud that I could hear.

We set a time for a follow-up transmission, 0400 Sunday morning. At that point I would have a better idea if Captain

Dragomir's ambitious plan had legs. I asked for the takeoff and landing requirements of a C-45 on the off chance Dragomir's pie-sky plan got cleared.

"1400 feet coming in heavy, 1500 going out light."

It was more than I expected but we still had enough. I made no mention of Princess Stela and her son. The boy king would remain a well-kept secret.

Oh knock it off, Schroeder. Like *legal brief* and *military intelligence*, a *well-kept secret* is a contradiction in terms. It was when, not if, Frank Wisner would learn about his son.

Lucian drove us back to Captain Dragomir's borrowed pagoda in Sibiu. I assumed it was borrowed because, like the brick house in Secaria, there were no framed photos or memorabilia to indicate it was his. Revolutionaries can't afford the luxury of a permanent residence. And, yes, I was beginning to believe that spit'n'polish Captain Dragomir of the Romanian Palace Guard was a genuine revolutionary.

Good for him and Godspeed. I was still on the next flight out of here.

The Captain wanted to read me the latest version of his call-to-action speech which, from the sheaf of papers on his desk, looked to be about two hours long. I wanted to talk about our alleged landing strip.

"How long will it take to hardpan that field and when do you plan to start?"

Dragomir grinned at my petulance. "Two days, and we start tomorrow morning."

"We're going to need about four hundred and fifty meters end to end."

"I understand. We will work around the clock."

"What if it rains?"

"There is no forecast of rain for the next forty-eight hours."

Smart aleck had an answer for everything.

"I take it from your question that you were able to establish contact."

"Loud and clear." The Captain prompted me with his eyebrows. "Sunday," I said, "0400 hours."

He filled in the rest. "At which time you will report your assessment of the success of our operation on Saturday night, a report Frank Wisner will use to determine whether to grant our request for money and munitions."

"Something like that," I said to a man who was looking far too pleased with himself. "You know, Captain, I'm thinking that a crowd on the final night of a grape harvest festival might've had a glass of wine or two. Or ten."

I gestured to the sheaf of papers covered with the Captain's florid scrawl. "They might not be in the proper frame of mind for a long-winded lecture on the glorious history of the Romanian monarchy."

An accepting shrug from Dragomir. I was beginning to glim the different shadings of the Romanian national gesture. Accepting, dismissive, sore, fatalistic.

"If the natives really are fed up with Soviet tyranny, Captain, you don't have to build a bonfire. All you have to do is strike a match."

Captain Dragomir sat at his desk and wrote this down with his fountain pen. "Whom are you quoting?"

I was quoting myself so far as I knew. But citing Harold Schroeder of Youngstown, Ohio was unlikely to stoke the revolutionary fervor of the local populace.

"Abraham Lincoln, the 16th President of the United States,."

Dragomir nodded and made a note.

"Captain, about this Saturday, I'm confused. Why would the authorities award you the prime speaking slot at the close of the festival?"

"The Deputy Mayor is scheduled to close the festival. We will see to it that he is interrupted."

"Oh."

Interrupted. Not kept from reaching the podium but interrupted in mid-speech and carried off over the strenuous objections of the local gendarmes. Shit. This was shaping up to be a firefight.

Dragomir's raised chin challenged me to object to this new development but I couldn't bring myself to do it. PS and I had agreed to participate. And we both knew these two-bit barn dances never go as planned. I would make sure to keep Stela and her son out of harm's way.

"I have another quote for you, Captain."

"But my speech, it is too long!"

I returned his smile. "This one's short, what you call 'pithy.'"

Dragomir picked up his pen and searched his hen-scratched page for an empty space.

"The British Special Air Service has a motto that applies to your situation quite nicely. To you yourself as a matter of fact."

The Captain eyed me from an oblique angle. Was I about to indulge in sticky and unprofessional sentiment?

I told him the SAS motto anyway.

"Who dares, wins."

Chapter Twenty

Saturday evening was balmy in every sense of the word. Thin clouds veiled the moon, the sky glinted pearl gray. The teeming throng that crowded the cobblestone square in Sibiu's old town was tipsy, not drunk. Not yet. Princess Stela and I stood behind a crudely constructed wooden stage where three gypsy men played crazy-fast music on violin, drum and guitar. Young couples danced, older folks clapped to keep time.

Stela wore a simple black skirt and a bright lavender blouse with short sleeves. Dracula's silver cross hung from a chain around her neck. She looked scary pretty and vice versa. Her son was nearby, out of sight, in the care of Captain Dragomir's pretty young maid.

To our right was a handsome black and gold filigree iron bridge crossing a cobbled street below. It seemed the perfect perch for Captain Dragomir to give his speech. Not so, explained PS. The span had been favored for centuries by politicians for just that purpose and was now known as 'The Bridge of Lies.'

The crowd got frisky when the buxom young Queen of the Fest ascended the stage and tossed them yellow roses from her bouquet.

The crowd got grumpy when the Deputy Mayor, a small whiskered man wearing a black suit and a scarlet sash, stood to the podium to call an end to the festivities.

And they got uproariously happy when a big man in peasant garb, having sneaked across the back of the platform on hands and knees, stuck his head in between the Deputy Mayor's legs, stood up and promenaded the flummoxed little man back and forth across the stage.

Captain Dragomir took the Deputy Mayor's place at the podium to scattered applause. The big man in peasant garb used the moment to drop to one knee at the back of the stage and dump the Deputy Mayor into the waiting arms of two of Dragomir's men. They bound and gagged him.

The Captain gave a powerful, and relatively brief, speech, his voice filled with fire and brimstone. Stela translated for me. Dragomir celebrated Romania's ultimate nationalist, Vlad Tepes, the *dracul* who drove the evil Turks from the homeland.

It gets muzzy after that. I had only a couple glasses of that cat's piss they called Riesling but it felt like someone had slipped me a mickey because the rest of that night was an out-of-focus Salvador Dali film. I can't swear that any of it – Dragomir leading the crowd off to storm the Mayor's office, locals dragging the Deputy Mayor behind by his scarlet sash – really happened.

The only memory I can swear to is Captain Sorin Dragomir holding Prince Vlad aloft and shouting, "Our glorious past lives again. Behold the new King of Romania!"

The boy king didn't whimper, squirm or bawl. Could be I'm bats but the back of my brain holds a snapshot of the son of Princess Stela Varadja and Frank Wisner waving his pudgy hand to the eager crowd.

The response was volcanic. Bugles blared, the earth shook, the crowd roared itself hoarse. Could be Captain Sorin Dragomir was onto something here.

I came to in the sitting room of Dragomir's pagoda, in a well-upholstered chair, my stocking feet propped up on an ottoman. I checked my head for wounds. No blood, no squishy tissue. What the hell and then some.

Princess Stela placed the back of her hand to my forehead. "You are still hot."

"How would you know? Your hand's cold as ice."

Not the snappiest comeback of all time but passable for a man who just woke up in a plump chair with his boots gone.

"What the hell happened?"

"Your eyes roll up and you fall over."

"What? Did I hit the deck?"

"No deck, I catch you."

"You?"

"Yes. I am strong."

No shit. "Guess I was more tired than I knew, but I feel fine now. How'd I get here?"

"Sorin's men, they carry you to the truck."

"They should have splashed water on my face, stood me up."

"They did so. You could not stand."

Weird. And a little nerve wracking. I had put my carcass through a lot of abuse in my scant twenty-eight years. Could be my carcass was telling me to knock it off.

Then again, perhaps I was simply undernourished.

"I could do with some cream cheese and caviar on toast about now, a thick T-bone on the side, blood rare, hold the mushrooms."

"You are funny man," replied Stela, not smiling.

"Ha ha funny or funny-in-the-head funny?"

PS smiled just enough to indicate that she understood the question but gave no satisfaction. I settled for a ham sandwich and a beer.

Captain Dragomir breezed in a bit later. I expected to find him flushed with Scotch and victory but he was cool and composed and well turned out in a gray-blue military tunic with a braided collar, brass buttons and epaulettes you could set a drink on. He asked how I was feeling. I assured him I was in fine fettle.

"That is most welcome news because tonight will be critical," he said, patting one of my woolen socks. "You must accompany us."

Stela shot me a dark look as only she could.

I had been Nurse Nancy'd by unlikely females before – Lizabeth, The Schooler's moll comes to mind – but I found it hard to believe the Vampire Princess was suggesting I should recuperate in my comfy chair when my participation in, and consequent approval of, Captain Dragomir's late night raid on a Romanian Army garrison was her only real hope of a flight to freedom.

Her glittering black eyes continued to bore a hole in my forehead. I will never understand women if I live to be one million years old.

"I plan to accompany you, Captain," I said, turning away. "But I'm not going into battle unarmed."

Dragomir's face lit up and he hurried out of the room, leaving me alone with PS.

I asked why she didn't want me to march off to battle.

"You are no use to me when dead."

"Don't worry. I'm a devout coward."

She clucked her tongue. "A coward who jumps from aeroplanes."

"I got talked into that. I said I was a coward, I didn't say I was smart."

"You are dumb coward?"

"Sure."

"Good."

"Why is that good?"

"Dumb cowards live longer than smart heroes."

I hoisted my beer.

Captain Dragomir returned with a flat cedar box and a bulky rucksack. He presented the box to me with both hands. A shiny brass plaque read: 'To Captain Sorin Dragomir, in grateful appreciation. FGW.'

I opened the lid to reveal a long-nosed, pearl-handled .44 caliber Remington six shooter nestled in a bed of crushed velvet.

"It's a cavalry officer's service weapon from the Civil War, given to me by Frank Wisner on the day he departed Bucharest."

"Wow."

I couldn't very well refuse this five-pound hand cannon, all I was packing was a steak knife. But how in the hell was I supposed to carry it?

That's what the rucksack was for. Dragomir removed a leather belt holster complete with a strip of rawhide meant to cinch the holster around your thigh. I thanked the Captain for his generosity. All I needed now were spurs and a ten-gallon hat.

Dragomir's men began to arrive, in civvies. They didn't change into uniform. A couple carried their spiffy Lee-Enfields but more had shotguns or hunting rifles slung over their shoulders.

"We are guerilla fighters tonight," said Dragomir to my puzzled look.

The Captain herded his men into the pagoda's small backyard. I laced up my boots and followed them out. It was ten p.m. or so and the night had cooled. We stood around on the spongy grass and listened to our fearless leader say his piece. He wasn't a fire and brimstone Baptist this time, more like an Episcopalian.

I didn't understand a word he said but I knew it wasn't going over well. Something bloody and gruesome had occurred in the storming of the Mayor's office. I could smell it on the men. They were fired up and ready to wage war.

The discussion grew heated, one of the men shouting *acum, acum, acum!* The Captain kept his cool, explaining himself in a way that settled them down. When he was done he hooked my elbow and hauled me back inside for a glass of peat moss.

"They want to march now, *acum*, before the army garrison hears about our uprising and mans the parapets."

"Makes sense."

Dragomir poured us each a slug of Scotch. I took the glass he offered and drained it. It tasted bad but it felt good.

"But I do not want to march as yet," he said. "I want them to learn what has happened, to talk about it amongst themselves, to decide which side they want to be on. Now that the revolution has begun."

"Sounds good, Captain, just one question. Who is *them?*"

Dragomir eyed me as if I were daft. "The soldiers in the garrison."

"Of course."

History is up to its eyebrows in rabble-rousing strongmen who are good at only one thing - whipping their followers into a frenzy and marching them off a cliff. But the Captain had the smarts to hang back for a minute or two, to delay his attack for strategic advantage. He was an impressive leader, this Dragomir.

It looked like Frank Wisner's hoped-for indigenous anti-Communist resistance movement was underway, unbeknownst to Frank, the CIA and the President of the United States of America.

I would have to find a minute to let them know.

Chapter Twenty-one

We marched the two miles to the Romanian Army garrison though our dozen fighters could have squeezed into the beds of two pickup trucks. We carried burning torches made from tightly-wrapped rags soaked in pitch. I wore the Remington six shooter in my new belt holster.

The torches were a big hit. We marched out of Dragomir's pagoda about eleven-thirty that Saturday night and proceeded down the narrow cobbled street beneath the Bridge of Lies. The old folks had gone to bed but young men were still winding down the festival on street corners, smoking, passing bottles back and forth.

I understood why the Captain didn't want his men in uniform. Or in trucks. We weren't an anonymous militia racing through town, we were the home team. Men joined us at every intersection. None asked who we were, none asked where we were headed. We were the home team with burning torches.

Every few blocks a partisan would present the swelling crowd a basket of rods or sticks or rusty old scythes which our recruits stumbled and scrambled to grab hold of. We marched on at a good clip.

This shindig was probably a bit more inebriated than Frank Wisner had in mind but it wasn't bad.

We strode past ancient three-story homes with peaked tile roofs. When the street widened half a mile later we passed newer, smaller homes with flower boxes and postage stamp yards. Few late night revelers were out and about in this neighborhood and some of our recruits were sucking wind and falling behind.

We were running out of steam as we approached a major thoroughfare half a mile later. Dragomir, who had not acted as Grand Marshall so far, pulled out a parade whistle and gave it three blasts. The recruits weren't sure what this meant but it perked them right up.

The Captain shouted "*Companie, opri!*" which I translated as 'Company, halt' because that was what we did.

Dragomir waded out onto the boulevard and whistled oncoming traffic to a halt. He waved us through, we turned left. The four-lane street was crowded on both sides with tall apartment buildings. Some had balconies. Balconies full to bursting with lustily cheering partisans. To this day I don't know how the Captain pulled that off.

We marched west, new spring in our step. Our ranks swelled. The garrison was some eight blocks further on. We arrived with a whooping, chanting drunken throng of over a hundred men. Maybe two hundred.

The garrison took no notice of us, remaining dimly lit behind twenty-foot walls. Looked like they knew we were coming though. The sentry box in front of the main gate was lit, empty, door ajar.

I gave the joint the once over. It was big, with a couple three-story steel and concrete office buildings inside the walls, likely used by Romanian officers and their Soviet minders. The windows were dark on this Saturday night I was happy to see, the brass weren't up late frantically cabling Moscow. But the garrison wasn't the collection of ramshackle barracks I had expected to find. It was formidable.

Captain Dragomir had said he had men inside. Now, it seemed to me, would be a good time for them to get busy.

We stood there stupidly, our torches guttering low, some of the men gently swaying as if on the deck of a ship at sea. I caught Dragomir's eye. He smiled, and lipped his whistle.

He sounded two blasts, one long, one short. The motorized gate winged open a moment later. No hostiles opened fire. We followed our fearless leader inside the compound.

A small group of soldiers rushed up to greet the Captain and tell him stuff and gesticulate wildly in the Romanian manner. Dragomir listened, asked several questions and listened some more. His slow motion style of command was making me nervous. We had penetrated an enemy encampment. We should be wreaking havoc by now.

But the behavior of the soldiers seemed to indicate that havoc had already been wreaked. They gave each other quick sideways looks, took a step back and saluted Captain Dragomir as one.

He accepted their tribute humbly, then gave the Romanian command for 'As you were.'

We followed the soldiers deeper into the compound. There were barracks further on, low-slung wooden buildings that formed a quadrangle with a grassy square in the middle for mustering troops.

And troops there were this Saturday evening, fifty or so. They barely noticed the arrival of us torch-bearing revolutionaries, however. They were too busy getting their pictures took.

Our eager insurgents slowed to a crawl at the eerie scene taking place in the quadrangle. A photographer was posing soldiers for keepsake photos.

Two tall pole lamps provided the only light so it was quite a shock to see what the photographer's flash captured, like a bolt of lightning on a black night.

Two young soldiers, one on either side, were mugging at the lens. In between them was a dead Romanian officer, impaled from behind, on a wooden stake. As more flash photos were taken it became clear that there were three such officers from which the enlisted men could chose.

The lower legs of the victims, I noticed as I got closer, had been bent back at the knee and bound to their thighs. The victims had been hobbled in this way so that gravity and the impaling stake could do their grisly work without resistance.

God.

That wasn't the worst of it. The victims were arranged in a V with the commanding officer planted at the tip. He was the most popular photographic subject. He was also, I noticed from his blinking lids and twitching lips, still alive.

Not right. Not even close.

I shoved my way to the head of the line, pointed the barrel of the Remington at the man's heart and put the poor bastard out of his misery.

The shot rang out like a cannon round. Blood gushed from the commanding officer's nostrils and his carcass sank several inches down the stake.

I turned around, my five-pound six shooter firmly in hand in case anyone cared to object to my course of action.

Our anti-Communist insurgents and the Romanian Army conscripts took a moment to look around and ponder this new development, then erupted into deafening cheers.

Chapter Twenty-two

Four a.m. is a wonderful time of day, still and calm as a glacial lake. Lucian had driven me to our improvised landing strip so that I could radio STINGRAY at the appointed hour.

I inspected the strip as I donned my phones and fired up the J/E. It looked like the steam roller had mashed the ag field into decent shape. There was no give in the dirt when I stepped on it and Lucian's truck hadn't left any ruts.

I checked the pocket watch Captain Dragomir had loaned me and keyed the mike at the tick of four.

"This is TIMBER calling STINGRAY. Come in STINGRAY."

I got a reply on my third try. "This is STRINGRAY, over."

Now that I had the floor I got tongue-tied. My words were being recorded or transcribed verbatim and would be replayed or repeated at the highest levels of the U.S. government.

The charter of the OPC awarded Director Frank Wisner ironclad confidentiality. But STINGRAY worked for the USAF, which reported to the Joint Chiefs, who reported to the Commander in Chief.

Think, genius!

"Operation proceeding…"

No, more positive.

"Operation successful."

Now what?

"Await further instruction…"

No, numbskull, no time to waste.

"Strongly recommend ongoing support for…further undertakings."

Weak!

"*Future operations.* Strongly recommend ongoing support for future operations."

STINGRAY took a beat to set up his droll reply.

"Copy."

We hadn't pre-arranged the next dance step. I hadn't told STINGRAY to tell Wisner that I needed a quick answer on Captain Dragomir's request for anti-tank weapons and a pot of gold because that had seemed an outrageous demand on top of an outrageous demand. I'd been thinking like an enlisted man, not the officer in charge.

Dragomir had said the nearest Red Army base was three days distant. He'd have to take delivery of the money and munitions by tomorrow night in order to have enough time to truck his regulars and new recruits to his designated ambush spot in the mountain gorge. The ambush spot where Vlad Tepes Draculea had massacred the invading Turks centuries before the United States of America was even a twinkle in George Washington's eye.

I was disappointed in myself. I felt like a frayed wire connecting a powerful generator, Sorin Dragomir, to a large capacitor, Frank Wisner. With any luck Dragomir's surging current would complete the voltaic arc.

Which is a tortured way of saying I hoped Frank Wisner would divine the Captain's clock-is-ticking message despite my failure to transmit same.

Frank Wisner had. STINGRAY confirmed that our 'request for provisions' had already been approved.

Whew.

And wow. Who'd have thunk it?

I told STINGRAY that the landing strip exceeded the required length and that it needed to be approached from the west because of tall trees at the eastern end.

"And it's hard dirt, not asphalt."

Long pause from on high. "Roger."

I waited for instructions, conscious of how profoundly absurd it was to be listening for important words to appear from 30,000 feet while perched on the front bumper of a hay truck parked in an ag field in a valley in rural Transylvania.

I was happy to be here though, happy to be far away from the army garrison and that grotesque tribute to Vlad the Impaler. I told myself at the time that I had seen worse during my behind-the-lines service in World War Two. But that wasn't strictly true.

"Tomorrow, 2200 hours" came the reply. "Co-pilot COYOTE will make contact five minutes prior, weather permitting. Fuel dictates a ten minute window."

"Copy."

"Command requests security assurance."

"Security in place."

"How will runway be lit?"

He would ask that. I told him torches, what else could it be? Then added the kicker.

"Will need to smuggle two high value assets on board."

It took a static-choked ten minutes to work out the details but I signed off feeling that STINGRAY and I had hammered out a winning plan.

Weather permitting.

Chapter Twenty-three

Princess Stela bid us goodnight at about half past seven the following evening.

I was sitting in the parlor with Captain Dragomir, going over his last minute tick list. Stela entered with Cosmina, Dragomir's young maid and the boy king's nanny. The pint-sized monarch was snoozing on her shoulder.

Stela wished Dragomir good luck. He nodded.

I knew the Captain had instructed two of his men to remain behind and look after Princess Stela. He knew she would kill to be on that supply plane with her son when it took off in a few hours time.

Turned out he was right.

"And now we must put young Vlad to bed," said Stela and whispered off on slippered feet, Cosmina scurrying behind.

Stela had assured me she had an escape plan in place. I didn't press, figured she'd seduced some young fool into helping her to sneak out the window and roll on down the road.

I was clear with her about one thing. We had a short runway, no additional passengers would be permitted. Not even the boy king's adored nanny.

Princess Stela assured me this would not be a problem.

I had given her a hand-drawn map detailing her hiding place on the thickly wooded far side of the landing strip, the side opposite the road.

The C-45 would taxi to the end of the runway and turn around. She and the boy were to scramble up a rope ladder tossed from the cockpit after Dragomir and his men offloaded the cargo on the opposite side of the plane.

It was high risk. Anyone looking under the plane's fuselage would spot their approach even in the dim torch light. I was counting on the Captain's men being preoccupied by two things that delight men everywhere.

Guns and loot.

I had a date with COYOTE for 2200 hours. At 2000 hours Dragomir herded six of his men into the back of a troop truck they had commandeered from the army garrison. It was a small number for a big mission. Maybe the other core members of his cadre were done in by the exertion of the previous night's activities.

Sure, Schroeder. More likely Sorin Dragomir only had six men he could trust to handle a fortune in gold.

We began the twenty-mile trip to our improvised landing field, the Captain, wearing knitted leather driving gloves, at the wheel. I rode shotgun.

I assumed, that is to say hoped, that Stela and her son had enough of a head start so that we wouldn't overtake them on the road. They'd have a hell of a time getting to their hiding place with Dragomir's men prowling the perimeter.

The Captain was in a cheery mood, singing snatches of patriotic songs and one burst of "God Bless America, land that I love!"

Why not? He was about to assume an important role. He was about to become the spear point of Western Civilization's attempt to pierce the Iron Curtain. By his own account his success might lead to anti-Communist insurrections in a number of Balkan countries.

Little wonder Frank Wisner had signed off on Dragomir's request for twenty-five thousand dollars in gold. Frank Wisner wouldn't have blinked at five times that amount.

We arrived at the landing strip forty-eight minutes early. I was still carrying Captain Dragomir's pocket watch which I intended to give back to him before I boarded the plane.

I looked across the runway to Stela's designated hiding place, hoping she was hunkered down with the boy king. Shit, the kid was only three. What if he started bawling?

Don't sweat it, Schroeder. PS will stuff a rag in his mouth if she has to.

Dragomir's men set about lighting the landing strip's perimeter, using plump little smudge pots filled with kerosene instead of torches.

After that we spent fifty long minutes listening to crickets chirp. I radioed COYOTE at 2210 even though he was the one who was supposed to initiate contact. No reply.

Dragomir's men muttered darkly and shot me looks. It was all I could do not to shrug. The Captain remained silent.

A light rain started to fall and I felt something I didn't expect to feel. Relief. This operation always had a creepy funhouse feel to it. I still wanted out of here and I still wanted Captain Dragomir to succeed. Yet I felt relieved as the rain fell.

And then the J/E lit up.

COYOTE wanted to know if they could land. I told the Captain to drive the troop truck onto the landing strip, speed up, then hit the brakes.

He did that. The truck tires didn't sink down but about a quarter inch.

I passed this information along to COYOTE. He had twang, this flyboy.

"Roger that, TIMBER. We din't just buck through a hunnert miles o' thunderheads to bang a U'ey. Clear the decks, we're rollin' in."

"Roger dodger, you old codger."

Always wanted to say that on the radio. It looked like we were going to do this thing after all.

The C-45 roared in and touched down without much difficulty. It taxied to the end of the runway and turned around at the stand of trees.

I was surprised to see that it had been painted black and bore no markings of any sort. They didn't want to display the USAF roundel on a secret mission of course, but Beech made a civilian version of the C-45 that was used by mail haulers and such.

Amateurs. A mail plane would have been a more effective disguise. Black screamed cloak and dagger.

I ran up to greet the crew and gave them the all clear. They opened the cargo bay. The truck rumbled up to offload the supplies.

I was supposed to give Stela a flashlight signal when the offloading was complete, her cue to come forward.

But when the loading was done and the truck eased away from the plane all hell broke loose.

Half a dozen jeeps roared out of the stand of trees behind the strip, lights blaring, mounted machine guns firing.

I raced for a clump of bushes by the road, figuring the C-45 would be a target.

But there was no gunfire toward the plane and no gunfire from the plane.

I hit the dirt and crawled behind the clump of bushes.

Captain Dragomir had two men flanking the truck, one on each side, and another bringing up the rear. They carried automatic rifles captured at the garrison. They would have been better off with their Lee-Enfields. They struggled to operate their new weapons and were quickly cut down.

I felt that familiar wall come down. The one that protected me from the shock of combat. The eerie calm that said *this is something you can worry about later. Now is not the time.*

The kill squad shot up the truck's tires instead of concentrating their firepower on Dragomir and his companion in the cab, who was squeezing off a few piddling pistol rounds.

The other two men were in the tarp-covered bed of the truck, cowering or dead.

The kill squad wasn't in uniform. They were driving GAZ-67s. They wanted to take Sorin Dragomir alive.

They were NKVD. Beria wouldn't trust the *Securitate* with a job this big.

A deep voice spoke over a bullhorn. I recognized the language as Romanian. I surmised the content as 'Come out with your hands up.'

Captain Dragomir did just that, to my shock and dismay. He marched resolutely toward the man with the bullhorn, his hands held high.

I noticed something odd about his attire. He had doffed his jacket and gloves before he climbed out of the truck. Shame on me for doubting him.

Two men jumped out of the lead jeep to grab him as he approached.

Dragomir reached behind his back and whipped out the handgun he had wedged in his belt and fired four rounds at the man with the bullhorn before the machine gunners cut him to ribbons.

The head man clutched his throat with one hand and reflexively squeezed the bullhorn trigger with his other so that his death gurgle was broadcast out across the runway.

The Blue Caps were shocked to silence as their commander toppled from the jeep.

Then the second-in-command seized the bullhorn and started barking commands.

I suppose a true hero would have unholstered his six shooter, raced into battle to avenge his leader and gone out in a blaze of glory.

But the thought never occurred to me. If Dragomir's remaining men didn't get killed here they would be captured, interrogated and killed later. I was the only one left who could tell his story. How Captain Sorin Dragomir, loyal monarchist and fierce anti-Communist crusader, had martyred himself for the cause.

That's what I told myself anyway.

Dragomir's companion in the cab hit the dirt as instructed and was cuffed and carted off. The Blue Cap with the bullhorn addressed himself to the back of the truck as the GAZ-67 machine gunners trained their weapons in that direction.

I would like to report that these last core members of the Captain's cadre followed his example. I would especially like to report that they broke open the crates containing the anti-tank bazookas and went to town on those GAZ-67s. But they did not. They surrendered meekly.

I have always had a healthy skepticism of leaders. Big egos and wisdom don't often come in the same package. But leaders do come in handy once the shit hits the fan. Dragomir's men knew their leader was dead and that took all the starch out of them.

I looked to the sky. Thick clouds blacked out the moon and stars. I inched forward on my belly and felt the dirt runway. The pinprick rain hadn't done much damage, it was still hard packed.

Then I looked up from the dirt. I looked up to see two small figures duck under the belly of the plane and approach the light from the cargo bay. Princess Stela and her son.

What was she *doing?* The chaos of the last few minutes had been the perfect opportunity for her to clamber up the rope ladder on the far side of the plane and into the cockpit.

The Blue Caps, the two who had jumped down from their jeeps to grab Dragomir, rushed over to intercept Stela and the boy. They wore black leather coats and held Makarov pistols. The bigger one rattled off an angry stream of Romanian.

PS calmly ushered her son behind her and replied in a different language. Russian. The men lowered their weapons. A heated argument ensued. Commissar Second-in-Command stalked over to join the fray. The boy king began to whimper.

Stela set down her suitcase, picked him up and held him to her chest with both arms, her voice lower now, but firm, not pleading.

If she was the one who had blown the whistle on our covert operation why would the NKVD be giving her the third degree?

But if she hadn't, why would they abruptly turn away and allow her to climb up the step stair into the cargo bay. Which is what they did.

I was feeling a little left out, lying on my belly in the dirt while the cargo door got shut and sealed. At least they didn't fire up the propellers.

We might wait it out, the C-45 crew and me. They knew I was nearby. The Reds had gotten what they came for. They showed no interest in attacking the plane. They might disappear into the night and leave us sadass Yanks to lick our wounds.

Unfortunately the rain went from a gentle brush stroke to a Gene Krupa tom tom solo about then. I dug out my J/E, put on the phones and made a quiet call to COYOTE.

He answered instantly. I told him I was going to attempt to run across the landing strip.

"Deploy the rope ladder from right cockpit window. If I'm hit make no attempt at rescue. Take off as conditions dictate."

"Roger, TIMBER. Best o' luck."

I got my gun in hand and waited till the three Blue Caps disappeared into the troop truck, then put my head down and darted across the runway.

I could have dispensed with the darting. In fact I could've done a buck and wing while accompanying myself on accordion and the kill squad wouldn't have noticed. They were busy as ants on an all-day sucker, swarming the troop truck, exclaiming and shouting. If you can whoop in Russian they were doing that. They had, apparently, found the crate of gold sovereigns.

Co-pilot COYOTE, a blue-eyed scamp with sandy hair, sought to keep things light after he hauled me in through the open window. He pressed his finger to my lips, looked over to the pilot and whispered what co-pilots are supposed to announce in a loud voice.

"Clear."

They fired up the props. I staggered back to the cargo hold, took a jump seat and looked out a porthole window.

We throttled down the hardpan runway. It held up well despite the downpour, even the smudge pots stayed lit. Sorin Dragomir had done everything right.

I did not return Stela's happy smile as we torqued into the black sky for a long flight to an unknown destination. The Princess had a lot of questions to answer.

Boy, did she.

Chapter Twenty-four

We flew all night save for a quick refueling stop in northern Greece. We shared flyboy fare – salami on a hard roll and a coke.

The drone of the engines put little Vlad to sleep soon after takeoff. Stela held him on her lap. He was a handsome lad with light brown hair and rosy cheeks. He looked more like his dad than his mom.

I wanted to have a little chat with the Princess so I asked the loadmaster sergeant to go chat up the pilots for five or so. He nodded and climbed into the cramped cockpit. I looked over at Stela in the jump seat across from me. She met my stare defiantly.

"They knew me," she said.

"The Blue Caps?"

"*Da.* They were knowing all about Sibiu."

"Then why the hell did they let you board? You took part in the uprising!"

She winced and held up her hand at my raised voice, as if I was some loudmouth drunk. Pissed me off.

I leaned over and growled, "Answer the damn question Stela."

"I explain it to them. If I am arrested I am, I become a…how do you say? A saint who is killed?"

"A martyr."

"Just so. A martyr to the people. But if I am to go on areoplane I become a…how do you say?"

"You know how you say."

"A traitor?"

"Yeah," I snorted, "just so."

I leaned in some more. "Why did you duck under the plane? Why didn't you climb up the rope ladder on the other side?"

"I did not have this ladder. When came all of the gun shootings your brave pilots hid away."

Hate to say it but that sounded believable. Flyboys were notorious for feet of clay on terra firma. I would have to give COYOTE an enormous ration of shit.

The Princess had all the right answers but my fevered brain kept replaying the same scene. Captain Dragomir being torn to pieces by machine guns as he fired his service weapon at the enemy.

The enemy. A slippery concept on this occasion. Sorin Dragomir's enemy was Soviet Communism. In the abstract. In the particular it was Princess Stela Varadja. He had kidnapped her son. So I kept pressing, asking her who she had recruited to help her and her son slip out the window and down the long road to the airstrip.

"Lucian, he was from Palace Guard, like Sorin. He fears the Blue Caps, wants to go away, go away to America."

"And you promised him a flight out?"

"*Da.*"

"And what happened to him? Where did he go?"

"When the shootings started he ran away."

"And if he hadn't fled, how did you intend to get him onboard the plane?"

Stela shrugged .

I had no way to confirm this story but Lucian, who had driven me in his hay truck to the unfinished airstrip, did seem a bit of a nail-biter. He'd spent so much time checking the mirror for a tail that I twice had to grab the wheel to keep us from veering off the road. That Stela didn't make any excuse for her callous behavior inclined me to believe her.

I didn't ask her any more questions that night. I wrapped myself in a blanket against the cold, stretched out my legs and nodded off.

We landed at a military airbase just before dawn and were immediately bundled into a large van with a tall bespectacled man who introduced himself as Stanley. I didn't know if he was CIA or OPC or State Department and I didn't ask. No point. I was just along for the ride.

We were seated with our backs to the driver. There were no windows. It was a polite way of being blindfolded.

Stanley sat across from us in the back of the van. He seemed a bit puzzled at my traveling companions, a woman and a small child. All I had told STINGRAY was that I was bringing along two high value assets. When I introduced Stanley to the fetching Princess Stela Varadja he slid me a glance.

I replied with a weary head shake. *This is not what you think it is.*

He made polite inquiries about our flight, not wanting to debrief me in the presence of the mystery woman. I figured that would take place at the CIA station in…"Where the hell are we anyway?"

A mischievous grin from Stanley. "You'll see."

We drove about ninety minutes, the last thirty minutes or so filled with stops and starts and honking horns. Little Vlad got cranky despite Stela's attempts to soothe him. She looked beat.

"I'll take him," I said. She handed him over gladly.

The kid couldn't have been over fifty pounds but he weighed a ton. He writhed in my grasp. I had to hold him at arm's length to keep him from clawing my face. I hoisted him high above my head and smiled up at him as he bawled.

"Hey there, big stuff, I hear ya. You've been bounced around from pillar to post."

I tossed him up a few inches and caught him. He stopped bawling. I did it again, higher this time. He smiled.

I waited until we were stopped at another intersection. The van had a high ceiling, high enough for me to stand up. So I tossed the boy king up high, jumped to my feet – Stela's look was sheer horror – and caught him at waist level as he plummeted downward.

Young Vlad looked glassy-eyed for a moment. Then he giggled.

"Ya see," I said, "you get to like it."

The van parked a few minutes later. Our driver opened the side door and we crawled out. My legs felt wobbly when they hit the pavement. We were in a narrow back alley behind a four-story, polished stone building of classic Renaissance architecture. A stunner.

The driver handed me Stela's suitcase and got back in the van. There didn't look to be an entrance on this side of the building but Stanley led us to a rust colored steel door cut into the stone. He used two keys on two locks. We entered a small chamber where we faced another steel door. Stanley inserted a pin key into a metal pad next to the door.

We waited. Stela with her sleeping son on her shoulder. Me flexing my neck and shoulders, trying to shake off the long trip. The steel door opened. Damned if it wasn't an elevator.

We crowded in. Stanley pushed a button – there was only one – and up we went. When the door opened we entered a wide, plushly carpeted corridor.

This weren't no CIA station. I saw only two doors in the long hallway. One close, on the right. One far, on the left.

Stanley led us to the close one, its hinges on the outside, no handle, no keyhole. It popped open when he stuck a plastic card into a slot.

We walked into a foyer with a kitchen behind it. A kitchen containing more marble and granite than Westminster Abbey. To the left was a living room with red leather chairs, white linen sofas lined with gold braid, and a crystal chandelier for Chrissakes. The bay windows were covered with flouncy lace.

I marched over to the first window and threw open the drapes. Pink dawn bathed the basilica of St. Peter's Cathedral.

Holy shit. Rome!

Stanley smiled at my goofy grin. "They say this was Mussolini's bachelor pad, his *imbottitura di scapolo*."

"Really?"

"That's what they say," said Mr. Stanley. His thick black frame glasses made his eyeballs look like fat goldfish in a bowl.

"And what do you say?"

"Our Italian friends have a stormy relationship with the truth."

We were warmly welcomed by a tiny middle-aged housekeeper a moment later. She shook our hands vigorously and cooed over little Vlad.

I expected Stanley to take this opportunity to escort me to a back room and ask endless questions while he took copious notes. But he asked only one question as he pulled me along on his way out the door.

"What is the condition of our friend?"

Amateurs. Me included. This operation had been such a yank job that no one had taken two seconds to give Dragomir a code name.

"Our friend, if you're referring to Captain Sorin Dragomir, is dead."

Stanley nodded cheerily and said, "Duly noted."

It was all I could do not to slug him.

"Take a day to recuperate," said Stanley, patting me on the back in fatherly fashion. "Maria will take good care of you."

He didn't tell me not to leave the apartment as he let himself out the vacuum-locked door with his plastic card. No need. Place was a cell with lace curtains.

Chapter Twenty-five

Maria cooked up scrambled eggs and something that looked like bacon but wasn't and something that looked like toast but was smaller and crunchier. Whatever it was it hit the spot.

After breakfast she showed us to our separate quarters, each with its own bathroom. I let Stela have the larger room, Benito's boudoir as it were.

Maria told us to pile our dirty clothes outside our doors, then she retired to her room further down the hall. I gave PS and her son first crack at the hot water and wandered off to case the joint.

The windows in the living room opened out. The pantry was well stocked. So was the liquor cabinet. The keyless door was beyond my ken.

Five years ago I would've knotted bed sheets and rappelled down the side of the building to show my independence. But we had plenty of food and booze and a good cook. Yeah, it was involuntary confinement, but it beat a Romanian barn stall all to hell.

I took a hot soak in a Roman tub. The coating of grime on my body turned the water brown so I drained the tub and took a scalding shower. I dried off with fluffy towels and donned a monogrammed robe. Somebody had a sense of humor. The monogram read *BM*.

I studied my face in the mirror. The swelling was down, the bruises now more gray and yellow than black and blue. Finding the bathroom fully stocked, I shaved off my scraggly beard - which took forever - brushed my teeth and combed my hair with something that was either hair tonic or aftershave. A new man!

I dropped my stinking heap of clothes in the hall and eyed the king size bed. It called to me, murmured sweet nothings in my ear. But something was wrong, something was missing.

My little arsenal sat atop the mahogany bureau. What else, what else?

Dragomir's pocket watch, that's what. I had stuck it in my pants pocket for safekeeping. It would not do to have Maria run it through the wash cycle. I went back to the stinking pile and retrieved it, put it on the nightstand next to me and sacked out at precisely 8:39 a.m. Romanian time.

My eyes popped open three hours later. I went to the bathroom and splashed myself awake. Maria had deposited my freshly laundered clothes on the bureau next to my little arsenal.

I should have shoved all that stuff in a drawer but I'd been too tired to think straight. I could only imagine what Maria thought. What kind of nut travels with a steak knife, a sap and a century-old six gun in a cowboy holster?

And I could only imagine what Frank Wisner would think of me when I greeted him in a flannel shirt and moleskin pants suitable for duck hunting. An outfit he himself might have left behind at the stone cottage.

I pulled on my clothes, shoes and socks and followed the aroma of strong coffee down the hall. I saw an odd tableau in the living room. Maria the housekeeper was down on all fours wrassling with young Vlad, who fought her playful advances with grim determination.

Stela stood by a bay window in her slip and, the late morning sun made clear, nothing else. She had one high-arched foot planted on the sill, and was bending over to embrace her knee.

I wanted to question her further in order to make sense of the odd sequence of events that had brought us here. But now was not the time. Watching the Princess do ballet exercises in her underwear would be, shall we say, unhelpful to my concentration.

I went to the kitchen, poured some mud and returned to my room, unnoticed.

The coffee, as in Romania, was strong. How is it that hard charging, high achieving Yanks drink coffee so weak you can see the bottom of the cup while Italians and Romanians down pitch-black jet fuel all day long and never get anything done?

They oughtta do a study. In the meantime I had a bigger bone to chew on.

I had assumed the traitor who compromised the operation was Guy Burgess or one of Wisner's poorly-vetted new hires. But the U.S. had invaded sovereign territory on a covert mission. The Reds could have blown the plane to bits and we couldn't say boo. Why didn't they?

Who wanted on that plane as much as I did?

Princess Stela Varadja.

Was her heated confrontation with the Blue Caps playacting for my benefit?

I mulled it over. Stela was a survivor, sure, but a cutthroat killer? I couldn't picture it.

If betraying the operation was her only ticket out, maybe. Mothers will do most anything to save their kids. But the operation *was* her means of escape. Her only other motive to betray us that I could think of was a fanatical devotion to the cause of World Communism. And that didn't make a lick of sense.

Could be the NKVD kill squad didn't attack the C-45 because they knew they didn't have to, because they knew they could let it be. The rules of engagement for the C-45 crew would have been the same as the OPC mission briefers had instructed me. 'Do not fire unless fired upon.'

If the Blue Caps knew that going in, they would know the C-45 crew wouldn't use their weapons even when the kill squad took down the truck. They would know they could ignore the plane and concentrate on getting what they wanted - the cargo. Let the plane crew return home in defeat.

No one in Romania, Stela included, knew the OPC rules of engagement. The rat, therefore, was in D.C.

That was where my black coffee logic led me anyway.

I spent the rest of the afternoon in less seemly pursuits. Picturing the Princess and me at the bay window together, the basilica of St. Peter's rimmed in scarlet, our cheeks pink with wine, performing strenuous and acrobatic ballet exercises.

Maria served us a late dinner that evening. *Vitello piccata,* which was tart with lemon and sweet with wine, and *orcchiette* pasta, which looked like tiny ears. It was delicious though I couldn't say why. It didn't have a speck of tomato sauce.

We sat at a small round table squeezed into the back of the kitchen, the only dining area in the big apartment. It really was a bachelor pad.

Little Vlad, who sat propped up on a pillow across from me, looked vexed by these strange vittles. Maria had cut his veal into bite-sized pieces but the boy king wasn't interested.

His mother gently prompted him to eat his food. Nothing doing. She picked him up and put him on her lap. He squirmed. She tried to feed him a spoonful of the *orcchiette*. He turned his head away. She tried again. He pushed her hand away, hard, scattering pasta shells all down his front.

Stela gave a little shriek. The boy slithered out of her grasp, hit the floor and scuttled madly toward freedom between chair legs and crossed ankles.

Stela jumped up, ready to give chase, but Maria scooped up the boy as he crawled out from under. She scolded him in rapid fire Italian while she rocked him like an infant. He stopped squirming, and began to cry.

Maria looked a question to Stela, who paused, then nodded briskly and resumed her seat. Maria carried the sobbing boy king off to bed.

The Princess and I finished our meal in silence. I assumed she was stewing about her son but resisted the urge to say something soothingly stupid. I cleared the plates when we were done. Stela took the bottle of Chianti and our two glasses to the living room. She set them down on the cut glass coffee table and filled them full.

It was a pleasant moment between us. A bit of unspoken teamwork you might expect from a couple who had been together awhile. I joined her on the white linen sofa, a dangerous combination. White linen and red wine.

"I never thanked you," she said.

"For what?"

"You took big risk to save us. Your CIA does not want us, we are worth more to them if dead."

"Three-year-old boys should not be martyrs."

Stela patted my hand.

She spun tales of life in the Palace during the war as we drank our wine. Expecting a dreary picture of life under enemy occupation, she talked instead of the months when Frank Wisner ran the OSS station in late '44. How they conspired to rescue downed Allied flyers right under the nose of the *Wehrmacht*, and how the Palace briefly returned to the glory and elegance of the pre-war years when Bucharest was the Paris of the Balkans.

"We were doing important work, in fine style. It was so satisfying," she trilled, raising her glass, "so intoxicating."

Her English, I noticed, improved when she got tipsy. We clanked and drank, huddled closely together on the divan.

She slid off her shoes, set her slender ankles on the coffee table and flexed her toes, the nails freshly manicured and painted with clear polish. I admired Princess Stela's dainty white feet for a time.

I knew where this was headed, had been anticipating it all day. But now that the train was about to leave the station I hesitated. And not just because I didn't want to lie to Frank Wisner.

He was on his way to Rome, that would explain why I hadn't been debriefed. This had been Wisner's operation top to tail and it was obvious he wasn't going to trust some tweedy goof like Stanley to ask the questions for him.

And it wasn't that I didn't trust Stela. I didn't but it wasn't that.

What I really had doubts about were me and her together. I'm a man who enjoys a stiff drink or two or three. Four is where you get into trouble. I figured Princess Stela and me together were nine, maybe ten. I was afraid that after one night with her and I'd end up a wretched stewbum wandering back alleys in the Bowery, filtering shots of Sterno through scraps of moldy bread.

Metaphorically speaking.

So I asked Princess Stela a question she wasn't used to hearing. "Shouldn't you be looking after your son?"

That concluded our night of passion. Stela grabbed her glass of wine and stalked down the hall. I watched her go with some regret, surprised at myself for making the right decision.

I poured myself another splash and thought about the report I was going to have to make to Frank Wisner.

He wasn't going to like the airstrip part but it wasn't all bad news. I had witnessed the locals' fury at the puppet government and seen a Romanian Army garrison surrender without a firing a shot. That the mission was blown by some D.C. pinko wasn't my fault.

My only unauthorized walk in the park was snatching Stela and her son out from under Captain Dragomir. Which made me feel fortunate that my grilling would come from Wisner himself. Anyone else might question the wisdom of bringing a known NKVD field hand into U.S. protection. But Frank Wisner knew Princess Stela and would understand.

Sure he would. What devoted career man and loving husband doesn't enjoy a surprise visit from his former mistress and bastard son?

Chapter Twenty-six

Stela and I avoided each other for most of the following day. We both knew who was coming to visit tonight. Maria had prepared an enormous tray of appetizers instead of dinner.

I holed up in my room, reading an old LIFE magazine. The cover was a photo of the hero of the Berlin Air Lift, 'Captain Candybar,' a USAF pilot who came up with the idea of dropping candy to the kids of that ravaged city, using hankies as parachutes. Cute.

Frank Wisner arrived that evening about seven. He looked beat from his long trip but he greeted Stela and me heartily. "And who is this handsome young lad?"

Man, was he in for a big surprise.

Wisner asked Maria for a glass of ice water. "And no gas." He asked Stela and me if we were enjoying our stay. We said that we were.

"Good," said Wisner and turned to me. "Where can we talk?"

Frank took a glass of ice water from Maria and followed me down the hall to my room. He plunked himself down on the plump red cushion of the room's only chair. I closed the door and sat on the foot of the bed.

Wisner paid no mind to my goofy duds, just studied my face.

"They really went to town on you, the Magyars."

"It was an enthusiastic interrogation, sir, but I count myself lucky," I said. "I'm surprised you know about that."

"We didn't drop you in blind, we had sources in place."

"Yes sir."

"Though we lost track when you and Stela fled the stone cottage."

Huh?

"That was a smart move on your part, to send up a J/E flare from the airstrip."

"Thank you. But that was Captain Dragomir's idea."

That the OPC had lost track Stela and me after we fled the stone cottage suggested that one of Stela's Soviet minders was a source and that Sorin Dragomir wasn't. Which made no sense whatsoever.

Supposition and speculation, Schroeder. Noise. Tell the boss man what you know and shut your yap.

I ran it down. From my capture by the Magyars to my transfer to the stone cottage and our subsequent escape to Sibiu, to Stela chewing out Dragomir for the kidnap of her son to the Captain's successful uprising in Sibiu. I told him what the Princess was up to in the cottage with her NKVD minders. If Wisner was surprised he didn't show it.

I didn't mention how PS managed to get herself on the plane despite the objections of the Soviet secret police because I still wasn't sure what went on there. I would let Wisner know as soon as I did.

I also left out the grisly scene in the quadrangle of the Army garrison, out of respect for Sorin Dragomir's memory. I didn't believe he had anything to do with that though we never discussed it. I chose to believe he was innocent of that atrocity.

The C-45 crew had already been debriefed so Wisner knew about the kill squad disaster at the airstrip. He didn't know how Captain Dragomir met his end however. I described his heroics in detail.

Frank Wisner hung his head when I was done. "Son of a bitch."

"He was the genuine article sir."

Wisner nodded solemnly and shifted gears. "What the hell happened?"

"Someone blew the whistle on us."

"I know that! Who?"

"I might have a possible but I need to ask a question. What were the rules of engagement for the plane crew?"

"The usual."

"'Don't fire unless fired upon.' Which the plane wasn't, even though the kill squad had plenty of firepower."

"You're suggesting the mission was compromised stateside."

"Yes sir. By someone who knew our rules of engagement and instructed the Blue Caps to concentrate on securing the cargo and not waste ammo on the C-45."

Wisner grunted. "Who's your candidate?"

"Guy Burgess sir. I was thinking of Guy Burgess."

"I've heard the rumors, Schroeder, but this mission was self contained. We didn't brief MI6."

So much for that theory.

Wisner paused to glug down half his glass of water. "How'd you come to be captured by the Magyars?"

"My fault. I sent the Captain and his platoon back home after we took some hostile fire on our recon mission."

"And you proceeded alone?" said Wisner, chin down, eyebrows up.

"No sir. Two of his men accompanied me."

"And?"

I hesitated. It felt like I was squealing on Dragomir.

"Unfortunately one of the Captain's men shot the other one in the back and knocked me out." I continued before Wisner could interrupt. "In the man's defense the Magyars had kidnapped his daughter."

"Ah," said Wisner with a bitter, wizened smile, "Romania."

I wanted to dispute his obvious conclusion that the traitor was one of Captain Dragomir's inner circle, those dark fierce men who had followed the Captain through hell and high water. But I had nothing to say that was worth hearing.

"I knew it," said Wisner after a time, looking oddly pleased. "There is a living, breathing anti-Communist underground out there. We'll just have to do better job of counterintelligence. Save for one nigger in the woodpile the operation might well have been a success."

"But isn't that the thing about top secret operations, sir?"

"What's that?"

"It only *takes* one."

We walked back down the hall. Maria had set her platter of appetizers on the marble counter that separated the kitchen from the living room. She was stirring up a pitcher of martinis.

"Tanqueray," smiled Stela to Wisner. "And Cinzano."

"Excellent."

Maria poured three martinis from the kitchen and set them on the marble counter, not about to sashay around with a tray like some cheap cocktail waitress.

We helped ourselves to the food and drink. Maria went to the living room where young Vlad was perched in a chair ignoring the picture book in his lap, his eyes on Frank Wisner and Princess Stela. Maria tried to carry him off to bed but he fussed and fought.

"Let him be," said Stela. "He will not know what we say, he does not speak *engleză*."

"Yes I do," said the boy king, drawing laughter from Frank. "Cosmina taught me."

Stela flinched at the mention of Vlad's nanny, the only mother her son had ever known.

She and Wisner took their drinks over to the sofa. Maria entertained young Vlad. I remained at the marble counter, enjoying a chunk of cheese wrapped in shaved ham. I chewed, I pondered.

A forgotten detail had been dredged up in my debriefing. How the kill squad hooted and hollered when they discovered the truck's secret cargo. Gold. They had not expected to find gold.

A rat in D.C. would have told them about the gold. A rat in Romania wouldn't have known about it. Dragomir would not have shared that news with anyone.

I had been right the first time. Stela was the traitor. She'd hit the Daily Double - made her escape with her son while getting revenge on his kidnapper.

Maybe. But it was weak tea. More speculation and supposition. I needed something concrete to convince myself. I ate and drank and cast my mind back, looking for stuff that didn't fit.

It didn't take long.

Lucian, PS's supposed rescuer. She said herself he was a coward. Why then would she rely on him to stage the all-important rescue of herself and her son? It didn't read right, but I still had bupkis. Think, you dink!

No, don't! Open your eyes and shut your yap. Wait for the ball to drop.

I studied Stela, hoping to spark a memory. She was all things gracious and demure in the presence of Frank Wisner, much as she had been with me during our sumptuous dinner in the stone cottage. That thought got chased by another thought that disappeared around a corner.

No doubt Stela wanted to reveal to Wisner that Vlad was his son but Maria and the boy king kept upstaging her. PS didn't want to make her big announcement, I assumed, while young Vlad chased a rubber ball across the room on all fours, barking like a dog.

Princess Stela conveyed her displeasure to the housekeeper with an expression that would have stopped a clock. An expression I remembered well.

It was during our dinner at the cottage, after the Princess excused herself from the table to freshen up and instead slipped into the bedroom of Ilinca, Dmitri's Soviet comrade. Stela had worn that same expression of grim and angry purpose when she returned from Ilinca's bedroom

When I'd asked what she'd been doing, Stela said she was making sure that the sedative with which she'd dosed Ilinca was doing its job.

But nothing that Stela did that night after she returned from Ilinca's bedroom made sense. From her rushing me out to the carriage house and then rushing back to the cottage to collect her things and change clothes, to her violently retching at the side of the road.

I take that back. Her retching made sense.

Stela should have changed her clothes while I was still inside the cottage in case Dmitri or Ilinca came to. I had been too busy ogling the GAZ-61 to realize that at the time.

Best I could figure Stela saw that Ilinca was stirring when she visited her bedroom and decided she would have to kill both her and Dmitri to make certain they wouldn't rouse themselves and sound the alarm. Stela did that when she returned to the cottage to collect her things.

Slitting throats is a messy business, the carotid artery being so close to the pump. That's why she waited to change clothes.

And still I had nothing.

Unless she still carried that beaded purse, the one that held the sap I'd used to crown Dmitri. Dollars to doughnuts she'd kept it, and it held a straight razor. It's comforting to have a weapon in enemy territory.

It was my turn to excuse myself to freshen up. Not that Frank and Stela would notice my absence. They were reminiscing happily on the white linen couch, heads down, voices low.

I slipped into Mussolini's bedroom and closed the door. It was a teen boy's wet dream. Floor to ceiling mirrors along one wall, ankle-high gold carpeting, a life-size marble reproduction of *Venus de Milo* and a bed the size of a hockey rink.

I found Stela's beaded purse in the top bureau drawer and dumped the contents out on the bed. No razor. I turned the purse inside out, looking for spots of dried blood. No joy. I examined the purse's contents. Same deal.

Clock's ticking, Schroeder, what now? Where would the Princess hide the murder weapon? Somewhere close at hand, but also a place where Maria wouldn't stumble on it when she tidied up the room, as she'd done this morning.

Well, Stela might keep the razor in her purse overnight, then tuck it away in a more secure hiding place once Maria had changed the sheets.

I got down on my knees, ran my hand under the mattress, groped around for half a minute and snagged it. A dainty little number with an ebony handle.

That she had a straight razor stashed under her bed should have been enough but I wanted hard evidence to convince myself that Princess Stela was a cold blooded killer. If she could kill Dmitri and Ilinca with her own hand she was capable of something worse.

I opened the blade slowly. It was gleaming clean. But some of the victim's spurting blood might have wicked into the handle cavity. I pounded the open handle against my palm.

All I got were a couple drops of water. PS had rinsed out the damn thing.

I went to the bathroom and hunted up a Q-tip. There was one last possibility. I gently poked the cotton swab into the hinge between the handle and the blade. I let it sit there for the count of ten.

When I removed it the Q-tip was dark pink.

Chapter Twenty-seven

I went to my bedroom and got the Remington and its holster from the bureau drawer. No, I didn't plan to shoot anyone, I wanted to return it to Frank Wisner. I removed the bullets so he wouldn't notice one was missing, took a pillowcase and stuck the gun and holster inside and carried my awkward bundle down the hall to the living room.

Wisner and Stela were still huddled on the white linen sofa, a bit closer together than they had been. Maria was in the kitchen stirring up another pitcher of martinis. The boy king was slumped over in the armchair, fast asleep. Outside the bay windows the basilica of St. Peter's was lit by floodlights against the night sky.

And not two weeks ago I'd been shelving books in the back stacks of the Cleveland Public Library.

"Schroeder, what have you got there?" said Frank Wisner, happily.

I sat down on the wing of the L-shaped sofa. Princess Stela clenched her cheeks in a smile.

"It's something that used to belong to you sir. Captain Dragomir loaned it to me. I thought you'd like to have it back."

No flicker of recognition from Wisner. That changed when I removed the six gun from its holster and presented it to Frank with both hands.

"Good Lord," he said, "good Lord."

I'm guessing memories of the war years came flooding back, leastwise Wisner's eyes grew moist as he stared at his parting gift to Sorin Dragomir.

I chanced a glance at Princess Stela. She still had her phony smile in place but her eyes were solid ice. Could be she didn't appreciate my distracting Frank from their boozy reminiscence with a treasured keepsake from the kidnapper of her son.

But then she wasn't going to like anything I did tonight. I got up to fetch a fresh martini and flirt with Maria but she sat on a stool in the kitchen, rubbing her feet, in no mood to talk. I poured myself a drink and stood there like a stooge, looking at nothing.

I didn't really care that Princess Stela had killed her Soviet minders. I might have done the same if I thought it necessary to make our escape. But it wasn't necessary, not really. She could have cut the power to their transmitter instead of their throats. What PS did was eliminate witnesses in case the NKVD intercepted us on the road to Sibiu. If nabbed she would claim I'd kidnapped her, and finger me as the neck slicer.

Princess Stela was the rat who blew our mission and got Dragomir and his men slaughtered.

I knew that, felt sure about it save for one tangle. Stela supposedly sneaked out the bedroom window with her son so that Lucian could drive her to her hiding place at the airstrip before the Captain and his contingent arrived.

Not likely. Stela wouldn't have trusted cowardly Lucian to come through in the crunch. More likely she would have used him to sneak a letter to her NKVD contact in town. A letter detailing where she was being held and when the CIA supply plane was due to land, but not where. She wouldn't give away the store right away. I imagine Lucian had to shuttle a few letters back and forth before Stela and the Blue Caps worked out a deal.

Thus Stela would have waited until *after* our departure to leave the pagoda. The Blue Caps would have swarmed the joint, rushed PS and her son out the door and killed anyone in their way. Lucian, Cosmina, anyone.

The tangle I couldn't unknot was how the Blue Caps got Princess Stela and the boy king to their hiding spot on the far side of the landing strip before Captain Dragomir rolled up in his truck. We hadn't been overtaken by any fast moving Soviet jeeps on that winding highway.

True. But we had bypassed a few dirt roads that climbed straight up the mountain. Sheep trails or toboggan runs. A four-wheel GAZ-67 could have powered up and over those peaks and beaten us to the airstrip with time to spare.

I was, I must admit, impressed. Back in my wayward youth I had managed to play both sides against the middle myself, on a small scale. But Stela Varadja was straddling the middle stripe of a four-lane highway, leveraging the two most powerful nations on earth to her benefit and doing a damn fine job of it. So far.

I took my drink and the pitcher of martinis back to the couch. I set down the pitcher on the glass coffee table. Frank Wisner looked at their two empty glasses and said, "Your timing, Schroeder, is first rate."

Seemed like he'd said that to me before, at his Maryland farm. I hoped he was right. If I didn't torpedo Princess Stela this evening she would beguile her way into some important OPC posting where she could do real and permanent damage. She was dirty, no question, but it would take more than a bloody Q-tip to convince Frank Wisner. I was still low scrotum on this totem.

"Princess Stela has been singing your praises, young man. She tells me she could never have rescued her son without your able assistance."

I couldn't resist. "Or attendance for that matter,"

"Come again?"

"I was not aboard the C-45 when it prepared for takeoff."

"Well, that wasn't Stela's fault, certainly," frowned Wisner.

I looked at Stela. She met my gaze over the rim of her martini glass. She would have already told Wisner how she talked her way past the Blue Caps. I could say that was mere playacting and that she would have been only too happy to leave me behind but...

"No sir, I guess not."

We sipped and chatted for a few until PS turned to look at her sleeping son with maternal concern. "I should now be putting him to bed."

Ah, here it comes. The big reveal.

"Yes, he finally wore himself out," said Wisner. "He's a ball of fire that boy."

"Just like his father," said Princess Stela, pointedly.

"I never had the pleasure. Your husband was stationed in Prague as I recall."

"For a time. Then to Zagreb. I did not see him for most of a year."

"Is that so?" said Frank Wisner, surprised. And oblivious.

Princess Stela and I shared a little moment just then. Our last.

Her quick glance said, *Can you believe this guy?* Or, more completely, *Funny how blind people can be when an uncomfortable truth is staring them right in the face.*

I acknowledged her with a tiny shrug. It's too bad she was such a shit because I did admire her style.

She sighed. "The boy is your son, Frank."

Frank Wisner took a long moment to absorb this shock, then turned to me, eyes ablaze.

Why was this my lookout? "Princess Stela shared this information with me," I explained, "but I didn't feel it was my place to say anything. Sir."

Wisner pivoted to Stela. "How can you be sure?" he demanded, as if a Princess obsessed with bloodlines would be careless about questions of paternity.

She crossed to the arm chair and picked up the slumbering boy king and carried him back to the white linen sofa. She placed him in Frank Wisner's arms and left it to him to note the familiar large brow and angled ears.

I had a dark thought as Wisner reached the obvious conclusion. He was now theoretically subject to blackmail from Princess Stela. Or me. And he had the power to make us both disappear. I knew he wouldn't do that – Beria would, Wisner wouldn't. But the fact that Frank Wisner held the same unchecked authority as Lavrenty Beria made me queasy. The history books are full of well-meaning leaders who start out good and end up wicked. The Angel Lucifer was God's right-hand man before he decided to go into business for himself.

Young Vlad awoke in his father's arms. He didn't fuss or squirm, seemed, in fact, right at home.

"Hey there, cowboy" said Wisner, putting his finger in the boy's chubby palm. "My name is Frank, pleasure to meet you."

"My name is Vlad," he replied in a tiny stern voice, as if offended by the informal greeting.

"Yes, Vlad, of course. Such a powerful name."

Princess Stela smiled beatifically at this sweet moment. I might have joined her save for the realization that I had now slid down another notch on the totem pole.

The boy king's eyes got droopy. Wisner returned him to his mother, who rocked him to sleep.

"I will see to it that you are well taken care of," said Frank, suddenly all business. "In exchange for which you will work for us."

"I will accept," said Stela. "But not in Paris. Paris is no fit place for to raise a child."

"I agree. What did you have in mind?"

"A small city, with fine schools."

"Such as?"

"Copenhagen."

Frank snorted. "And why would I waste a woman of your talents on Copenhagen?"

This exchange caught me by surprise. If Stela wanted to do real damage she would seek a posting to a major capital. Maybe grooming her son to become the next King of Romania really was her first priority.

Maybe not.

"I will find you a place in London," declared Wisner. "Where royalty is always welcome."

Princess Stela did not object.

No good deed goes unpunished. It looked as if my attempt to keep the boy king from becoming a political trophy had led to a Commie rat being posted to the nerve center of European intelligence. And the home of Guy Burgess.

I poured gin and vermouth down my gullet as I watched mumsy-wumsy and popsy-wopsy fawn over their fair-haired boy. Might as well get blotto, I had nothing. I was about to pour myself another when young Vlad suddenly came to in his mother's arms.

He writhed and squirmed. She clutched him tight, he fought harder.

"Why don't you let me take him for a minute?" I said. Stela shook me off.

"Oh, let him hold the boy for God's sakes," said Wisner.

Stela handed him over. "Not long, he needs bed."

I stood the boy king up on my knees and looked him in the eye. He didn't struggle, he didn't cry. Why did he resist his mother's touch so fiercely?

Simple, Schroeder. The boy had seen what happened to his beloved nanny when the kill squad arrived at the pagoda.

I had the evidence I needed. I had an eye witness who was beyond reproach. All that remained was to ask the question.

"Hi, Vlad, it's me, Hal. I first met you with Cosmina, remember?"

The boy king didn't answer. Stela jumped up.

"She was a nice lady, Cosmina. How is she?"

Vlad's face crumpled and he started to cry. Stela snatched him back.

I gave Wisner a hard look. He came through.

"Let the boy answer the question, Stela."

I asked young Vlad again about Cosmina.

He answered tearfully, in Romanian, before his mother hauled him off.

I looked to Wisner. "What did he say?"

Frank's big sturdy mug was contorted, out of joint. "He said they shot her."

Chapter Twenty-eight

I filled in the blanks for Frank Wisner. How Stela slit the throats of her Soviet minders. How she betrayed our supply operation in exchange for a plane ride out. How she staged a confrontation with the kill squad at the airstrip that was intended to schnooker me into thinking she was on our side. By the time I was done Wisner was muttering darkly to his martini glass.

I didn't attempt to advise him. What do you say to a man who has just discovered that the mother of his son is a murderous traitor. He didn't have long to agonize in any event. A moment after Maria bid us *Buonanotte* and shuffled down the hall, Stela reappeared, her cheeks red with gin and anger.

"I am responsible for my son, and for survival of my lineage!"

Okay. No dispute there.

"I was under guard, with long way to aeroplane."

Yeah. So?

"I knew *Sovietici* would get us to there."

"You told me it was Lucian who helped you," I said.

"I did not say the truth."

No shit. "Why did the *Sovietici* agree to let you flee?"

"I promise more secrets for them."

Frank Wisner cleared his throat to speak. The long day had taken its toll, he sounded like an outboard motor with a clogged fuel line. "How did you know...the plane crew... wouldn't fire at the NKVD?"

"And risk their aeroplane?"

I jumped back in. "And I suppose the chance to get revenge on Sorin Dragomir didn't figure into your decision."

"He kidnapped my son! Why do you now cry tears for kidnapper?" yelled Stela. "And he had no...how do you say?... no friends, no..."

"Collaborators," suggested Wisner.

"*Da.* No *collaborators* in Bucharest, in Cluj, in Constanta. Sorin Dragomir was vainglorious fool!"

Stela Varadja didn't add 'Just like all you men' but Frank Wisner and I heard it just the same.

Her point about collaborators in the cities was well taken. Had she made it earlier I might have rejected Dragomir's plea for gold and munitions. Stela and I could have doped out another way to smuggle her and the boy king to freedom.

And what way was that, Schroeder? Wisner might well have dispatched a plane to retrieve me, but in Stela's mind, Frank would never permit his former mistress to climb aboard. The Vampire Princess was right. She took her only way out.

I could see Frank Wisner sorting through all this in his lawyerly way. He couldn't turn Stela over to the authorities for prosecution. And he wouldn't return the mother of his son to Communist Romania. In the words of Bill Harvey he was 'a gentleman of the old school in the wrong line of work.'

"London will remain your destination," said Wisner finally. He gestured for Stela to come and stand before him. She did so, eyes downcast, the humble penitent.

Ha.

"I will arrange for you a small apartment and a job to pay for it. A menial job. You will have no telephone privileges and your mail will be opened."

"I will have minder?"

"Yes," replied Wisner, icily, "but you're used to that. I will see to it that young Vlad is properly educated, at schools of my choosing. And if you keep to the straight and narrow for a number of years, I might consider giving you an employment opportunity."

"Thank you, Frank," said Stela, barely audible.

"Get some sleep, we leave first thing."

Princess Stela Varadja whispered down the hall in that ballet dancer way she had, her feet barely touching the ground. And why not? She had won, Sorin Dragomir had lost.

I was reminded of one of Wild Bill Donovan's pithy maxims. 'There is bad intelligence, but there are no bad sources.' We don't deal in good and evil, in other words, just truth and fiction.

Frank Wisner would find a way to use Stela's considerable skills. She wasn't a Commie rat after all. Princess Stela was an all-purpose rat.

Chapter Twenty-nine

I staggered into the lobby of the Mayflower Hotel more dead than alive after a Rome to Paris to London to Shannon to Gander to New York to Washington D.C. crossing. Three days and nights in the sweaty embrace of 'the romance of winged flight.' Give me a stateroom on a liner every time.

The pigskin valise that Wisner provided before I left Rome contained new socks and underwear, a black wool topcoat and a shiny new set of lock picks. All the necessary *accoutrement* for the young-man-about-town.

Plus a gun. Wisner included the Civil War Cavalry Officer's Remington .44 he had given to Captain Dragomir who had then loaned it to me.

I got it back. Wisner said I'd earned it.

I checked in at the front desk. "Welcome, Mr. Schroeder, we've been expecting you." I signed the ledger and gave the bell captain a buck to see to my suitcase.

Then I crossed the lobby to the Towne and Country Lounge, lust in my heart. The joint was jumping at four o'clock in the afternoon. Reporters cadging free drinks from press flacks most likely. The big election was only days away.

I searched out Winston behind the bar. He made brief eye contact, looked skyward, made more eye contact. Something was up, report to my room.

I sighed and trudged off to the bank of elevators. My room key read 640, same as before. Made sense. The spy suite, swept for mikes on a regular basis. No doubt Bill Harvey was waiting to interrogate me, sitting on my bed with a bag of doughnuts.

But the bed was unoccupied when I opened the door.

"Welcome home" said the last man in the world I expected to see. He was seated in the club chair by the window. Major General William J. Donovan.

"Thank you, sir."

"How was your journey?"

"Very long, sir."

He nodded. "Worst part of the job, travel, never cared for it. But it gives you time to think."

The great man had changed in the two years since I'd seen him. The wide-set eyes now a bit sunken, a slight tremor in his voice that hadn't been there before. Hair white as snow. I made small talk, asked him what he had been up to.

He rattled off news about a bunch of private initiatives, Committees to Save This and That. I didn't listen very closely, I could tell his heart wasn't in it. Retirement from active duty did not suit Wild Bill Donovan.

Our conversation was interrupted by a ringing phone. I hesitated.

"Answer it," said Donovan.

I did. It was Winston.

"I took the liberty of sending up a pitcher of Manhattans and a tray of hors d'oeuvres, Mistah Hal. I wanted to let you know."

"Thank you, Winston, well done." A waiter wheeled in the goodies not thirty seconds later.

General Donovan declined a cocktail. I suppose it was rude of me to pour one for myself but Carrie Nation and her hatchet couldn't have stopped me at that point. I was keen to tell him about my recent cockeyed mission but Donovan closed that door before I could open it.

"We can't discuss your trip."

"But sir..."

Donovan held up his hand. "I was a civilian in '46 as well, yes. But it's different now. There are competent people in charge, professionals. They deserve your silence."

Frank Wisner worked for Wild Bill during the war. Sounded to me like this was Donovan's laying on of hands.

"Would you like a bite, sir?"

I wheeled the tray over. Not a cucumber sandwich in sight. Donovan helped himself to a pickled egg and a handful of beer nuts. Apparently he and Winston had done this before.

"Did you know that your father worked for me?"

I was shocked to silence.

"He was a translator on my office staff during the Great War. I barely knew him at the time but he did me a service later on."

I backed up and sat on the edge of the bed. Donovan crossed his legs and laced his hands behind his head.

"I was not a popular choice for OSS Chief on the Hill. Congress wanted someone more 'sophisticated' to better cozy up to the British gentry of MI6. They didn't want a dumb Mick in other words. If I wanted a serious budget from Ways and Means I had to impress the bastards going in. Your father helped me do that."

"Sir, my father runs a candy store in Youngstown, Ohio."

"Is that right? I never knew what he did for a living." The old lion pointed to the pitcher. I poured him one. He took a sip and continued.

"Your father had been brought along to some German Bund meetings by his brother. He didn't take them seriously, a chance for married men to get out of the house and drink beer.

But the meetings after Pearl Harbor turned serious. They had, your old man soon discovered, a fundraising network that stretched from Pittsburg to Chicago. And safe houses, hidden boat docks on Lake Erie."

Donovan leaned forward, took another nip, sat back. "Two days before my scheduled testimony I received his registered letter. And it was my distinct pleasure to reveal this network of fifth columnists to a closed session of the House Ways and Means Committee."

And the old man never said a word about it. I was beaming ear to ear when Wild Bill dropped the hammer.

"Allen Dulles wants a favor."

I was flattered of course. The top guns of OSS teaming up to ask a favor of little ol' me. But I'd been asked favors before and they generally led to a lowering of my life expectancy. I wasn't going back out again. Not for Wild Bill, Allen Dulles or Abe Lincoln back from the grave.

But it wasn't like that.

"Allen knows politics better than I do and it's all politics now. He thinks Dewey is vulnerable since Truman got religion on the Red Menace. Dewey's camp is planning a big rally in the VFW Hall on the Sunday before election day, with the hero of the Berlin airlift as the guest of honor."

"Captain Candybar?"

Donovan nodded. "Dulles told Dewey's campaign manager that you'd make a nice addition to the rally."

Me?

"It would be the end of your career as a field agent of course. Do you still have ambitions in that regard?"

"Not a one, sir."

Donovan grunted. "Yes, it's different now."

I asked if Frank Wisner knew about this request for me to appear at a political rally.

"No. The Chief of OPC doesn't get involved in politics."

"Not in this country anyway."

A pause, then a bark of laughter from Wild Bill.

"You can tell Frank I put the arm on you. And you have my word that no mention of your latest...adventure will be made."

Donovan wasn't as out of the loop as he let on. And could be Wild Bill wasn't completely sold on Wisner's professionalism. It wasn't a 'mission' or an 'operation.' It was an 'adventure.'

I didn't ask about my end. There's always a payoff in politics, provided the front-runner stayed that way. I told the General I would give it a go.

Donovan's request answered a nagging question. Why had Frank Wisner gone to all the trouble and expense of my frantic six-legged plane trip when a train to Naples and a leisurely ocean crossing would have done just as well?

Bill Donovan nibbled his drink and stared out the window. I couldn't imagine what else he might have to say.

"You father traveled to D.C. in November of '44, waited in my office all day," said the General after a time. "He demanded to know if you were still alive and when you were coming home, insisted your tour of duty had expired. I said you were still alive to the best of my knowledge. And I told him why we hadn't brought you home on schedule."

"Why was that, sir?"

"We were too close to victory. And you were too damn effective."

And with that Wild Bill Donovan got up, shook my hand and walked out the door.

I poured myself a second Manhattan and mulled it over. Hard to believe that jolly-jolly Uncle Jorg was a fifth columnist, though I did recall long silences around the dinner table in those days. Mom wiping a tear for no reason, Uncle Jorg no longer a weekend visitor. Then a brick through the front window late one night. Dad was already sweeping up when I got there. 'Some drunk,' was all he said.

I eyed the telephone on the desk. I owed my parents a phone call. I've been putting it off because Mom had been pestering me. 'Even your crazy kid sister settled down and got married.'

I would call them after the rally. It was time to cash in my chips – intel analyst or field agent instructor. A grown-up job. Then I'd call 'em.

I wasn't a total shit. I picked up the phone and dictated a telegram, telling Ma and Pa Schroeder I had returned to D.C. in one piece and would call soon.

Chapter Thirty

My suite at the Mayflower had a dressing area off the bathroom with a full-length mirror. I had checked my dress-up duds with the bell captain before my trip. They were hanging in my closet when I returned, cleaned and pressed.

I stood in front of the mirror for a longer time than I'd care to admit, trying to decide whether to wear my black suit with the narrow lapels that made me look like a small town mortician. Or my double-breasted navy blue blazer with fake brass buttons that made me look like an insurance salesman out for a big night.

Captain Candybar would doubtless be turned out in his dress blues, a silver oak leaf cluster gleaming on his chest.

I chose the black suit with a white shirt and blue tie with red polka dots.

The Dewey rally started at seven. I went down to the Towne and Country Lounge about five-thirty but Winston was not in residence. Just as well. Much as I craved strong drink I had a beer and a quick bite instead, then walked the six extra-long blocks to the VFW Hall on Vermont Ave.

I was still the 'Hero of Mahlendamm Bridge.' No reports of my disastrous trip to Romania had made the press. Goings-on in Transylvania were well down the list of pressing concerns for Americans in November of 1948.

The hall was cavernous. Men were already trickling in, mostly Great War vets with enameled corp and regiment pins on their caps. The curtain was down, the proscenium hung with red, white and blue bunting and a big Dewey-Warren banner. To the left of the stage stood three newsreel cameras flanked by floodlights.

A tall man who looked as if he'd lived the last fifty years on nothing but cigs and black coffee hurried up to me.

"You Schroeder?" he said, his breath strong as a train trestle. I nodded. "I'm Al, been a change of plans."

"Oh?"

"You and the Captain were s'posed to grin, wave and go. But the newsies wanna talk to da heroes. So we agreed to a brief Q&A. General interest, where you're from and whatnot."

"They're going to want to know why I'm supporting Dewey. And I don't know diddly about his foreign policy."

"Here's all you need to know: Governor Dewey loves America, Governor Dewey hates Communism. And you think that a Dewey Administration – a *President* Dewey, is the best choice to preserve America's freedom and liberty."

"What the difference?"

"Heh?"

"Between freedom and liberty."

Al shut his eyes and opened them again. "Don't be a smartass."

He gave me a quick once over. "We'll get you a decent tie. Makeup's in the green room," he said, shoving me down the aisle toward the stage.

Makeup?

I wandered around backstage until a stagehand pointed me toward a small room in the corner. The door was open. Captain Candybar sat on a stool, his back to the dressing mirror. He had a paper bib around his neck as a frizzy-haired girl patted his chiseled mug with pancake makeup.

It was a difficult situation in which to radiate manly self-assurance but the Captain managed it. He looked like a hero - wavy blond hair and a dimpled chin you could park a twenty-five cent piece in.

"Pull up a stool, Schroeder," he said. "You're next."

I was surprised he knew my name. The makeup gal went to work on me while Captain Candybar lit a Camel and put me in the know.

"The cameras are below stage, so look down, not up. Work the mike from an angle so you don't pop. Keep your answers short and sweet, and no jokes. Heroes don't crack wise."

I'd been gee'd up to dislike this guy but I found I had the opposite reaction.

"And one more thing. When you get sweaty under those klieg lights pat your forehead with your hankie, don't wipe it. Smears the makeup."

"Very *good,* Captain," said the makeup gal.

Al the press flack darted in about then, handed me a red silk tie and matching handkerchief, then turned and left without a word. A brass band started up a Sousa march. The Captain clapped me on the shoulder and made for the door.

"Those cameras out there," I said, "they don't look right."

The Captain turned at the doorway. "How's that?"

"They don't look like newsreel cameras."

The Captain unzipped a hundred watt smile. "We're working without a net tonight, Schroeder."

It took me a minute to decode his comment. Oh shit, oh dear. That wasn't a newsreel crew out there. We were going to be on television. Live television.

I donned my red tie and handkerchief and told my hands to quit shaking. I went over the lines Al had given me. I looked in the mirror and checked my teeth for spinach. The makeup made me look like I'd been embalmed.

I told the face in the mirror to grow some gonads. Told him he'd faced down murderous foes and grim death. It didn't help. I had butterflies the size of barn owls.

The speechifying commenced. A VFW bigwig was introducing the candidate. I left the green room. It was dark behind the curtain, lit only by a solo spot with a blue gel. An odd juxtaposition to the bright lights and glory on the other side.

Captain Candybar was watching from the wings but the candidate was nowhere to be seen. I didn't mind endorsing Dewey for President, I didn't have much use for Truman. But it would have been nice to meet the guy.

I went and stood behind Captain Candybar to peek a look. The rousing introduction of Governor Dewey produced only a polite round of applause. The grizzled vets looked to be a tough crowd.

Dewey started out low key, said his thank you's and poked fun at his reputation as a cold fish. He had a powerful baritone that filled the hall. Then he launched into an hour-long stemwinder that was interrupted several times by applause.

Well, 'interrupted' may be the wrong word. Dewey would come to the end of a stirring call to action, pause and wait till the audience supplied the expected ovation. He was hitting all the patriotic high notes but the vets were cool to him.

Could be it was because Dewey was in that awkward, in-between generation – too young to serve in the Great War, too old for action in WWII. He wasn't one of them. Which was why Captain Candybar and I and were here.

Al the press flack scuttled over to me. He was chewing an unlit cigarette and muttering to himself, unhappy that his boy was laying an egg. "Get ready," he said, putting a hand in the small of my back. A fat bead of sweat ran down my spine.

"And now, my friends," said Governor Dewey, "I have a little surprise for you, some last minute guests who would like to make your acquaintance. The Hero of Muhlendamm Bridge, OSS agent extraordinaire Hal Schroeder!"

Al shoved me, blinking, into the blazing light. The vets seemed to know who I was, the applause was solid. I grinned and waved. I walked over and stood next to Dewey and waved some more.

"And the man they call Captain Candybar," said Dewey. "The hero of the Berlin Airlift, Captain James Jenkins!"

Dewey and I looked left, the direction from which I'd entered and the wing where the Captain had been standing. A few titters from the crowd caused us to look in the other direction. When we did the vets let loose with hoots of raucous laughter.

The Captain had entered stage right while we were looking left and, by putting his finger to his mouth and tiptoeing across the stage, had the crowd in the palm of his hand before he ever spoke a word.

Dewey clasped both our hands, held them up and shouted, "These are the kind of men who will serve in a Dewey White House!"

The veterans gave us a thunderous ovation.

I hate the entire ridiculous hero rigmarole. But I loved every second of that ovation.

Governor Dewey thanked the crowd, shook our hands and left the stage on a high note. Press flack Al stayed behind to birddog the newsies. They wanted to talk to Captain Jenkins.

Jenkins fed them a couple well-chewed anecdotes in between praising the Governor's *unimpeachable strength of character* and his *lifelong dedication to the cause of constitutional democracy.*

All they trusted me to say was that Dewey hates Commies.

I did get to answer a question eventually, the one that the Dewey campaign wanted asked. Did I really think the United States was losing the Cold War?

I said that I did, but that a *President* Dewey could turn the tide of history and preserve our God-given right to life, liberty and the pursuit of happiness.

Not sure where that last bit of cornpone came from but Captain Candybar gave me a wink and Al immediately thanked the members of the press and started to usher us offstage. We had hauled Thomas Dewey's ashes out of the fire.

"Mr. Schroeder! Excuse me, Mr. Schroeder!"

What was this now? My eyes searched out the location of the familiar voice. She was at the back of the pack, Miss Julia, my fetching tormentor.

Al tugged at my sleeve but I was flush with victory. I brushed his hand away and called on the intrepid girl reporter.

"Are you the same Harold Schroeder who worked as an undercover operative for the FBI in December of 1945? The man hired to infiltrate the Fulton Road Mob?" she shouted for all to hear.

I hemmed, I hawed, I jacked my jaws.

"The mob that successfully robbed the Federal Reserve Bank with the help of three Irish hoodlums? Hoodlums who have never been apprehended?"

How in the name of J. Edgar Hoover did she know about the Mooney Brothers? They never made the press reports.

Captain Candybar interceded. "Young lady, I don't know who sent you but I can assure you that my friend Hal Schroeder is a straight shooter and a patriot. His service behind German lines made our successful wartime bombing runs possible. His courage at Muhlendamm Bridge paved the way for our victorious airlift over Berlin."

I was Sancho Panza to his Don Quixote in other words. Fine, he gave me cover to slink offstage. I peeked through the curtain to see if the baying newshounds were coming after me but they were still clustered around the Captain, who was signing autographs.

Press flack Al appeared and jabbed a bony yellow finger at me behind the curtain. "What the hell was that?" he hissed. "You're s'posed to be an authentic American hero!"

"Sorry."

Al wandered off, muttering obscenities. I stood there in a daze, prize porker to canned ham in record time.

I thought I'd gone round the bend for sure when I saw Miss Julia come marching backstage, reporter's notebook in hand. Didn't she know I was duty bound to kill her?

"I wanted to give you a chance to answer my questions, set the record straight," she said, pencil poised.

"How 'bout you answer *me* a question? In our first interview you got me to endorse Dewey, now you're pitching rude questions at a Dewey rally. Who the hell are you working for?"

"Myself. I'm trying to make it in a business that thinks I should be covering baby christenings and flower shows."

I cast about for villains. Harvey and I had parted on bad terms.

"Did Bill Harvey put you up to this?"

"A good reporter doesn't reveal his sources."

"Don't quote me scripture, missy, answer the damn question!"

"Bill Harvey was not my source."

"Was it Hoover?"

Julia laughed at me. "And you don't get a third question."

Shit. This raised two very unpleasant possibilities.

"Tell me where I was wrong," said Julia.

I should have read her the riot act but I couldn't muster it. She was just doing her job. And she smelled good.

"You got the gist," I admitted. "I was a bitter young shit on the make who managed to cover his tracks. Till now. But the 'Irish hoodlums' were just dumb kids dragged along by yours truly. Leave 'em alone."

"In exchange for what?" said Julia.

"I'll give you all the gory details your little heart desires," I lied. "After the election."

"I'll expect your call on Wednesday," she said crisply, handing me her card.

I looked it over. "Is this your home address?"

"Yes."

"Your building have a doorman?"

"No."

"Then move."

"Why would I do that?"

"You've gone and ticked off some powerful people."

"I'm used to that."

I chewed my lip. How to say this?

"Julia, despite your relentless campaign to destroy me, I like you." She fanned her face in mock humility. "But the people you've ticked off aren't city council candidates or utility board commissioners. They're among the most powerful men on earth. You need to be very careful."

Julia studied me carefully. "On *earth*?"

"Yes."

"I've ticked off foreigners?"

"I believe the term you want is 'foreign powers.'"

Julia bit her lip most fetchingly.

"I don't have any inside dope, Julia. All I know is that sometimes who gets elected President of the United States is more important to our enemies than it is to us."

Chapter Thirty-one

I decided to walk those six extra-long blocks back to the Mayflower in order to clear my head. I hiked west on K Street. The White House figured to be somewhere nearby but I couldn't catch a glimpse of it.

The night had taken a turn for the worse, a jagged wind whipped pinprick rain. I put my head down, my collar up and trudged on, telling myself that nothing much had happened.

I'd been asked a few embarrassing questions by a cub reporter, been robustly defended by Captain Jenkins and hadn't been pursued by any other reporters. The press was zeroed in on the big election and I didn't matter a whit in the larger scheme of things.

But Miss Julia had exhumed a corpse I would have just as soon stayed buried. She knew details of the Federal Reserve bank heist that never made the papers.

She had an inside source. And I had two possibles in mind.

Both men harbored a deep and abiding hatred for yours truly and who could blame them? But only one of them was likely to follow me down a dark alleyway on a cold ragged night in an attempt to top me off.

I looked around for a dark alleyway to test my theory but K Street didn't co-operate. It was too early for the Shakespearean Act Five anyway. *When that ghost and the Prince meet/And everyone ends in mincemeat.*

We had just concluded Act Three, best I could tell. Prince Hal now had to determine the identity of the ghost. And whether this low rent production was tragedy or farce.

The rain stiffened into needles. By the time I arrived at The Mayflower twenty minutes later my mug felt like a cube steak.

I took the elevator up to the sixth floor, changed into dry clothes and rode back down.

I was unsurprised to find William King Harvey parked on a barstool at the Towne and Country Lounge. He wouldn't pass up an opportunity to have a hearty laugh at my expense.

But it wasn't like that. I almost fell over backwards when Harvey said, "That was a wrong thing that girl did to you."

"Excuse me?"

"A man gets precious few opportunities in life to enjoy the tribute of his colleagues. That was a wrong thing she did."

I figured this for a drunken jibe but Harvey didn't smirk and he had a cup of black coffee on the bar in front of him.

Christ. A sober sympathetic Bill Harvey was more than I could take at the moment. Where the hell was Winston?

I don't want to say he descended from heaven on cottony clouds amid beams of rosy light right about then, but that's the way it seemed to me.

"Good evening, Mr. Schroeder."

"And a good evening to you, Winston. One of your perfect Manhattans if you please."

"Certainly, sir."

I watched Winston perform his mixing, shaking and pouring ritual before I leaned in. "I've got a choice piece of dirt for you, Bill, but it comes with a price. You tell me some deep dark FBI secret first."

Bill Harvey did not reply, not right away.

Winston served me. I nipped at my cocktail while I waited to find out how much Harvey valued me. Was I a crystal blue cat's eye or just a plain ball bearing? I got a surprising answer.

"You remember Igor Gouzenko, the NKVD coding officer?"

"Think so. He defected in Ottawa, early '46 I think it was."

"That's when the press broke the story. But Hoover was briefed on the defection by the Canadian MPs in September of '45, just a few weeks after the A-bomb finished off the Japs."

"Didn't know that."

"You remember anything else that happened around that time?"

"Sure, Truman disbanded the OSS by executive order. October first, 1945."

"Something he would have had a tough time doing," said Harvey, nostrils flaring, "if Wild Bill Donovan had been able to report to Congress that the Soviet Union, our stalwart ally in war and peace, had an extensive spy ring in place to steal our atomic secrets."

Harvey lowered his voice to a rumble. "Igor Gouzenko provided hard evidence that GRU, Soviet military intelligence, had twenty agents in *Canada*, in 1945."

"Did Hoover brief Truman about it?"

"Post haste."

I was stunned to silence. How could Truman have disbanded the OSS after that briefing? I wrangled up my tongue.

"How, or why, did the story come out in '46?"

"Hoover leaked it himself."

"Wasn't that around the time Hoover was lobbying for the Bureau to assume all intelligence activities foreign and domestic?"

Bill Harvey dug wax from his ear with his little finger. I took that as a yes.

I kept my end of the bargain. Truth is I would have told him details of my Romanian misadventure anyway. Harvey worked counterintelligence, he needed to know that the Vampire Princess was now an independent operator in the employ of Frank Wisner. But I wouldn't tell him why. I wasn't going to peach out the boy king.

I ran down the chain of events. When I got to the part about Stela blowing Dragomir's operation, Harvey surprised me. He was full of surprises this evening.

"Then you have your culprit in the roll-up of the ex-pats in Bucharest."

"I braced Stela about that. She said Wisner would never have given her such sensitive intel. Which is true."

"She may have come at it from the opposite direction," said Harvey. "The expats didn't check in to the Bucharest Hilton wearing OPC name tags, Harold. They would've had safe houses, local support. The underground Stela knew from her days rescuing downed pilots."

"But they rolled up the whole lot, not just a few strays."

"Drink up," said Harvey. "You don't think good sober."

I finished my Manhattan and set the glass on the bar. I wasn't sober, I wasn't drunk. I was right where I needed to be.

"You're sayin' that, since they worked together saving pilots, Stela and Wisner's Bucharest networks were one and the same."

"That's what I'm sayin'."

Man oh man. And I thought I was a proxy assassin. "But Wisner had to suspect that Stela's hands were bloody on the Bucharest deal."

"What are you carpin' about? She saved your sorry posterior didn't she?"

Touché.

"Think long term, Schroeder, big picture. Frank Wisner didn't really expect you to succeed anymore than he thought his ex-pats would run the Reds out of Romania. You were part of his 'indigenous anti-Communist' shakedown cruise. He took your report as good news, as progress."

I was developing a new appreciation for this drunken wildebeest. Harvey was a nice counterpoint to gung ho Frank. While it pains me to quote the bastard, J. Edgar Hoover's rude assessment of Wild Bill Donovan seemed a better fit for Frank Wisner. 'He has all of the answers but few of the facts.'

Then Harvey lowered the boom. "Hoover was willing to let sleeping dogs lie, but you've gone and embarrassed the old coot. You campaigned against Truman and pissed on Dewey's big night so now both camps hate you. Wisner will drop you like a hot rock and Allen Dulles and his black knights are drawing straws to see who gets to stuff you in a duffel bag and drop you off the Arlington Memorial Bridge."

"C'mon, Bill, is it really bad as all that?"

"Depends."

"On what?"

"On how bad a boy you were back there in Cleveland."

"Any suggestions?"

"Get the hell out. Go to Ireland. No extradition treaty."

"And I have friends there."

A wry smile from Harvey. "Do tell?"

"Nice idea, maybe later. Right now I need to uncover Julia's source, find out who's got it in for me."

"All right, do that," said Harvey. "We backed the Christian Democrat candidate in Italy's big election last spring. The NKVD mounted a last-minute smear campaign. If this girl's source is trying to pull that crap around here I'd like to know about it."

Harvey gestured at my empty glass. "You good?"

I met Harvey's pop-eyed stare, which is something like facing the high beams of a runaway Mack truck that has careened into your lane on a mountain road.

"Better than good, Bill. I'm perfect."

"Then pay the tab, assbite." He waggled his eyebrows. "We're going upstairs to play a little game I call *Let's Pretend.*"

We rode the elevator to the sixth floor. Harvey was carrying a bulging leather valise. I found out why when we got to room 640. He informed me that I would now be under round-the-clock surveillance by the FBI.

"Why shag me? Julia was the one who did the damage."

"For all the Director knows you and Julia worked this together."

"Makes no sense, Bill. What do I have to gain from humiliating myself?"

"Hoover's not a lawyer, Schroeder, he's a cop. He tracks behavior, then looks for motive. The Q&A was over, you were being ushered off stage. Yet you stop to call on an unknown reporter. The Director will wonder why."

"I called on her because I knew her."

"But you wouldn't have called on her if you didn't know her."

"Probably not."

Harvey smirked. "You see how this shit gets complicated?"

He plopped his overstuffed valise on the bed, snapped it open and pulled out a package that looked like a gift box from a department store. He tore off the lid and passed me a box containing a brown uniform suitable for a maintenance man and a matching cap with a black bill.

"There's more underneath."

I removed the cap and uniform to see a pair of horn-rim glasses and a bushy paste-on mustache.

"What, no mutton chops?"

Harvey called me a bad word. I set the package down on the narrow glass table at the foot of the bed and noticed the name stitched above the pocket of the uniform shirt. *Tony.*

"I don't look the least bit Italian."

"That's where the mustache comes in."

I re-examined the bushy black soup-strainer. "I would rather be tortured by Communists."

"Suit yourself," groused Harvey.

"And where am I supposed to be going in this ridiculous get-up?"

"To visit Miss Julia, grill her about her source."

"And how did you know I wanted to do that before you spoke to me?"

Harvey squinted at me with half a grin. I caught a quick glimpse of Sorin Dragomir in Bill Harvey's easygoing self-regard.

"Because I am one amazing motherfucker."

Chapter Thirty-two

Harvey gave me his private phone number and left. I ducked into the bathroom to tap a kidney and change into my new duds. The pants were two inches too short, I'd have to wear brown socks. The shirt fit well enough, the cap was the problem. I tried wearing it at a rakish angle like Captain Candybar but it fell off. Time for a haircut.

I put on the pair of glasses and looked in the mirror. Not bad. I was a horn-rimmed intellectual with a sexy Italian name. Not a woman born could resist me. I put my wool topcoat in a drawstring laundry bag and carried it out the door.

Bill Harvey had a maintenance truck waiting for me at the service bay of the Mayflower. I stood on the dock, shot the shit with the driver and looked around. No Commie spies slunk around no corners.

The driver took me north and east a couple miles to Miss Julia's address on Seaton Place NE. The rainstorm had moved on, the night was calm. We weren't tailed.

I had him circle the block when we reached her apartment building just in case. Nobody followed. We parked in the alley behind her building. The only sign of life was a stooped ragpicker in a crumpled hat digging through garbage cans. I gave him a brief looksee but decided that no self-respecting federal agent would stoop that low.

I told the driver I would lock pick my way in the back door of the building.

"No need," he said, handing me an all-purpose skeleton key. Former FBI agent Bill Harvey had tended to operational detail.

I climbed the stairs to Julia's second floor apartment, apartment G. I knocked, nobody answered.

I smelled a rank odor from inside. The skeleton key didn't work on her door lock so I had to pick it, my hands shaking, fearing the worst.

I rushed inside to find that the smell was just leftover liver and onions, the skillet still warm.

I tossed the joint. Hey, it's what I do. Unfortunately Miss Julia returned with the evening paper not a minute later and caught me red-handed. She didn't laugh at my joke.

"I *told* you this apartment wasn't secure."

Julia picked up the phone. "I'm calling the cops."

"Bad idea."

"You broke into my apartment!"

"You ruined my career!"

"Hal, I'm a reporter, I ask questions!"

She dialed the phone. *Say something, genius.*

"I've decided Bill Harvey's wrong about you. You're not a Communist agent."

"A what?"

"You heard me."

"Why would he think such a stupid thing?" she fumed. "And what made you decide I'm not?"

"A hardcore Commie's not going to have a framed copy of Norman Rockwell's *Fourth of July* mounted over her commode."

"Maybe I put it up it to throw you off."

"Then you'd have hung it in the living room where everyone can see it."

Julia gave me a sour look but she set down the phone. Whew. Came an insistent tapping at the door.

"Julie, you are okay?"

Julia opened the door to a small spry old woman who was clutching a kitchen knife.

"Sorry if we got a little loud, ma'am."

The old lady ignored me. "You are okay here with this person?"

"Yes, Mrs. Rogash, I'm fine, thank you for your concern."

Mrs. Rogash shot me a hooded look and shuffled back across the hall. "She looks out for me," said Julia.

"I can see that. Now, since you've consigned me to the salt mines for the rest of my miserable life, the least you can do is offer me a drink."

"All I have is applejack."

"What's that?"

"It's what we drink in southern Virginia," she said with a droll look at my uniform. "Tony."

We sat on her saggy red corduroy couch and sipped moonshine so strong it made my eyes water.

"There are only two people I can think of who know about the Irish hoodlums and have a burning desire to see me dead. I figured one of them for croaked and I'm guessing the other would prefer to lay low. However I have learned from past experience that I am, occasionally, incorrect."

"You're funnier than you know."

I smiled and nodded. "My first suspect is Commander Frederick Seifert, formerly of the Federal Reserve Bank of Cleveland."

The man I had used as a hostage to rob the bank. It remains the worst thing I have ever done and he was entitled to exact his revenge in any way he chose short of murder.

"I'm familiar with Commander Seifert."

"Is he your source?"

"You tell me," said Julia, fighting back a yawn.

"I don't think so. The feebs let him retire shortly after...you know."

"After you robbed his bank."

"Yes. But Seifert's the old fashioned type. I don't see him trying to settle a score with a male rival by squealing to a girl reporter."

Julia looked at her wristwatch. "I'm late for an appointment."

I didn't like the sound of that. Who makes an appointment for ten p.m.?

"Then I'll make this brief. My second suspect, the one I assumed was dead, is Leonid Vitinov." No reply from Miss Julia.

"Stupid to write him off now that I think of it. My Control Officer in Berlin released Leonid to the NKVD after we exposed him as a Soviet double, thinking Beria would purge him. But Leonid was a fluent English-speaker with first-hand knowledge of American intelligence. Why croak the guy?"

"And this Leonid hates you because you exposed him?"

"Yes. And beat the crap out of him." Pause. "And stole his wife." Pause. "Who I later killed."

Julia put her hand to her mouth in shock.

"It was a terrible accident," I said, "but you can see how Leonid might not be too open-minded on that score."

"Hal, all I know is I was contacted by a man from the Committee for Free and Fair Elections."

"Uh huh. And the man who contacted you was short, suave and smoked expensive Turkish cigarettes."

Julia nodded, reluctantly.

"I suppose Leonid gave you some Federal Reserve Police contacts to corroborate his story."

"Yes, but they refused to be interviewed."

"You accused me of terrible crimes in front of the national press based on nothing more than allegations from a man unknown to you?"

"All you had to do was deny it! And if this Leonid was a Soviet agent stationed in Berlin how in the world did he know details of an FBI sting operation in Cleveland?"

"That's a long story," I said. "And you're late for an appointment."

The corduroy couch made a rude noise as Julia shifted her weight. She made no move to go.

"You're meeting Leonid, aren't you?" No answer. "What name's he using?"

"Terry. Terry Andrews."

"And he looked like a *Terry* to you?"

Julia glared at me. I needed her to make this meet. I should stop being a smartass maybe.

"Think of the story you can write."

"Sure. *How I Was Duped by a Soviet Spy.*"

"Leonid said he had another scoop that wouldn't wait, am I right?"

"Yes."

"That's his payday. The next story will be nailed down, with photos and affidavits. Something big, something fatal to the Dewey campaign. They'll want the Star to run it the day before the Presidential election, figuring the wire services will pick it up. By the time it's exposed as a hoax it'll be too late."

Julia looked at her watch, hesitated.

"And your story will be *How I Helped Capture a Soviet Spy.*"

"What do you have in mind?"

"To let Leonid make his pitch to you, then nab him when you part company."

"And you can do that without getting me shot?"

"I'll try my damndest, Julia, but I can't guarantee it."

"All right, let's go."

My kinda gal. But a thought occurred. "We can't."

"Why not?"

"This is a big meet. Leonid will be shadowed by Soviet agents. Which will make it next to impossible to bag him."

"If I don't show he'll call and arrange something else," said Julia.

"Uh uh. You've ticked off the FBI, he'll figure your phone's tapped. Leonid can't risk contacting you and we have no way of contacting him. Do we?"

"No, but he might leave a message at the Star."

"I guess."

"And who's to say this Leonid won't just give up when I don't show?"

I shook my head. "This is his last shot. Oh, he's got a back up reporter if you don't come through, but you passed his first test with flying colors. I'm guessing he'll give you tonight before he goes to Plan B."

I got off the couch and paced across the narrow apartment, turned around and paced back. Julia hadn't settled in here yet. The landscapes on the living room wall were yellowed leftovers from a previous tenant.

"Okay, the first rule of missed connections is to return to the initial point of contact. Where was it?"

Julia described Bonnie's, a homey diner in Georgetown with curtains on the windows. I pictured Leonid in the *Café Gestern* in Berlin where we first met. At a corner table, away from the window, facing the door.

"If there's no message at the Star," said Julia, "we'll go to Bonnie's Diner."

"Good."

"And what about his Soviet agents?"

"Lenny is not an agent in good standing. Plus he's an asshole."

"Meaning his back up boys will ditch him when I don't show for my ten o'clock."

Julia grinned at my wide-eyed surprise. "I'm a quick study."

She was that. Now all I had to do was figure a way to subdue a veteran agent on full alert. My .44 would be worthless, Vitinov would know I couldn't risk shooting him. Once he saw me he would know his mission had been blown and his life was over. Lavrenty Beria wouldn't forgive him twice.

My plan was for Julia to wait at Bonnie's Diner and hope Leonid showed. I would find an observation post and wait till the meet was over to make my play.

But what if Leonid sneaked out the back door? What if he...

"Yoo hoo, Hal, over here," said Julia, waving a hand in front of my face. "This is simple. Terry thinks I'm a bimbo infatuated with his oily charm. I know how to deal with him."

"I'm listening."

"There's a tavern on the corner. I'll bat my eyes at him and say I don't want coffee and lemon pie, I need a drink. You jump him when we walk over."

"That's very gutsy, thank you. Now all we need is a reason why you stood him up," I said. "Something trashy since he thinks you're a bimbo."

"Sure. Why not give me a shiner and I'll say I had a drunken fight with my sister."

"Right eye or left?"

Julia put her hands on her hips. "I can't figure you, Schroeder. I can't decide if you're a real life intelligence agent or just a half-assed joker."

I adjusted my horn-rim glasses and said something I had read in the back stacks of the Cleveland Public Library and had always wanted to repeat even if I wasn't quite sure what it meant.

"That, my dear Miss Julia, is what we intellectuals call a 'distinction without a difference.'"

I took a certain perverse pleasure in watching Julia struggle to bite back a giggle.

Chapter Thirty-three

Julia left her building by the front door and headed to the Evening Star offices on Pennsylvania Ave downtown. I donned my wool topcoat against the chill and left by the back door.

It was a quarter of ten on a Sunday night and quiet as a tomb save for a yowling cat. I heel and toed my way east down the alley. Conditions were ideal for detecting a tail – a clear night in a quiet part of town.

The FBI favors the tag team automotive method but I didn't spot any four-door Ford sedans idling at cross streets as I hiked west. I didn't hear any following footsteps, didn't see anyone behind me when I spun around. I could smell a shag, I swear. But I couldn't see one.

Miss Julia and I had made a plan. She would need a hat. She selected a black, close-fitting little number but I objected. The hat needed to be instantly recognizable. Julia shrugged, she was a one-hat gal. We decided on an orange scarf pulled up over the back of her hair and tied with a topknot.

Julia was to flag a cab to the Evening Star and check for a message from Leonid. At 10:40 she would walk the three blocks to the M Street streetcar line. I would hoof it to the next stop on the M line.

Julia would take a window seat on the right hand side. There were four possibilities. Julia had, or had not, gotten a message from Leonid, and had, or had not, been followed. If she had gotten a message she would exit the streetcar at my stop. If not she would keep her seat. If she thought she'd been tailed she would be bareheaded. If not she would wear her orange scarf.

Thus, if she stepped off the streetcar at my stop wearing her orange scarf we would hurry off happily to her rescheduled meet. If she kept her seat while wearing her orange scarf I would bound aboard and join Julia on her trip to Bonnie's Diner.

I wanted to see that ugly orange scarf in other words. I wanted to know we weren't being shadowed. The spy game has a simple scoring system that's independent of politics and war. Whoever holds superior knowledge at the end of the contest wins.

I was excited. As an observation agent my WWII service consisted mostly of hiding in mudholes. But now, as an operational agent, I would get to use actual tradecraft.

I checked Captain Dragomir's pocket watch. 9:48. I was about twelve blocks from my destination. I had a few spare minutes to call Bill Harvey's private line.

Leonid would be State Department certified as a special attaché to the Soviet Ambassador or somesuch, meaning he would have full diplomatic immunity, meaning the worst we could do was deport him.

But Bill Harvey wouldn't let any of that bother him.

I got to R Street and looked around for a phone booth. No Ford four-doors sat idling, no stealthy figures lurked. The hair on the back of my neck stood down. I wanted a phone booth to avoid being overheard but none presented themselves. The only establishment open at the late hour was a corner tavern, Swoozy's Joynt. I swoozed in.

An intelligence agent is supposed to have keen powers of observation. But I had been preoccupied, hadn't noticed the neighborhood's storefront churches and catfish stands. I hadn't noticed but the patrons sure noticed me. I was the only white face in the joynt.

I had been to a shinebox before, in both Cleveland and Youngstown. They always have a killer jukebox, everything from Delta blues to Louis Prima. The key was to pump nickels into the Wurlitzer and let your hep choice of tunes show you belonged.

But the jukebox sat silent this evening. Swoozy's dozen or so patrons were listening to a glowing Philco that sat behind the bar. A fire-breathing speaker with a gospel cadence had them mesmerized. While I couldn't make out much of what he was saying his tone was unmistakable. He was angry. Angry at folks who looked like me if the hard stares of the patrons were any clue.

There was a pay phone at the back of the bar. A pay phone on which a large man in a Panama hat was having a heated conversation.

I squeezed onto an empty stool near the door and ordered a draft from a tall black woman with hoop earrings and a regal bearing. Was this Swoozy? She poured me a beer, set it down and ignored my dollar bill. My money wasn't welcome here. Neither was I.

I leaned back and looked down the bar at the phone box. Panama Hat was in full harangue, in ragged counterpoint to the radio preacher. I needed to talk to Bill Harvey right now. There was a big man on the pay phone and another phone behind the bar that money wouldn't buy. What then?

I got my wallet in my left hand, put my right hand in my gun pocket and strode the length of the bar, hoping a bit of misdirection would do the trick, hoping my out-of-state driver's license would pass for an FBI buzzer.

The big man in the Panama hat was dripping sweat though the room was cold. He gave me a yellow-eyed once over as I approached, then returned to his argument. Someone was late with a payment. Whether Panama Hat was the creditor or the debtor I couldn't say. He would have to work it out later in any event, I had a Soviet saboteur to apprehend.

I whipped open my wallet while hoisting my .44 from my pocket and holding it at my side. "Agent Schroeder, FBI, I need this phone."

The big man didn't look at anything but my face. "Wait your turn," he growled, "*ofay*."

This brought a wave of guttural approval from the patrons behind me. Someone turned down the radio. Panama Hat and I were now the evening's entertainment. He was going to be a job of work. He stood a head taller and went about two-fifty.

I took my time stowing my wallet and gun. Then I tore the receiver from his big paw, stepped forward, grabbed his wrists and said the eight most powerful words in the English language.

"I have a problem, I need your help."

That took the starch out of him for the moment. I spun away and addressed the patrons of Swoozy's Joynt, two of whom had left their barstools and were headed my way.

"I'm a federal agent attempting to keep Communists from sabotaging the Presidential election this Tuesday." This went over okay so I added, "I need the telephone and a ride downtown. I'll pay ten bucks."

No takers. The patrons were waiting on the big man in the Panama hat. He was behind me now, presumably yanking a razor from his shoe.

"I do some gypsy haulin'," he said to me in a voice deep as the sea. "Make your damn call."

I turned around. "Sure thing, thanks." I patted my pockets and cleared my throat. "You got a dime I can borrow?"

His name was Cleve, the big man in the Panama hat. We got along just fine. He didn't ask any questions as we drove southwest down Rhode Island Avenue, I didn't tell any lies. His gypsy cab was a dark red Plymouth coupe from the late twenties. It ran nice and smooth though I could see pavement rushing by through rusted out floorboards.

My phone call to Bill Harvey's private line had gotten me a chirpy girl at an answering service. I told her that 'Tony' needed to meet Mr. Harvey outside Bonnie's Diner and gave her the address. I said it was urgent. Twice.

She said she would give Mr. Harvey the message when he checked in. Private line my ass.

The Plymouth didn't have a mirror on my side so I kept a vigil out the back window. Cleve drove slow, then gunned the sputtering coupe through an amber light at 9th Street. Well done. Maybe I could I recruit this guy as my backup in the likely case that Harvey didn't show.

Nah, too many ways to go wrong. And a crying shame. I'd pay good money to see the dapper little Russian's face when he got a load of big Cleve.

We drove down to M Street. The silence between us grew heavy. Cleve had questions that wanted answers. He couldn't very well return to the bar without a tale to tell. He had saved my bacon, I would tell him what truth I could.

"I'm not FBI."

Cleve grunted.

"You probably figured an FBI agent wouldn't be worrying about a shag job on his home turf. Or borrowing a dime to make a call."

Cleve hawked a loog out the window. I was making a fool of myself. I said my piece, not knowing where I was headed till I got there.

"A Soviet agent is attempting to turn the Presidential election with a last-minute smear story. His name is Leonid Vitinov. Leonid Vitinov. I'm trying to intercept him before that happens. I'm lone wolfing it, except for a girl reporter. My name is Hal Schroeder. Her name is Julia Hammond."

"Why tell me?"

"Not sure. I guess there's a chance Julia and I will both be killed and no one will know why."

"Who you want me to tell?"

"Well, if you see a story in the paper about our mysterious and gruesome deaths, tell somebody at the Evening Star. Preferably a girl reporter, Julia would like that."

"Awright." Cleve made a soft right onto M Street.

"You can pull over here."

He curbed the Plymouth at M and 19th. I handed him a twenty. He pulled a fat roll from his jacket pocket. I told him to keep the change.

"'Preciate that Mr. Schrader..."

"Schroeder, Hal Schroeder. And the Soviet spy is Leonid Vitinov."

"Right. You g'wan tell me who you working for?"

My apple pie answer surprised me. "I'm workin' for you, Cleve, I'm workin' for you."

Chapter Thirty-four

Julia had her orange scarf on when the streetcar pulled up, which meant no message from Leonid and she hadn't been tailed.

I boarded, paid my fare and took a quick inventory of the other passengers. A couple loudmouth teens out past curfew, a sleeping drunk in a filthy raincoat and a colored lady in a maid's uniform who looked beat from a long day's work.

I sat down next to Julia. We were off to Bonnie's Diner in hopes Leonid was waiting for her, sitting in a back booth, tapping his foot.

Julia and I started in again about what she should say to 'Terry' to explain missing the appointment but, sitting there, the back of my neck got itchy. For some daft reason I thought about my old pal Col. Norwood, MI6 Berlin Station Chief. About his description of the Four Powers at Versailles after WWI, how they haggled endlessly over the wording of a peace treaty, ignoring the down-at-the-heels vagrant at the table. The vagrant who would come back to haunt them.

I asked Julia if she had a compact with her. She did. I told her to powder her nose and position the mirror so I could observe the slumbering man in the back row.

He was short. His raincoat was streaked with grime but his felt hat, though crumpled, looked clean as a whistle, right down to the little bird feather in the band.

I felt a clutch in my lower intestines. This was the ragpicker in the alley. This was Leonid. The fastidious little man couldn't bring himself to dirty up his fine felt fedora.

"Don't turn around, Julia, but did the grimy man in the back row board at your stop?"

"Yes, I think so. Why?"

"It's him, it's Terry."

Julia stiffened. I squeezed her hand.

I had been very stupid. Once again. This operation was Leonid's last shot at redemption. He wouldn't have trusted Julia to show up alone. He would have been stalking her every move.

Had he made me?

Of course he had. Leonid would recognize me in a blizzard at a thousand paces. With his eyes closed. But I had superior knowledge for the moment. Leonid didn't know that I'd made him.

Big deal. I wasn't going to get the drop on him here. And I had Julia to worry about now that Leonid knew she had betrayed him to his blood enemy. Would he attempt to slip up behind us and do the deed?

Nah. Much as Leonid would love to blow my head off it would interfere with his assignment. He had a smear story to peddle.

The Russian knew the first rule of missed connections too. He would assume we were on our way to Bonnie's Diner, up to no good. He would exit the streetcar before it reached the diner and move on to his backup reporter.

I couldn't let him do that. I would have to jump off the streetcar after he did and chase after him, leading to a shootout on a dark street. Or to Leonid disappearing into the night.

Damn. I'd spun the wheel all the way round and landed on double zero. I would have to march to the back row and take my chances.

The streetcar was steaming west toward Georgetown, passing darkened stops. The loudmouth teens, now that I gave them a second look, were wearing button down shirts under their windbreakers. Georgetown undergrads, headed back to the dorm.

The colored maid had her head against the window and her eyes closed. We weren't stopping anytime soon unless Leonid pulled the ring cord which, not wanting to attract any attention, he wouldn't do. But I needed to get Julia off the car in case my encounter with Leonid did not go well.

"Julia," I said under my breath, "I want you to pull the ring cord as soon as we approach a major intersection, someplace you can grab a cab and go home."

"Why? What are you going to do?"

"I'll walk you to the front like we're both leaving. I'll escort you down the steps and out the door, then duck down in the stairwell. Leonid will have his face pressed to the window by then, trying to make sure we both got off, which will give me a few seconds to slip back down the aisle and grab him."

Julia examined me closely. "That's a very stupid plan."

"I agree with you. Got any better ideas?"

"I'm not going, I'll wait here."

"No, Julia..."

"Hal, I'm a reporter. I report things."

"Not if you're dead, you don't."

The streetcar slowed down just then. I looked out the window. A young couple was waiting at the corner ahead. Our timing was plain lousy.

"Forget it, stay put," I said. "Leonid should make his exit right here."

"I thought you wanted to grab him on the streetcar?"

"I do."

"What's keeping you?"

"You are."

"The hell with me. Do your job."

This was not what I wanted to hear. I suddenly realized that I had very little interest in sacrificing my life so that Thomas Dewey could win an election. And who was to say the papers and wire services would run a sensational muckraking story on election eve? I had plenty good reasons to keep my seat and let Leonid duck out.

I heard the soft rustle of a shopping bag well behind me. Leonid would have carted a change of clothes around with him - clean topcoat, fresh shirt - for his late night sitdown with Miss Julia. He was moving toward the rear door, preparing to exit.

I got up and sprinted toward the rear exit as the streetcar rattled to a stop at the corner of M and 29th.

I would like to think that I did this because I wanted to capture and present to Bill Harvey an NKVD Major with intimate knowledge of Soviet spy networks in the U.S. and not because Hal the hero was afraid to look like a punk in front of a girl reporter.

I arrived a few steps late. Leonid had bulled his way out the rear door while the car was still moving. He tripped on the curb, steadied himself and took off running.

The rear doors snapped shut, snagging me at the elbows. I fought my way through and stumbled onto the sidewalk. Leonid had a good head start but I anchored the 880 relay on my high school track team. Piece o' cake.

"He's getting away," said a familiar voice at my ear. Miss J, who else? "Go, go, go!"

I went. I wasn't great at short sprints, my long legs took too long to get churning. But I could make up a lot of ground over a middle distance. A middle distance Leonid didn't give me when he turned left at the next corner.

It was glimmering dark on 28th street. Quiet, residential. No streetlamps.

Leonid was nowhere to be seen or heard, though I could feel the presence of the Napoleonic little prick. He was laying in wait behind a parked car, or tucked inside a doorway. I was backlit by a streetlamp on M Street so I stepped back, peered around the corner and waited for Julia to catch up.

"Where...is...he?" she said between breaths.

"Up the street."

"Why are you standing here?"

"Because I..."

But she was gone, darting across the street, keening like a banshee, giving me cover to turn the corner. In combat it's always nice to have a crazy person on your squad.

It was possible that Leonid had used this brief time to steal away up the street. That was the logical move on his part. Why then did it take such a monstrous effort to put one foot in front of the other? Creeping up the side street felt like climbing Breakneck Ridge.

Where was Julia?

She wasn't huddled on the far corner where I'd last seen her. The only sign of her was a pair of pumps that had been kicked off. Christ, she *was* crazy.

My eyes adjusted. I started to make out the dim outlines of parked cars and brick buildings. What was taking so damn long? I should've been dead by now.

I had my answer soon enough. The whizzing hum of a nine millimeter round fired from a gun with a silencer. It split a brick in the large house behind me.

No follow up fire commenced. A feint. Leonid was trying to make me dive for cover while he finished off Julia. I killed his wife, he owed me one. Julia's perfume would make her easy to find.

I didn't dive for cover. I crept across the dark street, .44 in hand. Being a hero requires this sort of ass-puckering activity from time to time.

All Leonid had to do here was kill people. I, on the other hand, had to protect Miss Julia, take Leonid prisoner without fatally wounding him and find a way to call Bill Harvey and tell him that there had been a change in plans. How was that fair?

I crawled under the fat chrome bumper of an Oldsmobile and looked up and down the brick sidewalk. I listened, hard. I heard the shuffling of shoe leather up the block.

Leonid, hunting Julia. I craned my neck again, couldn't see him.

Time to do something, Schroeder.

"Hey, Lenny." He hates it when you call him Lenny. "You know I can't kill you, you're too valuable. So let's square off in the street, you'n'me. I aim for your leg, you aim for my head."

No response from Leonid, but his shoe leather stopped shuffling. Probably trying to figure out where my voice was coming from. Speaking from underneath the hollow bumper bounced my voice around in all directions.

A clever diversion, for two seconds. Leonid resumed his shuffling.

"I changed my mind, Lenny," I said and rolled out from under the bumper and jumped to my feet in front of the Oldsmobile. "I think I will kill you."

I fired a round from my hand cannon into the sidewalk, shattering the quiet night and kicking up red sparks that presented a flash photo of Leonid Vitinov crouched on the sidewalk not ten yards away.

He looked much the same as the last time I saw him in Berlin. Stunned.

But he recovered quickly. His nine mill Beretta was steady in his hand as it rose up to greet me.

I remember thinking *why is a Soviet agent packing an Italian pistol* just before he squeezed off the first round.

It missed, badly. Something to do with an intrepid girl reporter in stocking feet rushing up from behind and slamming him to the pavement.

I rushed forward and scooped up the fallen Beretta as Julia grabbed Leonid by the hair and began bashing his face into the sidewalk. I said something I had never anticipated having to say.

"Jules, ease up. We don't wanna croak the guy."

She dropped his head to the pavement. I stripped off his belt and lashed his hands behind his back. Leonid offered no resistance.

I rolled him over. His eyes were blank, unseeing.

Shit.

I put my finger to his carotid. Leonid Vitinov was still ticking. I turned to Julia.

"What were you thinking, sneaking up the sidewalk like that?"

"I felt bad about putting you in the soup, I did what I could to help," said Miss Julia with a pretty frown. "I thought we were a team."

I guess we were at that.

Chapter Thirty-five

Lights had come on in the big houses on the block. Curtains were parted, the cops had been called. I threw Leonid over my shoulder and started up the block under watchful eyes. Julia padded alongside in stocking feet.

"Where are we going?"

"I have no idea where I'm going but I suggest you grab your shoes and go home." Distant sirens rent the night. "Now."

Julia kept trudging alongside. "We haven't broken any laws, Hal, I don't see the problem."

"We're breaking a law right now."

"What law?"

"The law against kidnapping a foreign diplomat."

Julia broke stride, I kept on, the little man's head bouncing off my back. He was groaning now. Another half-block and he'd be trying to scissor strangle me with his thighs.

I heard the squeal of tires behind me. I heard Julia say, "Holy shit."

The vehicle that roared up and smoked its whitewalls to a stop was a Cadillac Fleetwood flying a small American flag from its radio antenna. Bill Harvey was at the wheel.

How in the world?

I cranked open the back door and pushed Julia inside before I ducked in and laid the semi-conscious Leonid at our feet. Harvey gunned the Caddy north on 28th as the approaching sirens came together in an operatic climax.

Harvey didn't speak, just drove the hilly streets of Georgetown like a blue bat out of hell, puzzling his way north and east to a quiet street that dead ended at a stand of trees. 'Rock Creek Park' read the wooden sign.

Harvey swung the big car around, parked and killed the engine. I heard the squawk of a police scanner from underneath the dashboard. That was how he knew where to find us. Harvey had gotten my message after all and was on his way to Bonnie's Diner when he heard the dispatcher report shots fired in the 1200 block of 28th Street, Northwest.

There were other possible explanations why Bill Harvey showed up to rescue us in the nick of time, none of them good and all of them complicated. It was late, I was tired. The police scanner under the dashboard would do for now.

The D.C. cops were het up this Sunday night, the scanner spewed nonstop argle bargle. I guess they didn't get many shootings in hoity-toit Georgetown.

Leonid lay face down on the floorboards, cantilevered over the transmission hump. Harvey twisted around from the driver's seat. "He still out?"

"Not sure."

"We need to talk," said Harvey.

"Understood."

We should have locked Leonid in the trunk just then but I had one of my patented and unfortunate bright ideas. I grabbed the collar of his grimy topcoat and hauled the groggy little man, hands still lashed behind his back, onto my lap, sideways. Then I pulled the brim of his felt fedora down and clapped my hands over his ears so he couldn't eavesdrop.

Sitting on my lap, his eyes crossed and his hat pulled low, Leonid looked like a ventriloquist's dummy, like Mortimer Snerd with a full set of teeth.

"This your comrade from Berlin?"

I didn't bother asking Harvey how he guessed that. "Yes, Major Leonid Vitinov, NKVD."

"I know his thumbnail – father worked for the Czar, used his perfect English and knowledge of the West to bat his way up the ladder. Till you came along."

"Correct on all counts."

"Any chance he'll cross over?"

"Sure," I said, dandling Leonid on my knee. "He'll cross over and back again so fast it'll make your head spin."

"You sure about that? Why would he want to return to Beria at this point?"

"He doesn't, last thing he wants is to be shipped back to the Lubyanka."

Harvey glowered at me, something he was quite good at. "Then how do you know he won't play ball?"

"All I know is that if Leonid Vitinov becomes a useful asset to the USA after being captured by Hal Schroeder then, in his mind, Hal Schroeder wins. And that can't happen. Not now, not ever."

Could be Leonid heard me say that. Anyway his eyes popped open and his expression turned distinctly odd - flirtatious, come hither. It distracted me for an instant.

An instant Leonid used to strike, fangs bared. Only my instinctive recoil kept him from sinking his teeth into my nose as he intended. What he got instead was my lower lip, which he bit clean through.

And there we were, Lenny and me, engaged in a grotesque make-out session in the back seat. I was reluctant to pull away and lose a chunk of lip so I pushed him against the seat back and hammered his temple with my fist.

This was unwise on two counts. One, I was too close to get much heft on my punches and, two, it hurt me worse than it did him. Bill Harvey whipped out a leather sap but he didn't have a clean shot.

Miss Julia saved the day once again. She pinched Leonid's nose closed. He had to open his mouth to breathe.

I pulled back and Harvey put him out with a quick sap to the forehead. I dumped him back on the floorboard.

"Are you okay?" asked Julia.

"I sshink so," I burbled through a froth of blood, holding my lip in place with a handkerchief.

Bill Harvey took a mental snapshot of my distress. "I am going to dine out on this story till the day I die."

It hurt to smile so I nodded. Dutifully.

Harvey used side streets to crisscross back to Julia's neighborhood across town. He parked in an alley a block from her apartment.

"Stay away from the hotel," he said to me. "Call tomorrow, eight a.m. Use a rubber." Which meant find a pay phone.

Harvey turned to Julia. "Write what you want to write, but keep my name out of it and give us 48 hours."

"I'll give you 24," said Julia. "And your name is William King Harvey."

Harvey and Miss Julia faced off over the black leather banquette.

I didn't feel like playing referee so I tended to Leonid. He was face down on the floorboard, making whistling noises through his nose. Out like a light. Yet the belt that bound his hands behind his back was loose.

Tradecraft, Schroeder. Secure the prisoner, search for weapons.

I cinched up the belt, then groped Leonid from head to toe. I found an Exacto knife in his sock garter. The world turns but nothing changes. He'd had the same get-up in Berlin.

I handed the knife to Bill Harvey without comment. He grunted. I carried Leonid's limp body out of the back seat while Harvey opened the trunk. We dropped him in.

I gave Harvey Leonid's still-warm Beretta. Harvey drove off.

Miss Julia and I faced each other in the cold dark alley. The pinprick rain started up again.

"Now what?" she wanted to know, standing there, getting wet.

"If Leonid was planning to pitch you a hot story about Dewey why didn't we find any photos and documents on him?"

"Maybe they were in that bag he carried off the streetcar?"

"Maybe."

He might have set the bag down while he was stalking us on 28th Street. But not if it held his precious evidence, without documentation Leonid had nothing. He wouldn't part with the pigskin till he crossed the goal line.

"We need to get you stitched up."

"I'm not going to a hospital."

"Hey, I'm good with a needle and thread," said Julia, taking my hand, pulling me along. "And applejack makes a great anesthetic."

Chapter Thirty-six

She was good with a needle and thread, Miss Julia. I held my flap of lower lip in place while she stitched me up with a great deal of furrowed concentration and sharp warnings to *keep still*. Moonshine and an ice bag worked wonders.

We were almost done putting my face back together when I heard a knock at the door. The businesslike thump-thump-thump, thump-thump-thump of a person who was not going to go away.

I got up to go see, a needle and thread dangling from my lower lip. I stood to one side of the plywood laminate door. "Who's there?"

"It's me, Schroeder," said a male voice I knew but couldn't place. "Open up."

"Identify yourself."

No response. This was someone in the biz. He wouldn't give his name till he knew I was, in fact, Schroeder.

"I do fifty three times a day," said the voice.

Schram?! It was Special Agent Robert Schram of the Cleveland District Office of the FBI. He did fifty pushups, three times a day, or so he told me back in '46.

"What do you want Agent Schram?"

"I want you to open the damn door."

"Are you alone?"

"Yes. And I'm not leaving till I talk to you."

"I can hear you fine."

"Oh for Chrissakes."

I didn't know why I was playing so coy, I wasn't afraid of the man. He'd been my immediate superior when I was recruited to infiltrate Cleveland's Fulton Road mob. I opened the damn door. Schram eyed the blood-soaked hankie I was holding to my chin.

"The last time I saw you, you was bleeding like a stuck pig."

"I believe you had something to do with that, Agent Schram," I replied, amiably. He looked the same - gray, buzz cut, trim and angular.

"Yeah, sorry I socked you, Schroeder. I remember doing it, don't remember why."

Our last meeting had been at an Army asylum outside Cleveland where he'd been sent after his WWII shell shock finally got the best of him. I didn't remember why he socked me either.

"Ancient history, sir. Glad to see you doing better."

"No choice, had to. There were crazy people in there."

I smiled, briefly. "What are you doing here?"

"Sorry for the interruption, young lady," said Schram to Julia, remembering his manners all of a sudden. "I can wait out in the hall while you finish...whatever it is you're doing."

"She's sewing my lip back on and you can talk to me here or not at all." I didn't know what game was afoot but it never hurts to have a witness. Schram didn't care for my suggestion but neither did he leave.

I returned to the operating table – a hardback chair in the kitchen. Julia offered Schram a drink which he declined and invited him to make himself comfortable on the couch. He followed her into the kitchen instead.

"You a nurse?"

"No sir, I'm a farm girl with three brothers. I've patched up a few scrapes." Schram watched her work with a grimace and an inquisitive tilt of the head. "Since Hal is indisposed for the moment I wonder if I might ask you a question," she said.

"Ask it and find out."

"How did you come to find us?"

"Saint Lucy herself could tail Bill Harvey in that fatass hearse of his. Pardon my French."

"Saint Lucy?"

Schram took a beat to tee up the punchline. "The patron saint of the blind."

And there you have it, ladies and germs. Harold Schroeder had now, in his scant twenty-eight years, seen and heard everything there was to see and hear. Humorless, paranoid Robert Schram, a casualty of the brutal Leyte campaign in the Philippines, had told a *joke*.

Miss Julia finished me off with a deft triple knot and swabbed my mouth with a washrag doused in applejack. I was in heaven for half a second.

"The Director wants to see you," said Schram.

"Now? Tonight?"

"Yes."

"What about?"

"That's not for me to say."

The Director was, of course, J. Edgar Hoover. That he had sent the one FBI agent I had some respect for meant it was a friendly invitation, one I could refuse.

Sure I could.

I went to the kitchen sink and washed up, cleaned the blood off my shirt and coat best I could. They weren't going to let me sit down with the Bulldog with a gat in my pocket so I handed Julia my pearl-handled six shooter.

"Get some sleep. Put this under your pillow and don't answer the door."

For once she didn't argue. And that's how I came to meet the Director of the Federal Bureau of Investigation wearing fifteen stitches of white cotton thread in my lower lip and a brown maintenance man's uniform with a name patch that read *Tony*.

Schram had a trail car. Two feebs in a Ford Sedan Coupe were parked behind his Buick Roadmaster. He walked over and spoke to them briefly while I waited on the street. The one in the passenger's seat picked up the radio mike.

Our motorcade proceeded south towards Pennsylvania Avenue and the Department of Justice. My lip throbbed in time to the drumbeat in my temples. The warmth of the moonshine and Julia's touch were gone, it was cold out and I was off to meet the Bulldog, late on a Sunday night.

"You're a smart kid, Schroeder," said Schram at the wheel, driving fast on the deserted streets, one hand on the wheel. "We hate your guts but we give you that."

"Thanks."

"Did you spot our tail on the streetcar? I bet the Director five bucks you'd sniff it out."

I had not, but it seemed like Schram had a lot invested in my alleged criminal genius. Well, I *had* bested the Cleveland FBI and I suppose nobody likes being outsmarted by a dope.

I ran down the suspects in my head – the rowdy kids, the driver, the Negro maid.

"The maid. She looked tired after a long day's work. But she was going the wrong direction, heading into all-white Georgetown, not away from it."

Schram looked pleased, vindicated. But just as quickly his face tightened. "Let me be clear, Schroeder. That's how I got my mind back in order, I got clear on the facts."

"Okay."

"I want to know your angle in all this, your payday."

"Don't have one, Agent Schram. I'm not that smart anymore. Figuring all the angles, playing both sides against the middle...it plumb wore me out."

But Schram wasn't listening. He was looking in the rearview mirror and growling. "Dumbshits."

I turned around. The trail car had stopped at a red light. Schram took a hard right on two wheels. I clung to the door handle to avoid spilling into his lap.

"So what side did you come down on?" he shouted over the roar of the engine.

We weren't so different, him and me. Two men scarred by war who tried to make sense of it in any way they could. He went bats, I got greedy. That we were now engaged in civil conversation while tearing down a side street at sixty miles an hour was a stirring tribute to something or other.

"I came down on our side," I shouted.

"Why?"

The way he spat out the question gave me the feeling he was fed up, hellbent to outrun his trail car and keep heading south to Tierra del Fuego.

"Slow down and I'll tell you."

To my surprise Schram throttled back and let his trail car close distance. I repeated, in different words, what I'd told him in that puke-smelling Quonset hut in Parma, Ohio two years ago.

"They're all bastards, Schram, you know that. The chest-thumpers and the speechifiers, the Commissar General of State Security and the Director of the Central Intelligence Agency. They're bastards, they have to be," I said. "But at least our bastards get swapped out every few years."

Schram nodded along with my speech, then added an important clarification.

"Except for Hoover you mean."

Chapter Thirty-seven

I pictured the Bulldog sweating me under hot lights, his face an inch from mine, lips curled, breath foul, barking questions about the Fed Bank Robbery. And what bullcrap were Julia and I up to, embarrassing the Agency in front of the national press?

But it wasn't like that.

Two leather wing chairs sat in front of a desk the size of a pool table. J. Edgar Hoover sat behind the desk, his tie cinched up despite the late hour, shirt starched, hair parted. He had taken time to freshen up for my visit. Hoo boy.

This was about more than a few stray questions from a girl reporter. This was a full on sitdown at the adult table.

Frank Wisner's wartime affair with Princess Stela was a barely-kept secret. Hoover figured to know about Wisner's trip abroad and his arrival in London with the Vampire Princess. Did he know about the boy king and put two and two together? That would give the Director one helluva hole card.

Well, he wasn't going to learn anything from me.

An aide escorted me to the chair on the right. Hoover didn't look up from the important documents he was studying which, I noticed as I got closer, were late editions of several newspapers.

I sat there in silence for an eternity. Thirty seconds. When J. Edgar Hoover raised his meaty, marbled face and offered me a sawtooth grimace my blood ran cold. He really did look like a bulldog.

"Would you like a cocktail, Mr. Schroeder? I'm partial to Jack Daniels," he said in an accent I couldn't place, a potpourri of down south and nor'east.

"Me too. Sir."

Hoover's aide went to a credenza and used the small side of a jigger to measure something less than one fluid ounce into each highball glass. No ice. He served the Director first. I wasn't sure whether to drink mine or dab it behind my ears. Hoover looked me over but didn't comment on my odd appearance.

It was okeydoke so far. Except for that empty chair next to me.

"I'll wager you didn't know the Bureau's pre-decessor agency was founded by a direct de-scendant of Napoleon."

"No sir. I did not."

"Attorney General Charles Bonaparte was the grandson of the French Emperor's younger brother, the Prince of Westphalia. He established a force of special agents in 1908. He was quite a character, the AG."

Hoover leaned back and unbuttoned his suit jacket. He was wearing, at close to midnight on Sunday night, a vest. "Teddy Roosevelt once boasted to him that he made all his Border Patrol applicants pass a marksmanship test. Charles said that he had a better idea."

"And what was that sir?"

Hoover took a tiny nip of his JD neat. "He told Roosevelt to have the applicants shoot at each other and award jobs to the survivors."

I laughed along with Hoover's aide, who had doubtless heard this chestnut a hundred times. I was surprised. Even the Bulldog would have to slop on the charm now and then, if only for Presidents and Budget Chairmen. I was surprised that he thought me worth the effort.

"I have invited another guest to our late night stag party," he said.

A door opened behind me. I heard soft murmurs and the rustle of clothing being removed. In another circumstance it might have sounded amorous. The office was carpeted so I didn't get to enjoy the perverse pleasure of hearing my accuser's footfalls echoing up behind me. I didn't have to think very hard to figure out who it was. Hoover's aide pulled back the empty chair and Commander Frederick Seifert took a seat.

I had been determined to give J. Edgar as good as I got. If he gave me guff about the bank job I would say the press liked it well enough - two mobsters dead and most of the money recovered. If the Director had a problem with my performance he should have said so at the time.

But my bravado dried up and blew away when I saw the stooped figure to my left. Frederick Seifert looked an old man now though I doubt he was sixty. I had ruined his life by convincing him to open the door of the Federal Reserve Bank of Cleveland to The Schooler and my smartass self.

We robbed the joint, the only successful heist of a Fed Bank in history. That mob thug Jimmy Streets met his maker and the Mooney boys escaped to Ireland with fifty gees somehow made the whole sordid adventure jake in my mind. Just a high school prank, putting the principal's car up on blocks.

Only the principal in this instance lost his job and reputation.

Seifert refused the Director's offer of a cocktail. The chairs in front of the desk were positioned so that Seifert and I faced each other at an angle. Seifert looked at the wall. Nobody spoke.

Now that he had aged so I realized who Seifert had first reminded me of. Grandpa Jake, my father's father, who migrated from the old country just before the war, after his wife passed away. He wouldn't talk about how she died but we all knew it was something awful.

Nice, Schroeder. Nothing classier than stabbing Grampa in the back.

"Commander Seifert, I would like to take this opportunity to apologize to you for my...bad behavior in Cleveland...at your bank."

This was an extremely lame apology so I added, "I hope you can find it in your heart to forgive me."

Seifert looked at me for the first time. "I am indebted to the Director for the privilege of this meeting."

Seifert then turned to Hoover. "But forgiveness is not mine to give. That is between you and your God."

Cut. Full stop. Back up a step.

I needed to pray for forgiveness, true. Why then had Seifert addressed his remark to J. Edgar Hoover?

The way the Bureau played the story in the press was that the Federal Reserve bank job was part of their sting operation to roll up the Fulton Street mob. They wanted to take credit for my gunning down mobsters. G-men greasing Pretty Boy Floyd and John Dillinger had made Hoover a national hero.

But the bank job was The Schooler's idea, one I turned to my advantage. I looked over my shoulder to make sure Hoover's aide had left the room. He had. Probably recording our conversation from a nearby control room but never mind.

"Commander, *I* made the decision to rob your bank. The FBI had nothing to do with it. It was The Schooler's plan but I could have stopped it. And I did not."

This was something less than a full confession. I left out the I-was-looking-for-a-fat-payday part. But I couldn't get a word in edgewise once the two old boys got into it.

"So I was forced to walk the plank for an FBI sting operation that did not exist?" snapped Seifert.

"You let this green Marine talk his way inside and rob your bank," snarled the Director. "In fact he did us all a favor by exposing your incompetence."

It went on like that for a few minutes. Apparently Hoover had some longstanding grudge against the Federal Reserve Police. Seifert knew this and took offense. No question Seifert got the short end. Would he keep his mouth shut now that he knew the full story? I wouldn't in his shoes.

The Director leaned forward when Seifert put both hands on the armrests of his chair, ready to launch.

"I understand you got blindsided by all this, Frederick."

Hoover looked to me, his steely glare trapped in the jowly face of a debauched aristocrat. "I did as well, thanks to young Mister Schroeder."

Hoover returned his gaze to Seifert. "Which is why I made a personal appeal to the President, asking that you be permitted to retire honorably, and with a full pension."

Commander Seifert visibly deflated in his chair. After a long silence he said, "I didn't know that, John." He got up and shuffled off.

I felt forgiven by Seifert somehow. Or, more precisely, ignored. Which was fine by me. I braced myself for the second part of this potboiler, the Director's *quid pro quo*. Which, as I understand it, is Latin for 'where's mine?'

Hoover looked up from his newspapers. "Thank you for coming Mr. Schroeder," he said as his aide glided up behind me. "See that you get proper treatment for that lip."

The aide pulled back my chair and escorted me briskly from the room.

Chapter Thirty-eight

I left J. Edgar Hoover's office with a head fulla bees, I did. Special Agent Schram was waiting in an anteroom.

"How'd it go?"

"Okay. I guess."

"Don't guess, Schroeder. Learn the facts."

"Sure thing."

Schram didn't care for my sarcasm. A long, angled look of sour appraisal was followed by a lean in and softly spoken words. "I have been to the top of the mountain, son. I believe you know that."

"Yes sir." I assumed he was referring to his role as commanding officer of the 21st Infantry in the Philippines, during the gruesome battle of Breakneck Ridge.

"I didn't get to the crest until two days after we planted the flag. Had to get out and walk because we kept running over corpses. The walking was good. We found a Filipino who was still breathing and brought him around. You can't kill those goddamn Bikols with a stick."

Schram reached out and laid his big-knuckled hand on my shoulder. "But you know what the hardest part was?"

"No sir."

"The hardest part was climbing back down the other side, to level ground. That was...very difficult."

I wasn't sure what Schram meant but, judging by how hard he was digging his thumb and forefinger into my trapezius muscle, he meant it plenty.

"Do you understand what I'm saying?"

"No sir," I said, squirming, "not exactly."

Schram's face glazed over and his grip relaxed. I feared he had faded off like he used to do, but the old campaigner surfaced a moment later.

"You will, Schroeder, you're a smart kid."

And with that he was gone. Guess it was my night for cryptic encounters with older men.

I was escorted out of the anteroom by Hoover's aide and down a hall. He opened a small door to what looked like a broom closet. Steep stairs stretched downward to a dimly-lit tunnel.

"It will take you to 9th Street," said the aide, "the Director thought it best."

I climbed down to the musty tunnel, alone with my thoughts, and a few rats. Why hadn't Hoover asked me about the shooting incident on 28th Street? And why hadn't he pressed me for dope about Wisner and Princess Stela? Too crude? Too soon?

The only thing I knew for certain was that I had been played, made to feel guilty then given absolution. 'Hal did us a favor by exposing your incompetence,' said Hoover to Seifert. The Director had dumped me in a boiling pot, then promptly fished me out. I owed him now.

My first instinct was to find a cheap hotel and lay low. The newsies would be gee'd up this close to the election. They would want to ask me embarrassing questions about Miss Julia's embarrassing questions.

Tough shit. OPC Director Frank Wisner would be red flagging urgent cable traffic in London. *NKVD Major Leonid Litinov has gone missing.* Wisner might want to ask me a few questions about my old adversary. Something he would find difficult to do if I was holed up in the Fleabag Arms with a toilet on every floor.

I owed Frank Wisner. Frank Wisner was the one footing the bill. I would sneak into the Mayflower the way I sneaked out, delivery dock and service elevator. The skies had cleared, a nickel-bright half moon was high. I walked north on 9th Street.

Two blocks later a black Fleetwood glided up beside me. Bill Harvey leaned over and rolled down the passenger's side window.

"Hey there sailor, new in town?"

I got in, we motored off, American flag flapping from the radio antenna. Harvey turned right on G Street and parked the Caddy by the pitch-dark hulk of the National Museum of Something or Other. He killed the lights but kept the motor running. The purring heat felt good.

"The Director never works on Sunday. What gives?"

"Good question, Bill. I thought you and the Bulldog were on the outs. How'd you come to find me?"

"I'll give you a hint, smartass. Georgetown, not two hours ago. We're fleeing the scene but I wheeled into a dead end street. Why?"

I had wondered about Harvey's odd maneuver at the time so I shut my yap and thought it through.

"Okay, you spotted a car in the rear view mirror, you took evasive action but the car followed. You turned down a dead end street because you wanted to determine if the follow car was pursuit or a tail. An unmarked cop car in pursuit would follow you down the dead end street, an FBI tail car would peek a look and keep on going."

Harvey nodded. "The tail car followed us to the girl's apartment but the feds lost interest in me once you two stepped out of the Caddy. I swung around and hung back. When I saw you climb into Schram's Buick half an hour later I knew where you were headed."

It was interesting to hear an account of the pursuit from both the fox and hound. Hound Schram suggested that Harvey was a lumbering fox. Fox Harvey suggested that was part of the plan.

"That's a fascinating and informative account, Bill. I appreciate your taking time away from interrogating a senior

NKVD officer about all-important spy networks to bring me up to date."

"Up yours, Schroeder."

"And yours as well."

Harvey pulled a cigarette from his pack of Pall Malls, rolled it between his fingers. "Yeah, I got bad news. I couldn't rouse Leonid, had to take him to Georgetown Hospital."

"What?"

"He's a Soviet diplomat, fuckstick. He dies in the trunk of my car, my nine lives are up."

"He was playing possum!"

"I bent his wrist back to the breaking point, he didn't wince."

"Of course he didn't. What'd you tell the cops?"

"I pinched his passport, showed them his Beretta with the silencer and told them he was a Russian gunrunner posing as a diplomat. That should put him on ice till the election's over."

"Ha. Ten bucks says he's already sweet-talked some nurse into calling the Soviet Embassy. The Ambassador will spring him by morning, giving Leonid Vitinov a full day to peddle his story."

"That's not going to happen, Schroeder. We got a press officer now, knows every editor in town. He'll get the word out."

I told Harvey I didn't know that. In point of fact, I didn't know squat.

I didn't know why Frank Wisner plucked me from obscurity. I didn't know why Miss Julia got me to endorse Dewey, then turned around and jumped me at the Dewey rally. I didn't know why I was hauled off to Hoover's office and made to feel like his pet poodle.

Harvey lit his Pall Mall and settled back in his leather seat. "Ask yourself question number one, Schroeder. Who gets happy?"

I rolled down my window. Cold air helps me think. It took me a good long while to burrow my way through this steaming mound of manure but I came out the other end, smelling like a rose.

"Leonid Vitinov by way of J. Edgar Hoover," I said. "By way of Miss Julia."

"Explain."

I took a drink of cold air. "Once I knew Julia's source was Leonid, I figured he got details of the bank job from my pal Ambrose, who was kidnapped in Berlin and worked over by the NKVD. But that tough Mick would never spill his guts. So then I figured Hoover used an intermediary to give Julia the story. But why would Hoover want to dredge up that Bureau embarrassment?"

Harvey tapped cigarette ash into his overflowing ashtray.

"And Hoover doesn't really give a crap who's President, he's been through three already."

"Four," said Harvey.

"Four. What he does give a crap about is his new rival for hard power, the one with the unlimited budget and carte blanche for covert ops. Frank Wisner of OPC. Frank Wisner makes the Bulldog *un*-happy."

Harvey smoked his cigarette.

"I asked Julia who she was working for. She said 'herself', which I believe is true. Doesn't mean she didn't have help from the Bureau."

"You just said Hoover wouldn't dredge up the bank job fiasco."

"Hear me out, dammit."

Harvey leaned a fat cheek against an extended middle finger.

"Hoover knows everything. He knows I was responsible for the death of Leonid's wife in Berlin, knows the little prick would do anything to bring me down."

"So the Director fed Leonid dirt about your felonious behavior in Cleveland with instructions to pass it along to the girl reporter?"

I nodded.

"Makes no sense."

"Sure it does. Hoover needed a mouthpiece, Julia, who couldn't be traced back to him. Ditto the source. He needed someone with independent access to my lurid past."

"To do *what*?" demanded Harvey.

"Julia got me to admit we were losing the Cold War, which embarrassed Frank Wisner and OPC. She hung me out to dry at the Dewey rally, which embarrassed Frank Wisner and OPC. And now, after my latest misadventure with Miss Julia, I'm called to a baptismal session with J. Edgar and anointed, best I can tell, his on-call spy targeting Frank Wisner and OPC."

"Okay," said Harvey. "Now close the circle."

Did Harvey already know where I was going with this? Or was this just a cheapshit way of maintaining his all-knowingness? Well, take this pal.

"Leonid had one last blockbuster he wanted to peddle to Miss Julia. I assumed it was an anti-Dewey bombshell, Dewey being the more rabid anti-Commie. But the Reds don't care who's President any more than Hoover does. Truman and Dewey are Tweedle Dee and Tweedle Dum to them. What do they care about? Who do they fear?"

"J. Edgar Bulldog," said Harvey.

"Yes! Hoover's the only one with the smarts and the manpower to track down Soviet illegals. If the NKVD had twenty agents in Canada in 1945 imagine how many they're running in the States in 1948."

I paused. Harvey stubbed out his cigarette. I continued.

"I believe Leonid Vitinov's blockbuster story, the one he was going to give to Julia, is that the Director of the FBI collaborated with a Soviet spy in the final days of a

Presidential election in order to damage Frank Wisner, his rival for power."

I smiled smugly, anticipating Harvey's reluctant acknowledgement of my blinding genius. "Not even Hoover could talk his way out of that one."

"And why," said Harvey, "would an NKVD Major do business with J. Edgar Hoover?"

"Because Hoover's an authority figure Leonid can understand. The Soviets don't bother with any red line between police powers and espionage. The head of the NKVD is both spy and cop, not to mention judge, jury and executioner. In their minds J. Edgar Hoover is our Lavrenty Beria."

"Christ, Schroeder, that's low. And you didn't answer your own question. Why would Hoover dredge up the fed bank story?"

"Oh crap, who knows? It's ancient history, he doesn't care anymore."

"That doesn't sound like Hoover," said Harvey. "But that's not why I think your theory stinks."

I waited, impatiently, for my dressing down.

"Never underestimate the power of a good librarian. That's how Hoover got started, he invented the card file system at the Library of Congress."

"I'm hep, Bill."

"I got curious about the girl reporter after she put your name in the paper. When she ambushed you at the Dewey rally - a lowly stringer digging up obscure details of an old case in another city - I kept my CI researchers up late. Someone was feeding her, possibly the NKVD. But how would they know this shit?"

"I don't know, Bill. But something tells me you do."

Harvey pulled a folded photocopy of a newspaper article from his coat pocket and handed it over.

"What am I looking at here?"

Harvey turned on the Cadillac's dome light. I struggled to read the grainy print, certain I wasn't going to like it.

It was from *The Hibernian Bugle*, a Cleveland weekly, dated January 3, 1946, a couple weeks after the Mooney boys and I robbed the bank. The lead item in a column titled 'Comings and Goings' detailed the sudden departure of the entire Mooney clan for County Cork.

'Twas a proper sendoff indeed. Mrs. Aloysius Mooney, attended by her sons Ambrose, Sean and Patrick, hosted an open bar last Saturday at O'Brien's. Young Patrick, still on crutches from an unfortunate accident, impressed one and all by making a parting donation to Father Michael Kennedy of St. Malachi's Parish in the form of a crisp, newly-minted, one hundred dollar bill."

Oh Christ. Those idiots.

"The NKVD has librarians too," said Harvey.

"Where did your people find this?"

"At your previous place of employment."

"The Cleveland Public Library?" Harvey winked at me. "The Cleveland Public Library was Leonid's source?"

"Makes more sense than your convoluted crock of shit."

The sonofabitch had a point. "All right, say Hoover's not Leonid's source, he's not scheming to ruin me. Why's he call me in?"

"You've already answered that question."

I had at that. Rank opportunist Hoover saw a chance to gather me in his fatherly embrace while I was feeling like the world had turned against me.

"Well, it's not going to work. I'm not going to be his snitch."

"The Director won't like that, Harold."

"Too fucking bad. Is that why you're here, Bill? To enlist me?"

Harvey leaned back against the car door and pronged me with his thyroid eyeballs. He was good and pissed. I had questioned his integrity.

"I'm here, Schroeder, because I thought you had CI potential."

Counterintelligence? The purest form of intelligence gathering? Something I could actually do now that I was a blown asset? First I'd heard of it.

"And I just blew my chance is what you're saying."

I had happily tumbled into Harvey's jolly yarn. Drunken uncle doting on wayward nephew. But those bulging eyeballs told a different tale.

You're in deep, sonny boy, and you're on your own.

Chapter Thirty-nine

I climbed out of the Cadillac and started walking north toward the Mayflower. Bill Harvey drove off in a huff. Stupid of me to insult the man. I didn't have any friends to burn in Washington D.C.

The night had turned cold. Winter cold, Cleveland cold. I shoved my hands in my pockets and picked up the pace.

Something was eating me. If my elaborate Leonid-Hoover conspiracy wasn't true, if Leonid's source for the bank robbery info was *The Hibernian Bugle*, why did he want to meet with Miss Julia again? We didn't find any evidence that he had a follow-up story to sell. Unless it was in that missing shopping bag of his.

But I knew the answer to that. If Leonid's assignment was to deliver a smear story to whatever reporter would take it he wouldn't have wasted time playing hide and seek with us on a dark street. Not unless Leonid had decided to revert to amateur status, to settle a private matter.

I walked faster.

The loading dock of the Mayflower was alive with smells. The tang of oysters and blue crabs battled the sweet warmth of fresh-baked bread as delivery men unloaded trucks. My head swam. If this hellish night ever ended I was going to sit down to a two-hour breakfast followed by a light lunch, a late afternoon snack and a six-course dinner.

I hung back and waited for the trucks to leave before ducking through the back door and heading down the hall to the service elevator. An odd noise caught my ear. It seemed to be coming from the lobby. It was a noise on two levels, a gravelly murmur topped with static.

I could hazard a quick visit to the lobby. If there were any newsies still standing at this hour they'd be too drunk to recognize me.

As I got closer I noticed a small cluster of folks by the wall across from the reception desk. They were watching a television.

I'd never seen a television in action before. The screen was about ten inches across, straight-edged on the top and bottom and rounded on the sides. The picture was wavy and gray-green, as if shot underwater.

A man in a bowtie sat at a desk with a big microphone. He was reading copy, a news bulletin that he repeated.

"There has been a shooting at the Soviet Embassy on 16th Street. A passing motorist reported hearing three or four gunshots, followed by dark-clad man or boy fleeing the Embassy on foot."

Man or *boy*.

The fleeing suspect was short.

It was goddamn motherhumping Leonid Vitinov is who it was.

The PD wouldn't have been able to hold him for long no matter what cockamamie story Harvey fed them. The Soviet Ambassador would have come to collect Leonid, who would have fed his boss some cock and bull about how he landed in the hospital, knowing the real story would surface in short order.

Hence the shooting. A sentry at the gate, maybe a guard inside the Embassy as well. Leonid had no interest in returning to Lavrenty Beria. His business was here. With me.

I had outthunk myself once again. All my mental gymnastics about Leonid masterminding a Commie conspiracy to spike the Presidential election or ruin Hoover were wrong-headed. This was the oldest story in the book. A bitter man looking to settle a score.

Leonid didn't have a smear story to peddle. I had learned in Berlin that he wasn't a true believer in the cause of World Communism. Leonid was only a true believer in himself. And his old world code of honor.

I had dishonored Leonid Vitinov in every way imaginable. I had cuckolded him, outwitted him, killed his wife. Such disrespect would require elaborate vindication. Shooting me on a dark Georgetown street wouldn't begin to cover it. He had bigger plans.

Julia's humiliation of me at the Dewey rally was just the beginning. The follow-up would be Leonid killing someone dear to me, to avenge the death of his wife Anna. He would want to do this in my presence. The climax would, of course, be the tragic death of young Harold, in as protracted and painful way as possible.

But why had he waited? He saw me go up the back stairs to Julia's apartment after the Dewey rally. Why not act then?

Because Leonid wanted to make sure. When Julia got me to endorse Dewey, Leonid knew I'd made an ill-advised admission to an attractive young woman. I was smitten. But then Julia bushwhacked me at the Dewey rally, as instructed. Could be I'd gone to her apartment to yell at her.

Leonid had a ten o'clock appointment with Julia that night, an appointment he never intended to keep. When she didn't hustle out the door at 9:45 Leonid had his answer. I had talked her out of it, I was concerned for her safety.

Julia was dear to me. Game on.

My stupidity had saved us. My hare-brained scheme to snatch Leonid outside Bonnie's Diner got us out the door before Leonid could leave his observation post across the street, scramble up the fire escape and jimmy the back window. It must have been frustrating for the little man, about to ring up the curtain on his big production, only to have to chase down the street after that smart-mouth girl reporter.

Leonid and I both knew what I'd do now. I wasn't going to tolerate the killing of another female confederate. Anna was one too many. What I was going to do now was plunge myself headlong into Leonid's trap.

I had Julia's business card in my wallet. I went to the pay booth and called her number. It was busy, she'd probably taken her phone off the hook.

I considered calling the cops on the off chance they might station a squad car out front of her apartment. But if Leonid was already inside and saw the cops roll up...No, this one was all mine.

I might get to Julia's and reclaim my six shooter before Leonid showed his pretty mug. Not likely but what else did I have? The house dick. The house dick would have a gun.

"No sir, Mr. Schroeder, we are not permitted weapons," said the stout brown-eyed man in the black suit. "Many heads of state stay with us."

"Which is why you need a gun," I said, "to protect them."

"Heads of state provide their own security."

"Which means they don't trust you, the house detective, to carry a gun in your own house?"

I was trying to goad him into showing me his gat so I could rent it for a ridiculous sum. But all he said was, "You are correct, sir."

I hoofed it out of the hotel, grabbed a cab, gave the driver a fin and Julia's address. "And don't spare the horses."

The traffic was light, we flew across town. The cabbie didn't have a gun I could borrow either.

I had him do a quick around-the-block when we reached Seaton Place. No one followed, no one lurked. There's never a buzz-cut FBI tag team around when you need one.

There were lights on in Julia's apartment but no silhouettes in the windows. We stopped in the alley by the back door. I was about to climb out when a thought occurred.

"What's your name Mac?"

"Tommy."

He was middle-thirties, with shaggy brown hair that spilled over his collar.

"My name's Hal Schroeder, you may have heard of me." No sign of recognition from the driver. I held up another fin. "Tommy, I'm going to ask you a big favor. A young lady's life might depend on it."

Tommy eyed the fiver, saying nothing. He looked like he'd pulled a twelve-hour shift.

"I want you to wait five minutes then come up to apartment G as in George, hammer on the door and yell 'Police, open up!'"

I wanted a distraction so I could jump Leonid. He wouldn't plug us right away, he'd want to gloat.

"That's it?"

I liked it that Tommy didn't ask for details. "That's it. Apartment G, second floor, five minutes. I'll leave the back door open."

"I'll do it for ten."

I liked that too. I forked over my last bill. "You don't have a flak jacket handy do you?"

Tommy grinned, and squinted. "You're that hero guy, ain't ya? Some bridge in Berlin and all."

"Yeah," I said and climbed out. "I'm that hero guy. Be safer if you parked down the block."

Tommy nodded like he did this every day. I used the skeleton key on the back door and crept quickly up the stairs.

My legs got heavy as I approached the second floor. Was I that hero guy? Real heroes do things they don't have to do, things that get them killed. I could punk out now and no one the wiser. I'd been a selfish shit in the past, why stop now?

I didn't want Miss Julia to get killed of course, she was class A all the way. But if Leonid was already inside her apartment as he figured to be, dollars to donuts Julia and I were both goners.

Tough shit, had to do it. Tommy the cabdriver would be disappointed if the hero of Muhlendamm Bridge punked out. And I couldn't disappoint Tommy.

I heard music when I reached the second floor, a radio or a record player. The music was coming from inside apartment G. I assumed it was part of Leonid's well-laid trap, meant to make me think Miss J was winding down after a hard day.

I listened at the door. No voices. I inspected the door lock. No sign of a jimmy, but then there wouldn't be with Leonid.

Do it, Schroeder.

I knocked loudly, pretending to be soused. "Hey beautiful, it's me, Hal! Lemme in, lemme in!"

The door flew open after a moment. Julia, in a flannel nightgown, her hair up in curlers, scowled at me.

I scanned the room. No sign of Leonid. The music was coming from a radio in the parlor.

"You been in all night?" Julia nodded. "Back window locked?"

"Yes! What's this about?"

My neck got prickly.

They teach you at spy school that a good spy never attacks from the front so I was turning back toward the hall when the gun butt caught me at the base of the skull. I pitched over sideways.

I wasn't lights out but I hit the floor and stayed there.

Julia inhaled sharply but didn't scream, God bless her. We would need our privacy to sort out this little squabble.

I heard Leonid push the door closed behind him. I groaned loudly and rolled over on my back, nice and slow like, keeping my hands in plain sight, trying to get my eyes to work.

Leonid smelled like sweat, like he had run all the way here from the Embassy. Julia was whimpering softly, which didn't figure for a tough broad like her.

When Leonid swam into focus I saw why. It wasn't sweat he was covered with. He had a spray of fresh blood all down the front of his coat.

He must have commandeered the apartment across the hall to keep watch. Nosy neighbor ladies always have a peephole.

"Mrs. Rogash," said Julia in quiet horror.

"I had no intent to do her harm," said Leonid calmly. "But she chose not to listen."

"Why?" cried Julia. "Why did you come here?"

"Take two steps back," said Leonid, gesturing with his gun. He had a Red Army Tokarev this time, single action, semi-automatic. "And ask Mr. Schroeder that question."

Julia backed up two paces, towards the parlor. Leonid turned his back to the kitchen and backed up four paces. We were an isosceles triangle with Leonid at the vertex. I was on his left, Julia on his right.

I cursed myself for telling Tommy to wait five minutes. Despite his outward calm Leonid was off center, ragged, his gun hand shaky. He had a purple bruise on his forehead from when Julia slammed him to the pavement and Bill Harvey had sapped him a good one after that. And for all I knew the Embassy guard had winged him or Mrs. Rogash had stabbed him with a kitchen knife.

Leonid wasn't up to a big production tonight. He would be quick.

I had to move him in my direction. If I could distract him for half a second Miss Julia would do her part.

"Lenny's just ticked cause the grenade he gave his NKVD pal was the one that blew his wife to bits."

"On your feet Schroeder!"

"No thanks. I'm comfortable here." That didn't provoke any movement so I yawned, loud and long.

"On the floor, face down!" said Leonid to Julia.

She looked to me. I nodded. She proned herself out.

Leonid stalked over to me and stood just out of reach. He pointed his gun at my head.

"C'mon, Lenny, you've made it this far, don't screw it up now."

Leonid hesitated, I sighed. "First the speech, then the girl, *then* me."

But Leonid wasn't buying my bullshit this particular evening. I knew that because he fired his weapon at my head.

He missed, a lucky parlay of his shaky hand and my instinctive last-second roll to the left.

I kept rolling for all I was worth, hoping to topple the little man. But he hopped over me, twisted around and stood with his back against the wall, sucking wind.

Julia had sprung to her feet, ready to clobber Leonid with a four-cornered crystal ashtray from the coffee table. But his little hop and twist had saved him from another drubbing by the scrappy plowgirl.

I should have damn well stood up when he told me to. That way I could have bullrushed him and eaten his bullets while Julia made a run for it.

It was trickier now. He had us triangulated again, his back to the wall, the door to his left. If I jumped up Leonid would have time to cut me down in the two strides it would take to reach him.

Maybe not. The Tokarev was small bore, not much stopping power. I could still mash him against the wall and, with my dying breath, impale his trachea while Miss Julia dashed out the door.

Okay, Schroeder, you're fresh out of snappy patter. Do it. Leonid's getting his breathing settled and his gun hand steady. Do it now.

Tommy the cabdriver yelled, "Police, open up!" while hammering on the door so hard it slipped its latch and swung open.

I arched my back, pushed down hard and exploded to my feet.

We had a frozen moment just then, Leonid, Tommy the cabdriver and me. Not a one of us knew what to do, too much had changed in too short a time.

Leonid recovered first. He angled his gun back to its proper bearing. Me.

Which is where the greedy little bastard went wrong. He could have put a couple slugs in my midsection in the split second before I got to him. But Leonid wanted a kill shot. He fired at my forehead with a shaky hand.

I ducked, he missed. I drove my right shoulder into his chest and flattened him against the wall. His gun clattered to the bare wood floor.

I threw him down, sat on his chest and pinned his wrists. I wanted to kill him. Badly. But there were witnesses.

"I knocked a little early," said Tommy, matter-of-factly, "after I heard the gunshot."

"Well done, Tommy. You saved our lives," I said, keeping my eyes on Leonid. He looked done now, half dead.

"Jules, you okay?"

"Yes," she breathed.

"Then go check on Mrs. Rogash please. Lenny and I want to be alone."

Julia and Tommy left the apartment and closed the door behind them. Dinah Shore sang *Buttons and Bows* on the radio.

"You should have killed me when you had the chance," croaked Leonid.

I grinned. "That's my line, Lenny."

"You can't kill me now." He took a raggedy breath. Then another. "You are a hero."

"Only when other people are watching. We're alone now," I replied. "Do you remember dear old Col. Norwood's favorite line? 'No one asks hard questions of good fortune.'"

Leonid didn't appear to take my meaning so I said it plain. "The police department isn't going to give a shit how you died."

"What," he gasped, "do you want?"

"An answer to a question. Tell the truth, I let you live. Beria's gonna punch your ticket anyway."

"Ask…your question," said Leonid, barely audible.

It wouldn't do for Leonid to check out now. The question had been rattling around in the catch basin of my brain ever since I glommed Leonid's master plan. He knew something I didn't. Superior knowledge is the brass ring. If Leonid Vitinov kicked off with superior knowledge then Leonid Vitinov wins.

"My question, Leonid, is why are you so intent on avenging the honor of your wife, a woman who ditched you for a dirty Yank like me?"

Leonid struggled to speak, producing only bubbles of spit. I sat up on my haunches, easing the pressure on his chest. But I kept his wrists pinned.

"Anna did not…care for you. She wanted only a better life."

He was halfway right. Anna had asked me to arrange transport for her to New York. But our affection for one another was unmistakable, genuine.

Leonid's eyes filled with tears. "Anna wanted only a safe place…to raise our child."

Oh fuck.

What Leonid said made immediate and terrible sense. Anna had risked her life, and mine, to smuggle out a suitcase crammed with family heirlooms. At the time I'd thought she meant to sell off her silver-framed pictures and fine china for cash. But she didn't need money, I had her covered. What she needed was something to bequeath to her first born.

Anna was pregnant when I killed her.

Was I the father?

Time had been kind to me. The waking and sleeping image of Anna fleeing the live grenade, the one I tossed back from our truck at Muhlendamm Bridge, had faded from view. But I saw it again now. Anna's over-the-shoulder look at me as she fled the grenade that would take her life. The puzzled expression that said, *Why would you do this to me...*

WHANK!

I looked up to see Miss Julia holding the four-cornered crystal ashtray. One of its corners was smeared with blood.

I looked down to see Leonid with the side of his head gouged open, dead as a mackerel, a neck-slicer clutched in his left hand.

How had that happened?

Miss Julia looked down at me. "You okay?"

"I think so. Sure. How's Mrs. Rogash?"

"She's gone."

"Aww shit."

"Indeed."

Julia helped me to my feet, put her hand to my cheek and kept it there. "Hal," she said, "we need to find you a new line of work."

Chapter Forty

I was more than done with the hero routine but Julia had other ideas.

"It makes a better story if you did it," she said.

I had put Julia in harm's way and gotten her neighbor killed. Whatever she wanted. But what I'd told Leonid wasn't strictly true. The cops would ask hard questions of good fortune.

"This is a big deal, Julia, a double homicide, with one of the victims a foreign diplomat. We have solid evidence - Leonid's coat soaked with your neighbor's blood, her blood on his knife. Why give the cops a reason to doubt our story by making shit up?"

"Because I don't want to be known as the ashtray killer the rest of my life. Men find me scary enough as it is."

I agreed to do it her way. But it meant keeping the FBI at bay. By rights they should get the call, the killing of a diplomat being a federal matter. But G-men have secret potions for tracking footsteps and detecting partial prints and all like that. Better to have the local coppers barge in and trample the crime scene like a herd of cattle. I would make sure they treated Leonid's blood-soaked coat and knife with care.

We took a moment to contemplate Leonid's corpse splayed out on the bare wood of the entryway, his deep-set eyes staring skyward, his skull resting in a pool of purpling blood. I had expected to feel joy at vanquishing my stalwart foe. I felt satisfied he was gone, sure, but nothing approaching joy. It's a peculiar thing to say but somehow my youth – my wild, intemperate, fortune-kissed youth – died with Leonid.

We wiped Julia's prints from the ashtray and replaced them with mine. We quickly bogused up a story. *I got up to call the*

*cops, thinking Leonid was unconscious. Leonid came at me
with his knife, we struggled. I grabbed the ashtray and bonked
him.*

The yarn was well-ventilated. Why didn't I tie up the
suspect before leaving him unattended? How did I grab the
ashtray off the coffee table in the parlor when I was wrestling
Leonid in the entryway? But I would make it work somehow.

Tommy entered and surveyed the wreckage. "I gave the
neighbor lady mouth to mouth," he said, "but she was too far
gone." He looked down at Leonid. "What happened to him?"

"Go home, Tommy, go home to your wife and kids."

"I don't gotta talk to the coppers?"

"I'll handle it, you've done enough for one night," I said.
"Just keep it on the QT for now."

He turned to go with a quick wave and stopped. "How'd
you know I got a wife and kids?"

"You look exhausted."

Tommy laughed and banged off down the hall.

Julia got out her Kodak and said she wanted to snap my
photo for her story. I told her no.

"Hal, you were on television."

"Yes, but a photo in a newspaper is a document. It'll go into
a thousand file cabinets and come back to bite me someday."

"I can't do the story without your photo!"

"I'm in the Chaney High School yearbook, Class of '43."

I didn't really care about getting my picture in the paper, my
cloak and dagger days were behind me. But I wasn't posing for
one. Wisner would be cheesed off enough without seeing my
dopey mug on the front page.

I got through my late night sweat session at Washington
D.C. Police Headquarters in one piece. The graveyard shift
watch commander didn't really swallow my account of what

happened but he couldn't prove different. Miss Julia must have held up her end because the watch commander gave up on me about four a.m.

I got a few hours of blessed shuteye in an empty holding cell and a leftover baloney sandwich. The food in my Romanian barn stall was better.

Chief of Police Hyram Johnson was a beefy man with a Southern twang and thinning rust-colored hair. He wasn't interested in trying to poke holes in my story the next morning. He wanted the big picture. Who I reported to at CIA. Why a Soviet Embassy attaché had taken such an interest in me and a small time reporter.

I told him enough to make him scuttlebutt king of the PD lunch room for a week. Why not? My life was an open book.

The Chief plied me with coffee and donuts in a most congenial interrogation, in no particular hurry to turn me loose. I wondered who of my many admirers would finally kick down the door and spring me. William King Harvey? Captain Candybar? J. Edgar Hoover?

Turns out it was Chief Johnson's secretary. She breezed into his office following a cursory *tap tap* on the door to present him with a newspaper. I was sitting across from his desk, left wrist cuffed to the chair leg, right hand free to sip and chew.

The Chief read the front page and gave out with a low whistle. "Well," he said, "she shore din't waste any time."

"Who's that?" I asked.

"Your girlfriend," he said with a wink and showed me the headline in the early afternoon edition of the Evening Star.

CIA Hero Bests Soviet Spy in Desperate Fight to the Death!

Good Lord.

"I got a coupla G-men cooling their heels in the lobby who are just itchin' to talk to you."

No doubt.

"But I hate them stuck-up cokesackers. What say we smuggle you out the back door and send you down to E Street in Foggy Bottom."

"Where's that?"

"I thought you worked for Frank Wisner?"

"I do."

"That's where his office is."

How did he know that? Had Wisner called? So far as I knew he was still in London.

"Never been there," I said.

"Why not?"

It looked like Chief Johnson was angling for one last dollop of juicy gossip before he'd turn me loose.

"Because, Chief Johnson, I am what the Office of Policy Co-ordination terms a covert agent without portfolio."

The Chief liked this, but his eyebrows indicated he wanted more. I laid it on thick.

"I'm an off-the-books operative authorized to perform sabotage, subterfuge and, in extreme cases, subject to National Security Council sanction, termination with extreme prejudice."

Chief Johnson's eyes narrowed. "Are you funnin' me?"

"No sir." I gave him my best hard-eyed stare. "And we never had this conversation."

I was uncuffed and bundled out the back door in short order.

Chapter Forty-one

A cop in an unmarked car drove me to Wisner's surprisingly cramped and cluttered office about six blocks from the White House.

"Jesus Christ, Schroeder, you look as bad as I feel."

He said he had arrived home yesterday from London and had come down with the crud *en route.*

I was surprised to see him back so soon. I figured he would want to take some time getting Stela and the boy king settled. But I wasn't going to open that can of worms again.

I gave him a quick summation of events, how I came to have the stitches in my lip, how Leonid was intent on personal vengeance, how I killed him in self-defense. I felt bad about lying to him, though Wisner only half listened to my account. His mind was elsewhere.

"I don't take issue with your appearance at the Dewey rally, Schroeder," he said, his voice raw. "As I understand it you didn't identify yourself as CIA. You are free to express your political preferences as a private citizen, as are we all."

Wisner gestured to the copy of the Evening Star on his desk. "But this headline terms you a 'CIA hero.' There is no such animal. No active agent or operative can have a higher public status than any other. It damages our cohesion."

Very high-minded I'm sure. I had spent less than a week in D.C. all told yet its bleak cynicism had leached into my bones. I suspected that what Julia's cover story most damaged was Frank Wisner's sense of superiority to the crass, headline-chasing FBI.

"I understand your concern, sir. But becoming the CIA's Melvin Purvis was the last thing I wanted." Purvis being the G-man famous for gunning down Pretty Boy Floyd and John Dillinger.

I surprised the Director of the OPC with this remark. Leastwise he gave me a fresh once over. I sounded a little too big for my britches maybe. Wait till he heard my next little tidbit.

"Change of subject, sir. Last evening I was summoned to the office of J. Edgar Hoover. He wanted to discuss my dubious conduct back in '45, when I took part in a federal sting operation in Cleveland."

"The one you were asked about at the Dewey rally."

Wisner had been kept up. "Yes sir. We got that all squared away, best I can tell. However..." I paused to clear my throat and question my sanity. "I got the feeling that our meeting wasn't about me so much as it was about you and the OPC."

An almost imperceptible tightening from Wisner. "How so?"

"Well, by rights Hoover should have read me the riot act about my conduct during the Cleveland sting op – I more than botched it – but he was pleasant, welcoming. I got the distinct impression that I would hear from him again, that he was, well, recruiting me to be a source."

Wisner sat very still. "Did he ask you any direct questions related to OPC, your recent OS operation or our debrief in Rome?"

Three questions. But I do believe Wisner only cared about the last one. I pictured the headline in the Evening Star if J. Edgar Bulldog found out that Frank Wisner was the father of the heir to the Romanian throne.

CIA Chief Sires Commie King!

Someone once said 'Be quick with bad news, take your time with good tidings.' I took my time.

"Sorry, sir, I'm not sure what you mean by 'OS'."

"Offshore, overseas," snapped Wisner.

"Oh, of course," I said. "And no, sir, the Director asked me no such questions."

Wisner brightened at this reply and stood up. Too quickly apparently because he had to lean on his desk to steady himself. I got up as well.

"My driver will take you back to the Mayflower. Got everything you need?"

Alas I did not. But I wasn't about to ask the Executive Director of the Office of Policy Co-ordination for a wad of folding money.

The intercom buzzed. "I'll be in touch late tomorrow," said Wisner. "After the election results come in."

I showed myself out.

Wisner's driver was a pleasant young fellow who hailed from Twinsburg, Ohio just west of Cleveland. We talked about the Browns' terrific season - eight wins, no losses - as he drove across town. I suggested he drop me off behind the hotel in order to duck the newsies.

"I've got that covered, Mr. Schroeder."

Indeed he had. He drove down a steep ramp on the western side of the hotel and punched in a security code on a mounted keypad. A ribbed steel door rolled up, admitting us to the Mayflower's sub-basement. He parked by an elevator shaft, got out and keyed in another code. I heard an elevator car descending.

The young man watched my perplexity with a grin. The elevator car settled with a *ding*.

"They call this the King's Lift," he said as the door opened on an elevator operator in white and gold livery.

Wisner's driver waited until I climbed onboard, kept waiting till the door closed. The elevator operator cranked us skyward.

"I'm on the sixth floor," I said. "Why do they call this the King's Lift?"

"The concierge will explain sir."

We blew by the sixth floor and kept climbing to the top of the building. The door opened to reveal a small lobby with an inlaid marble floor and a soaring glass skylight.

A dark man in an expensive suit said, "Welcome to the Penthouse Floor, Mr. Schroeder. Mr. Wisner instructed us to relocate you for reasons of security. This floor is designed for use by heads of state, it is not accessible by the lower floors."

"Sure, of course." We heads of state need our privacy.

He showed me to the Woodrow Wilson Suite, a dazzling three room job with a wet bar, original oil paintings on the walls, Steuben glass bowls on the end tables and a private terrace overlooking the Capitol dome. What in the world had I done to make Frank Wisner like me this much?

"We took the liberty of hanging your clothes in the bedroom closet and placing your toiletries in the bathroom."

"Okay."

"Is there anything else you require, sir? Anything at all?"

I wanted nothing more than to take the world's longest shower and hit the sack but the concierge looked so eager to please that it seemed a shame to disappoint him.

"I could eat something."

"Certainly sir, we have an extensive room service menu."

"No doubt, but for some reason I'm dying for a corned beef sandwich on Jewish rye, brown mustard, not yellow. Can you do that?"

He nodded. Actually it was more like a bow. "Would you care for a beverage?"

"A glass of beer."

"What brand do you prefer?"

"I'm not fussy about beer."

"Pilsner glass or a chilled mug?"

"I'm not fussy about beer glasses either," I said, stripping off my vile-smelling topcoat.

The concierge managed to not look surprised, though I figured to be the first guest in the history of the Woodrow Wilson Suite attired in a brown maintenance man's uniform with a name patch.

"Shall we have your coat dry cleaned, Mr. Schroeder?"

"That'd be swell. But I'll need it by tomorrow morning."

"Very good sir. If you would like us to launder your ...uniform, simply leave it in the bedroom hamper," he said, gathering up my smelly coat. "You will find a terrycloth robe in the bathroom."

I would and did.

The corned beef was first rate, the beer cold, the bed so comfy I figured to sleep for a week. As I drifted off I tried to make sense of why I was ensconced on the Penthouse Floor of the Mayflower Hotel, my head swathed in downy pillows.

I didn't make much progress. I was asking a hard question of good fortune, true. But I wasn't all that interested in the answer.

Chapter Forty-two

They say that people who rise to great wealth from humble roots quickly become accustomed to the trappings of the good life.

No shit. You wake up at three a.m. with a taste for a ham and cheese omelet and a Bloody Mary and it's on a bedside tray in fifteen minutes and you're wondering why it took so long. After two nights in the Woodrow Wilson Suite of the Mayflower Hotel my humble roots were a distant memory.

I listened to the radio and visited the wet bar and sat on my private terrace and watched the sun set behind the Capitol dome.

It was very peaceful. There's a statue atop the Capitol that you don't really notice from street level. It looked like it might be an Indian brave.

I liked that you couldn't tell for sure. They fought a world war over what fiery totem got planted atop Berlin's Brandenburg Gate. Better to leave 'em guessing.

The FBI had come to call on Tuesday morning. They were oddly formal, and brief. On a short leash by J. Edgar, or intimidated by the surroundings. I answered their questions about the bloody demise of Leonid Vitinov, repeating what I had told the PD. They wrote down my answers, thanked me and left. Life in the Woodrow Wilson Suite was another world entirely.

I had been expecting a call from Frank Wisner once the election results came in. But the election was too close to call on Tuesday night.

Frank Wisner woke me up on Wednesday morning, by proxy. A young man, pale as his starched Mayflower tunic, apologized for the interruption. He was holding what looked like a walkie talkie that was plugged into the wall. He presented it with a bow.

"Hello?"

"Good morning, Mr. Schroeder."

"And a good morning to you sir." I looked up. The young man in the white tunic had vanished.

"Have you seen the election results?"

"Last I heard Dewey had a slim lead."

"That didn't hold. Harry Truman has won."

I listened to spitting static on the scrambled line and kept my yap shut.

"We will have to mend some fences," said Wisner. "I believe you can provide us a valuable service in the present circumstance."

I kept my yap shut.

"I would like you to consider being OPC's congressional liaison. I'm no good at that sort of thing, lobbying, testifying in closed session. I get flustered and lapse into lawerly mumbo jumbo."

Somehow I couldn't picture brawny Frank Wisner being unnerved by a committee of porculent windbags. "Sir, I am *not* a gifted speaker. I barely managed ten words at the Dewey rally."

"Americans like their heroes taciturn," said Wisner. "And congressmen prefer listening to themselves."

"Good one sir."

By rights I should have jumped at the opportunity, I didn't have any other hot prospects lined up. It would be nice to have a grown-up job, I might even get to ask Miss Julia out to dinner and pick up the tab. But I wasn't keen to be the Captain Candybar of the OPC. I asked for a day to think it over.

Wisner blew his nose.

"How are your accommodations?"

"Quite splendid, sir. Any chance I could live here?"

Frank Wisner chuckled and rang off. He thought I was kidding.

I ordered breakfast from room service. I read election coverage from the stack of newspapers the staff left at my door. I took a long soak in a hot tub. The day dragged on.

I was sorely tempted to sneak down to the T&C for one of Winston's perfect Manhattans. I could order one from room service of course but drinking a perfect Manhattan alone in your room is just plain sad. And the prospect of facing a mob of reporters shouting questions was unpleasant in the extreme.

I was reading Li'l Abner and the Katzenjammer Kids for the second time when the telephone shattered the plush quiet.

The front desk explained they had a Julia Hammond on the line, that she had been told, repeatedly, that Mr. Schroeder was not to be disturbed but that she had insisted, repeatedly, that I would want to speak to her. I told the front desk to patch her through.

I didn't care what bad-news-from-the-front Miss Julia was about to deliver. I just wanted to hear her voice.

"How are you getting along?"

"I'm a kept man at the moment, confined in splendid isolation."

"Would you like some company?"

"Yes, ma'am, I sure would."

"I could stop by for a cocktail."

"Be still my beating heart."

Julia giggled, I grinned. I missed her.

"Though I must tell you," she said, "I have an ulterior motive."

"Hey, join the club!" No girlish giggle this time. "What's this about, Julia?"

"My editor is after me to do a follow-up story on you."

Oh crap. "What sort of story?"

"What they call a 'feature.' A personality profile."

"I've already gotten a ration of shit for being called a CIA hero."

"Hal, I've got my foot in the door. This is my chance to bust it wide open."

"I understand, but if I'm seen to be buffing my own backside on this I'll be excommunicated."

"From what?"

"From the dark and devious priesthood of espionage."

"That's good. Can I use that?"

I sighed, I grumbled. "Knock yourself out."

"You sound angry. You mind telling me why?"

"Not so long as you're jotting quotes in your reporter's notebook, no."

"Then we're off the record."

"Off the record? What am I, Secretary of State?"

"At the moment you're far more newsworthy than the Secretary of State."

"And that's my doing?"

"Hal, we're talking about *good* publicity."

"I'm not a politician, Julia, I'm a spy."

This was a ridiculous statement of course. At this point in the proceedings I was a secret agent like Kate Smith is a toe dancer.

"I should never have let you talk me into...you know."

"I didn't have to try very hard," said Julia.

"What's that supposed to mean?"

"I wanted to write the story, not be the story."

"You explained that." A phone rang in the background. I heard typewriters clacking. She was at the office.

"And what did Hal want?"

Miss Julia had a point. I'd told her I was sick of playing hero and that was true. But playing a hero who got outmaneuvered by a Soviet agent and had to be rescued by a girl reporter figured to be a lot worse.

I sighed, I grumbled. "Talk to Frank Wisner at OPC. If he clears it we can talk."

"Frank Wisner, at O…"

"OPC. Office of Policy Co-ordination."

"OPC, got it," she said, sweetly. "Do you have Frank Wisner's private line?"

"I'm hanging up now."

So much for cocktails for two in a secluded rendezvous. Far above the avenue.

I felt bad for the intrepid girl reporter. There was little chance Wisner would give her the go ahead.

I plain felt bad. I'm a Catholic boy, I'd felt the black dog of guilt nipping at my heels ever since I agreed to take credit for dispatching Leonid. For some inexplicable reason I had felt it most acutely when I was repeating made-up details to the oh-so-polite FBI agents in my palatial suite.

I had sold myself a bill of goods, told myself I had mended my ways and now proudly trod the straight and narrow.

But that wasn't strictly true.

Chapter Forty-three

Being a hero can be annoying, as I've said many times. I didn't enjoy it except when I did. Free drinks, fancy hotel suites, thunderous ovations.

But I was now at another annoyance level entirely. The concierge had delivered the afternoon papers to my door. My picture was on the front page of the Evening Star in a story reported by Julia Hammond for the Associated Press.

I shared the page with Harry Truman. He was above the fold, holding up a copy of the Chicago Tribune and grinning ear to ear. The Tribune headline read **Dewey Defeats Truman**.

My photo was squeezed into the lower left corner. Just my mug, a caption and a 'story on page 3.' I was also on the front page of the Washington Post, the Washington Times-Herald and the Washington Daily News.

Miss Julia had stepped up in class. My picture figured to be in every paper in the country.

The photo looked about five years old. I'd never seen it before. I looked like a sap, a smirky half-smile on my face, but that wasn't the worst part. The worst part was the caption.

Hal the Hero.

Hero with a capital 'H', like I was a professional wrestler. Jake the Snake, Manny the Mauler, Hal the Hero.

Dammit to hell, Julia. Maybe you couldn't keep my dopey mush off the front page but you should never have written that caption.

I studied the photo. I was dressed in civvies, standing in front of a chalkboard. It looked like the photo had been cropped but I could make out the numbers *06/0* above my left shoulder and below that the letter *H*.

Think, Schroeder. You're standing in front of a chalkboard. 06/0 is a strange number.

Oh yeah. That's the way they write out the month and day in the military, because every box on every form has to be filled in. The photo was taken at Camp X, on my first day at spy school.

06/0 was part of the date. 06/09/1943. *H* was the first letter of my name.

The photo should have been classified. How had Julia's editor gotten his grimy mitts on it? My mind got to wondering.

I turned the page and skimmed the article on page three. Miss Julia had done a good job with the timeline of my career. OSS spy behind German lines, undercover agent for the Cleveland feds and 'extralegal' operative in post-war Berlin. Good one Jules.

The next paragraph had the subhead 'The man who saved my life.' I read the quote from Jeanne Pappas of Cleveland, Ohio.

Julia was one dogged newshound. It was Jeannie, my Jeannie!

"Hal was a crazy kid, all over the place. Sure of himself one minute, shy and nervous the next. Like most kids. What set him apart, I think, was that he was absolutely fearless."

Me? Jeannie came to my rescue on Kelleys Island knowing it was a million to one. Jeannie was the fearless one.

No, that wasn't right. Fearless is another word for stupid. Jeannie was brave, I was fearless.

In my wayward youth anyway. I felt like an old man now, making my way down an icy sidewalk with short slow steps. A little youthful *brio* might be in order.

I had done my duty, I wasn't going out again. But there had to be a better way to join the fight than trading on my phony hero rep on Capitol Hill, a better way to put what I had learned in the field to good use. A way that didn't involve cavorting with Mata Hari's or sending eager young freedom fighters off to slaughter.

I needed a serious sitdown with William King Harvey.

I had hoped to wow Harvey with my palatial digs but the deep pile carpeting betrayed me.

"Who the fuck are you supposed to be?" he said when the concierge presented him at my doorstep at the appointed hour of seven p.m. "Albert Einstein?"

The concierge looked up at me and darted a quick finger at his head.

I invited Harvey in and checked my appearance in the full length mirror on the back of the door, a last chance for Royals and Prime Ministers to adjust their finery before they ventured out.

I had been padding around the thick carpeting in my stocking feet. My hair was standing straight up.

I went to the bathroom and slicked it down. When I returned to the living room Harvey was nowhere to be seen. I found him on the terrace, peering down at the Capitol rotunda.

"Be a sweet perch for an assassin."

"Sure. But who's gonna waste a bullet on a congressman?"

Harvey gave me one clipped laugh. "Where's my drink?"

"It's on its way," I said with a sly smile. Bill Harvey had a treat in store.

We went back inside. Harvey flopped in an overstuffed, floral print chair and looked cross and out-of-place. "Good work on Leonid. He had it coming."

I mumbled my thanks and changed the subject. "Frank Wisner offered me a job this morning. Congressional liaison."

"Nice. How much?"

"He didn't say."

"What else did you talk about?"

"Don't you want to know if I'm going to take the job?"

"Are you?"

"I don't think Wisner wants to hire me."

"Why'd he ask you then?"

"Me, he doesn't want to hire *me*. He chewed me out for chasing headlines but now he wants to hire that grinning idiot on the front page."

"The poor hero in the penthouse suite?"

"Yeah. I hate that bastard."

"I'd drink to that," harrumphed Harvey, "but I'm empty handed."

I picked up the phone to call the T&C Lounge just about the time the doorbell bing-bonged. Winston wheeled in a linen-covered cart bearing a bowl of mixed nuts, an ice bucket, a cocktail shaker, glasses, assorted mixers and what looked like a dark brown apothecary bottle. Try as he might Harvey couldn't keep the astonishment off his face.

I had Winston, mixing cocktails, in my private suite.

"You gennemens are partial to a Jack Daniels' Manhattan so far as I recollect. But if you might allow me..." Winston picked up the brown bottle and showed us the hand-lettered label.

BN /127.

"We had a gennemen guest from Kentucky, from a family whose name you know, he was kind enough to leave us this gift." Winston uncorked the almost-full bottle and poured a tiny dram in a shot glass. "It's what they call single-barrel bourbon, uncut, unfiltered. Hol' that glass up to yo' nose."

I did. It smelled of vanilla beans and smoke. "Umm hmm."

I passed it over to Harvey who slugged it down. "Tastes good too."

I asked Winston what *BN* stood for.

"Those are the gennemen's initials," said Winston, discreetly.

"And the 127?"

"That's the proof."

"You're kidding."

"No suh."

Harvey gave me a caustic look, as if he expected me to put my hand to my bosom and exclaim, *Oh dear me, no, that's far too strong!*

"Shake up two, Winston," I said.

"Yes suh. Maraschino cherries?"

"Well it's not a proper Manhattan without a cherry, now is it?"

"Not rightly suh," said Winston with a quick blinding grin.

We watched Winston work his magic in silence. He set the chilled martini glasses on the coffee table and poured right up to the rims and just beyond, the icy surface tension keeping the drink from overflowing.

"I'll be downstairs, Mistah Hal. Give a quick call when you need another," said Winston and let himself out.

Harvey and I leaned over to sip our drinks, two birds at a birdbath. The cocktails did not disappoint.

"What else did you and Wisner gas about?"

"The weather, Bill. We talked about the weather."

Harvey told me to do something that is biologically impossible, then sat back and waited for the bourbon to do its work.

'Trust no one' is what they preach at spy school. But it's unalloyed bullshit, unless you fancy living in a cave with a crate of K-rations and a Browning automatic. At the end of the day you have to trust somebody.

I decided I would trust Bill Harvey. It had something to do with his fondness for food and drink. Hitler was a strict vegetarian who didn't imbibe. Harvey would go to his final reward with a pork chop in one hand and a highball in the other. And I admire that in a person.

"Could be I told Frank Wisner too much," I said. "I told him that Hoover called me in."

"He would've heard about that sooner or later."

"I also told him I got the sense Hoover was trying to make me his snitch."

Harvey shook his head, lugubriously. "Now you've done it."

"What?"

"You've gone and dangled your tender testes in between the two meanest yard dogs in D.C. Now that Wisner knows Hoover's courting you, he'll want to send you back with slop buckets full of disintel that'll have Hoover chasing his tail for years."

"You have a very active imagination, Mr. Harvey."

"Like how, smartass?"

I threw Harvey a brush back pitch.

"Well, like 'Hoover will want to know why you called on Julia at the Dewey rally.' Like 'Wisner will drop you like a hot rock and Dulles and his black knights will dump you in the Potomac.' Like that."

Harvey parked my beanball in the upper decks.

"We're wrong about everything in counterintelligence, Schroeder. Until we're right."

We nibbled our drinks and enjoyed the quiet.

"That mug shot in the newspaper was my OSS induction photo."

"That jibes with my latest theory."

"I'm done with guessing games, Harvey. Spit it out."

Harvey extended his pudgy legs and crossed his ankles. "Frank Wisner secretly authorizes the release of your classified induction photo. All bureaucrats like good press. But what he's really doing is lathering you up with pig fat."

"You're going to have to explain that one."

"Bear hunters up in northern Michigan have a trick I saw work a time or two. They smear their lead dog with bacon grease and turn him loose in the deep brush, hoping to scare up a big one."

"The big one in this case being J. Edgar Hoover."

Harvey grunted.

"And I'm the lead dog."

"Obviously."

Well, it beat being a prize porker. I guess. The fat bastard might be on to something. Maybe this was why Wisner was giving me the royal treatment.

Harvey fought to lean forward in his pillowy chair. "Lab techs at the Bureau will determine your newspaper shot was classified. Wisner knows that, knows Hoover will conclude that Wisner released the classified photo because he doesn't consider you to be a true member of the secret brotherhood. And Wisner assumes that Hoover will try to get you all hot and bothered about that insult to your sacred honor."

Bill Harvey gave up and let his overstuffed chair reclaim him. "Wisner will tell you to play along so you have motive, in Hoover's mind, to give the Director a shitpot of highly-classified OPC intelligence."

I stifled a yawn. "How you do go on."

"You'll see."

"I don't wanna see, Bill," I said, sober as a parson. "I'm no longer interested in working for Frank Wisner. I want you to give me a job in counterintelligence. You said I had CI potential."

"Convince me."

"We had a good network of White Russian informers in Berlin until Leonid peached them out to the Blue Caps. We had Nikolai willing to list all the Soviet illegals in country till our MI6 dearies got him tossed in the drink. We even had half a chance to launch an insurrection in Transylvania before Princess Stela blew the whistle."

I rattled this off with little effort, surprised I had all that cordwood stacked so neatly.

"And those leaks came from outside. What if the Reds penetrate the CIA at staff level? Just one mole turns every operation into bloody disaster!"

I reached for my drink. It was empty. Bill Harvey was similarly embarrassed. We eyed the dark brown jug on the cocktail cart. No need to bother Winston.

"Two fingers, neat," said Harvey.

Done and done. We marinated in blissful quiet in the Woodrow Wilson Suite, the car horns and sirens of the city a distant music.

"A fella could get used to this," said Harvey.

"Um hum."

Harvey looked heavy-lidded, half-asleep, but his words were crisp. "Do you know the difference between counterintelligence and counterespionage?"

"Sure."

"Dazzle me."

I took a wee nip and plunged ahead.

"Counterintelligence is playing defense against attempts at penetration by enemy agents intent on espionage, sabotage or intelligence collection. Counterespionage, on the other hand, is offensive-minded. It attempts to identify, contact and convert the enemy's own agents in order to use them against the sponsor government."

"Well said. And where do you fit in?"

"Beats me."

"Don't be a dumbshit. Why would I hire a battle-tested operative to fact check field reports? Like it or not, Schroeder, you're stuck with yourself." Harvey shifted on his overstuffed chair and farted loudly. "And I say that with some authority."

We nibbled our drinks. The evening sky outside the terrace purpled into night.

"I'm shipping out to Gay Paree next week," said Harvey after a time. "To sniff out Commie spies and turn them with promises of dancing girls and filthy lucre. Your job would be to run them."

"I'd be a case officer?"

Not something I had ever pictured myself doing. I hated my World War II case officer, the jerk kept trying to get me croaked.

A case officer is something like a football coach. You draw up the plays, give a fiery chalk talk, send your guys onto the field and pace the sidelines. On the plus side you don't have to worry about getting carried off the field on a stretcher. I could put what I'd learned to good use and live to see my 30th birthday.

"I'm in, Bill, with one stipulation. I want Winston to accompany me as my personal bartender."

"Can't do it, Schroeder, wouldn't be right," said Harvey, drink in hand. "We're still finding our way in this screwy world. Winston is right where he is supposed to be."

We nodded in solemn agreement.

I looked at the Steuben crystal bowl on the end table. It was engraved with a dozen leaping gazelles. The smaller, finespun bowl on the opposite table was rimmed with swan's necks that curved up like handles. Even Harvey knew not to use them for ashtrays.

I took a wee nip of *BN/127* and asked William King Harvey a question seldom heard in the Woodrow Wilson Suite of the Mayflower Hotel.

"You got twenty bucks I can bum?"

Chapter Forty-four

I was excited about the opportunity to be a case officer in a foreign capital. My only hesitation was Julia, which surprised me. I was supposed to be mad at her for turning me into a walking box of Wheaties. But if you can't ruthlessly exploit your friends for career advancement what good are they?

I called her at home. I had a double sawbuck in my wallet now. I would ask her out to dinner and tell her I'd been offered a job overseas and see if she gave a hang.

"I'd like to Hal but I can't," is what she said.

"Why not?"

"We'd be spotted together."

"You turn me into Hal the Hero and now you can't risk being seen with me?"

"It would look like we were on a date. I'm supposed to be objective."

"We could meet someplace out of the way."

"Hal, I'm sorry, I can't risk it."

"You said we were on the same team."

"We were, Hal. We were."

"So," I said, not taking the hint, not wanting the conversation to end, "how was Jeannie?"

"Who?"

"Jeanne Pappas, my high school sweetheart."

It had been profoundly disorienting to think of Julia, talking to Jeannie, about me.

"I called her at home, at dinnertime. She said she was busy. I said it was important and gave her my home number and told her to call collect."

"And she called back late."

"Yes, quite late."

When the old man was sawing logs.

"She seemed eager to talk this time but something cut our conversation short. I think it was a crying infant in another room."

Had Jeannie had another baby? I didn't know. I had been a good boy, kept my distance since our Kelleys Island adventure.

"Oh," was all I managed. That was followed by a long awkward pause. We were done.

"It has been a distinct pleasure to make your acquaintance, Miss Hammond."

"And yours as well, Mr. Schroeder."

Miss Julia took a moment before she hung up to say, "You know how I feel about you, Hal."

I didn't. Know how she felt about me. But that's the thing about women, you never know from one minute to the next.

And I never got to so much as nuzzle that perfumed neck.

Oh, boo hoo, Schroeder. Is the poor famous hero feeling sorry for himself?

Well yes, as a matter of fact, he was.

I was going to have to reject Frank Wisner's job offer tomorrow morning, check out of the Mayflower and return to my third-floor walkup in Mrs. Brennan's rooming house in Cleveland till it was time to ship out with Bill Harvey. Provided he could slide that by the powers that be.

Tomorrow, that was tomorrow. Tonight I had a taste for a thick juicy ribeye with cottage fries and a chocolate sundae chaser.

I dialed room service one last time.

Epilogue

I don't know what it is about me and women. Seems like every time I start to find my rhythm with a girl the Grim Reaper cuts in.

Jeannie witnessed two fatal shootings on a snowy pier on Kellys Island. Anna was blown to bits when an NKVD officer and I played hot potato with a live grenade. And Miss Julia had to split Leonid's skull after finding her neighbor's bloody corpse. These were all miseries of my making in one way or another. I wasn't a suitable escort maybe.

Killing a person for the first time leaves a nauseating stench in your nostrils and an aching hole in your gut. It's a hard feeling to shake. I suspect that Miss Julia didn't spurn my invitation to a night out because she thought it would damage her career. I suspect Miss Julia didn't want me around to remind her of that awful night.

I'd scoffed when my case officer Victor Jacobson called me a 'lifer' at our first meet in Berlin.

'Settled down in a cozy cottage with a doting wife, are you?' was his reply.

No, I was not. And I wasn't likely to find the homespun apple-cheeked girl of my dreams while riding herd on a bunch of career turncoats in Europe. More likely I'd become another balding, chain-smoking loner who works right through the weekend because he's got nobody to tell him not to. Another Victor Jacobson.

I wanted to be my own man on my own terms but that didn't mean I had to wake up alone on Sunday mornings. Sunday is a lousy day to be alone.

What the hell, I had time. I might still get lucky. Could be I already had.

But forgive me, I've gotten ahead of myself.

Bill Harvey had gotten authorization from the Director of Central Intelligence to hire me on as a case officer. I had Frank Wisner to thank for that. He could have insisted on claiming rights to his prize thoroughbred. But the gracious Southern gentleman wished me well when I told him I wanted to accept Bill Harvey's offer. Wisner even paid to have my meager effects Railroad Expressed from Cleveland.

Bill Harvey was not so generous. Counterintelligence, he explained, was 'back of the house' and a funding afterthought. Money was tight. We negotiated.

I was intent on a stopover in County Cork to visit the Mooney Brothers. I had debts to pay. To cover the extra cost I agreed to book passage on a bulk freighter from New York to Dublin. It was quite a comedown from the penthouse suite.

The *Shannon Gail* was a rusty bucket that took on water in rough seas, so much so that the 35,000 tons of barley in her hold started to ferment. By the time we docked in Dublin she smelled like a Friday night at Finnegan's.

I walked down the gangplank before dawn on Tuesday, November 16th, 1948. I took the train south to the city of Cork which, you will not be surprised to learn, is the county seat of County Cork.

I checked into the first rooming house I came across, a few blocks north of the train station. The lady behind the counter could have been Mrs. Brennan's younger sister, gruff and merry in equal measure. I parked my grip in a cozy room. The featherbed beckoned but I knew if I crawled in I'd wake up at three a.m. craving hot food and strong drink. I took a cold shower instead.

I returned to the parlor and told the lady of the house I was looking to find the Mooney Brothers - Ambrose, Sean and Patrick. She said they were close by, 'a wee stumble'.

"In a favorite pub no doubt."

"None other," she said with a twinkle.

I walked two blocks south as instructed. Well, I'll be damned. I had passed right by while looking for a place to flop. The Mooney Brothers Bar & Grill!

I ankled in and looked around. A jukebox blaring Tommy Dorsey, framed photos of Bob Feller and Bobby Waterfield and a recent Cleveland Press front page: **Tribe Wins World Series!** Polished brass rails and red checkered tablecloths. Home sweet home.

I sat at the far end of the bar, by the window with its café curtain. It was three o'clock or so, no crowd yet. Nobody but me.

I had handed fifty-thousand dollars in newly-minted banknotes to Ambrose Mooney on Whiskey Island in December of '45. The boys had earned their pay so far as I was concerned, but they wouldn't be the first young men to piss away a windfall.

And they sure as shit weren't going to turn a profit without a bartender to serve a thirsty man a beer. I looked around, I called hello. I parked my cheek on my fist and waited.

"Sir?" trilled a lovely voice. "Sir?"

I opened my eyes to see a riot of green eyes, red lips, white teeth and curly black hair.

"We discourage sleeping at the bar," said the prettiest girl in all the world.

This was Ambrose's lady love, had to be.

"Sorry. Had a long trip, I'm all in."

She cocked her head at my Yankee accent.

"I'm Hal Schroeder from Cleveland, Ohio."

"You are not."

"I'm afraid I am."

"No!"

"Yes!"

"Well jaypers," she said, extending her hand, "I'm Lilly."

We shook. Touching her hand sent a jolt up my arm.

"Uh, are the boys here?"

"Ambrose is in his office."

Sheesh McGeesh, Ambrose Mooney had an office.

"Okay, here's the plan. I'll go off to the little boy's room, you drag Ambrose out here with some question or problem and I'll sneak up behind."

"Perfect," she said with a dimpled smile. "Off you go."

Off I went on heavy legs. Young Hal would have seen something he coveted and schemed and plotted – *You know, Lilly, I'm moving to Paris and, gosh, I sure would like to show you around the City of Light.* But Hal the Elder would never do such a despicable thing.

The dope.

All such thoughts gave wing when I returned from the loo and saw Lilly and Ambrose together at the bar, she behind, he in front, leaning over to examine some bill or order form. It was a dull moment of daily commerce but something about the way their heads spilled into one another made it clear they were a matched set.

Lilly was good. She never once shifted her eyes in my direction as I crept up behind. She even raised her voice to cover my footsteps as I got close.

"What's a guy gotta do to get a beer in this shithole?" I said in a gravelly voice.

Ambrose spun around with a scowl on his face. A scowl that went away.

"I owe you a handshake, my friend."

Ambrose had offered me his hand after we sprung him from the Soviet Armory in Berlin. But it's bad luck to celebrate in the middle of an operation so I told him we'd do that later, then never got the chance.

"Yes you do, Hal."

I had always been *Chief* before, or *Boss*. But Ambrose was his own boss now. We shook hands, climbed onto barstools and started in.

He knew about my adventure in D.C., it was in all the papers. I promised to tell him the full story once his brothers wandered in. I congratulated him on his new business. He told me they'd been open for six months and weren't breaking even.

"I serve the best hamburger and French fries – fries, not chips - this side of the Atlantic, for ten feckin' pence. That's forty cents. I sell a few to the local swells but the working stiffs will drop a pound on beer and go home hungry."

"Maybe a hamburger is something new to them."

"That's the point! Stupid bloody Micks. I always thought meself an Irishman when I lived in Cleveland but here in Cork I'm feckin' Yankee Doodle Dandy."

The joint filled up as the sun went down. Old men in tweed caps, store clerks in bowties, salesmen wearing Derby hats and one-button suits. Not a woman to be seen.

Lilly had the gents lined up at the bar like trained seals hoping for a bit of herring.

"You'll do fine," I said, nodding in Lilly's direction, "so long as you don't let that one get away."

Ambrose followed my look and smiled to himself. "Don't worry, she's not going anywhere."

"No?"

"No."

They would make the most beautiful children.

Sean and Patrick arrived a short time later. They didn't want handshakes. They dogpiled me with sweaty hugs.

We adjourned to a table with brimming pints of Guinness. I had never partaken but I'd heard tell. I took a good pull. It tasted sweet and nasty by turns. It tasted, with apologies to Winston, like a carbonated Manhattan.

I couldn't tell the Mooney Brothers what really happened without breaking my pact with Julia but that was okay. They didn't want to hear the truth. What they wanted, in gruesome detail, was the story of how their old pal had dispatched Leonid Vitinov, Ambrose's vile kidnapper. They listened eagerly as Hal the Hero made shit up.

I might make an effective counterintelligence officer at that. You can hawk bogus crap in a loud voice all day long and it won't do you a lick of good, not till you tell the customer what he wants to hear. Effective counterespionage involves tailoring disinformation to what the end user is inclined to believe. We all participate in our own deception.

It's a transaction.

I owed Ambrose one more thing. A fancy wristwatch to replace the one I made him surrender to the Soviet checkpoint sentry in Berlin. I'd only had twenty bucks in my wallet when I went shopping in high-priced downtown D.C. But I found a souvenir shop near Dupont Circle.

While Ambrose was busy ordering food for the table I slipped the small narrow box his way. He frowned when he saw it.

"What's this now?"

"One way to find out."

I expected a rude guffaw when he opened the box to find a cheap wristwatch with an oversized face and a fake leather strap. Little gun barrels formed the hour and minute hands. The 3, 6, 9 and 12 were designated by blood-tipped bullets. And, on the oversized watch face, was none other than the grim visage of J. Edgar Hoover.

But Ambrose didn't bust out laughing. He held up the watch and admired it. "Ah jayz, Hal, it's feckin' grand."

A waitress served us hamburgers and fries. It was a hell of a feed. The patty was two inches thick, topped with cheddar cheese, pickles, lettuce, thick slices of tomato and onion and crowned with a puffy white bun. Ambrose attacked his with gusto.

"Zis good or what?" he said between bites.

I nodded, I swallowed. "Also intimidating."

"Eh?"

"Well, I'm thinkin' you might have a better shot at getting those mopes at the bar to try one of these newfangled hamburgers if the hamburgers aren't bigger than they are."

Ambrose looked to Sean, the smart middle brother. Sean pursed his lips to suppress a smile.

"Point taken," said Ambrose. "Arseholes."

Red-haired Patrick, who still looked about 19, hoisted his pint. "To our good mate, Hal."

We clanked and drank. The Mooney boys scattered to their duties after we finished eating. I made my way to the bar for another Guinness.

I got to watch Lily in action. She didn't linger long with any customer so as to spread the wealth. I noticed that she had a pencil tucked behind her ear and another pencil, a nub, that floated in the thick tangle of black curls that spilled down her back. I watched that nub of a pencil dance about as Lilly turned and tucked and stretched and knelt.

When the crowd thinned she poured me another pint, filling the glass three-quarters full, letting the creamy head settle for a minute, then topping it off.

I asked her how she came to know Ambrose.

She laughed. "They said you were keen to make jooks."

"Who?"

Lilly stared intently at my baffled mug. "You don't know, do you? They're so protective of me."

"Who is?"

"Me brothers."

Holy mother of God.

Of course. Their hair didn't match but their features were practically interchangeable.

"Where, uh, which one..."

"I'm the second child, a baby sister to Ambrose."

"But how...did you live in..."

She held up a calloused pink and white finger. I waited. She wiped the bar with a rag so as not to look at me.

"Our pa died of typhoid when I was twelve. We had to move in with Grandma Kaye, Pa's mum. She was a widow lady, lace curtain Irish with a fine house. She did not....well, she took a liking to me but she did not enjoy having three young hellions tearing about. Grandma Kaye made me mum a proposition. She would pay for their passage to the States, to join our uncle in Cleveland, so long as I was left behind to look after her."

"Your mother swapped you for boat tickets?"

Lilly looked up at me. "In a manner of speaking."

"Were you angry about that?"

"I was," she said, "but me mum did what she thought best. And now it's all come round."

I raised my eyebrows. Lilly answered by way of looking about the Mooney Brothers Bar & Grill. "Everyone is here who needs to be."

I took a swig and wiped foam from my upper lip. "And your mum?"

"She lives upstairs. She will be *so* wanting meet you."

No doubt. Things had worked out swell all in all. But I had almost gotten Mrs. Mooney's darlin' boys killed on two separate occasions. I wouldn't be a hero in her eyes.

I stood up. "We must do this again sometime, Lilly."

"I shall be here tomorrow, Mr. Schroeder."

I returned her smile. "Me too. And please call me Hal."

"A pleasant evening to you, Hal."

I left before I made a fool of myself and walked on air for a full block. Lilly was all too perfect and all wrong. And I was due in Paris in three days in any event. Still, no woman had ever pronounced my dull name in such a lovely way. *Ha-all.*

The cold damp air snapped me to. I put my hands in my pockets and trudged the last block. It felt good to be on to a new adventure, I looked forward to it. But Special Agent Schram's parting words of wisdom sat like an undigested lump in the belly of my brain.

Making it back down to level ground was the hardest part.

Wisps of fog from the Celtic Sea twined through the empty streets as I walked and pondered. What I think Schram meant was that it's not all heartbreak and horror up there on Breakneck Ridge. There's also the sweet tang of victory and a godlike sense of power.

Like life in the Woodrow Wilson Suite, a fella could get used to that. I'd had a good run of it lately. Could be I liked being Hal the Hero more than I let on. Hal the Hero might get bored sending young men into battle while he paced the sidelines.

They say good players make bad coaches. No patience. If I wanted to be a good case officer I would have to suffer an altitude adjustment, and learn patience.

Ugh. Times ten.

But I would do what I had to do.

I was too keyed up to sleep so I sat at the small sturdy desk in my second floor room and wrote my parents a letter. I apologized for not staying in touch. I told them I had an exciting job opportunity in Europe working for the government. They would know what that meant. I assured them it wasn't dangerous and I promised, scout's honor, to come home to Youngstown on Christmas Eve and stay till New Years.

No doubt you've heard about my exploits in D.C. I'm not quite the dashing hero the newspapers made me out to be but I hope that I have made you proud. That would make it all worthwhile.

The letter looked incomplete so I added a P.S.

Dad, Wild Bill Donovan sends his best.

I got a little blurry writing that. How in the name of God had I – juvenile delinquent, insubordinate OSS agent and on-the-make FBI sting operator – been privileged to act as liaison between these two fine men?

The answer was simple. I had been very fortunate, a lucky man in an unlucky world.

Poker, rummy and pinochle were the favored ways to pass the time on my first Atlantic crossing in 1943. A young Army chaplain, not much older than his captive flock of 19-year-olds, made note of this in his service on the deck of our troop ship. A remark I have always remembered.

"It's important to count your cards, gentlemen. Do so religiously."

He grinned as he surveyed us fuzzy-cheeked hatchlings shipping off to defeat the Axis Powers. We had no idea what horrors we would be asked to face or how important our sacrifices were to become. We had no idea how privileged we were to be there.

It took me a long time to understand that.

"Count your cards, gentlemen," repeated the young Army chaplain, hands on his hips. "But, when day is done, don't forget to count your blessings."

Amen, brother.

I got up from the writing desk and threw open a sash window to breathe the salty night air. I felt good, I felt complete, after a long race successfully run.

Only one thing nagged. Was Anna pregnant when I killed her with that hand grenade? Or did Leonid make that up to torture me?

I would never know the answer to that question. The Napoleonic little prick had won.

Leonid Vitinov died with superior knowledge.

The author's bio and information about John Knoerle's other titles are available at:

www.johnknoerle.com

Contact the author at:

bluesteelpress@att.net

www.ingramcontent.com/pod-product-compliance
Lightning Source LLC
Chambersburg PA
CBHW071005280626
47160CB00015B/920